# CHANCE

# CHANCE

## TEXAS BOUDREAU BROTHERHOOD

By
KATHY IVAN

# COPYRIGHT

Chance – Original Copyright © June 2021 by Kathy Ivan

Cover by Elizabeth Mackay

Release date: June 2021
Print Edition

All Rights Reserved

# CHANCE – Texas Boudreau Brotherhood Book #8

*No good deed goes unpunished.*

A glorified babysitting assignment escalates into more than Chance Boudreau bargained. When he meets Tina Nelson, their simmering attraction creates a dangerous distraction. But when Tina's past catches up to her, can Chance unravel the clues before she becomes a permanent casualty in a diabolic scheme?

"In Shiloh Springs, Kathy Ivan has crafted warm, engaging characters that will steal your heart and a mystery that will keep you reading to the very last page." Barb Han, USA TODAY and Publisher's Weekly Bestselling Author

Kathy Ivan's books are addictive, you can't read just one." Susan Stoker, NYT Bestselling Author

# BOOKS BY KATHY IVAN

www.kathyivan.com/books.html

## TEXAS BOUDREAU BROTHERHOOD

Rafe

Antonio

Brody

Ridge

Lucas

Heath

Shiloh

Chance

Derrick (coming soon)

Dane (coming soon)

## NEW ORLEANS CONNECTION SERIES

Desperate Choices

Connor's Gamble

Relentless Pursuit

Ultimate Betrayal

Keeping Secrets

Sex, Lies and Apple Pies

Deadly Justice

Wicked Obsession

Hidden Agenda

Spies Like Us

Fatal Intentions

New Orleans Connection Series Box Set: Books 1-3

New Orleans Connection Series Box Set: Books 4-7

Hello Readers,

Welcome to Shiloh Springs, Texas! Don't you just love a small Texas town where the people are neighborly, the gossip plentiful, and the heroes are…well, heroic, not to mention easy on the eyes! I love everything about Texas, which I why I've made the great state my home for over thirty years. There's no other place like it. From the delicious Tex-Mex food and downhome barbecue, the majestic scenery, and friendly atmosphere, the people and places of the Lone Star state are as unique and colorful as you'll find anywhere.

The Texas Boudreau Brotherhood series centers on a group of foster brothers, men who would have ended up in the system if not for Douglas and Patricia Boudreau. Instead of being hardened by life's hardships and bad circumstances beyond their control, they found a family who loved and accepted them, and gave them a place to call home. Sometimes brotherhood is more than sharing the same DNA.

This book is Chance Boudreau's story, and Chance was a handful, because he's both serious yet playful, and utterly besotted with Tina Nelson. While writing this book was a labor of love, it wasn't an easy book to write for a lot of reasons. But, between me and the rest of the Boudreau clan, we managed to get it done, and now you've got another Boudreau brother's story in your hands. I hope I did Chance justice in the telling.

If you've read my other romantic suspense books (the New Orleans Connection series and Cajun Connection series), you'll be familiar with the Boudreau name. Turns out there are a whole lot of Boudreaus out there, just itching to have their stories told. (Douglas is the brother of Gator Boudreau, patriarch of the New Orleans branch of the Boudreau family. Oh, and did I mention they have another brother – Hank "The Tank" Boudreau?)

So, sit back and relax. The pace of small-living might be less hectic than the big city, but small towns hold secrets, excitement, and heroes who ride to the rescue. And don't you just love a Texas cowboy?

Kathy Ivan

# EDITORIAL REVIEWS

"In Shiloh Springs, Kathy Ivan has crafted warm, engaging characters that will steal your heart and a mystery that will keep you reading to the very last page."

—Barb Han, *USA TODAY* and Publisher's Weekly Bestselling Author

"Kathy Ivan's books are addictive, you can't read just one."

—Susan Stoker, NYT Bestselling Author

"Kathy Ivan's books give you everything you're looking for and so much more."

—Geri Foster, USA Today and NYT Bestselling Author of the Falcon Securities Series

"This is the first I have read from Kathy Ivan and it won't be the last."

—Night Owl Reviews

"I highly recommend Desperate Choices. Readers can't go wrong here!"

—Melissa, Joyfully Reviewed

"I loved how the author wove a very intricate storyline with plenty of intriguing details that led to the final reveal..."

—Night Owl Reviews

Desperate Choices—Winner 2012 International Digital Award—Suspense

Desperate Choices—Best of Romance 2011 –Joyfully Reviewed

# DEDICATIONS AND ACKNOWLEDGEMENTS

To Chris Keniston and Barb Han, fellow authors who helped keep me focused, and worked with me on writing the blurb for Chance (and most of the Boudreau Brotherhood books).

To my sister, Mary. She knows why.

As always, I dedicate this and every book to my mother, Betty Sullivan. Her love of reading introduced me to books at a young age. I will always cherish the memories of talking books and romance with her. I know she's looking down on me and smiling.

**More about Kathy and her books can be found at**

**WEBSITE:**
**www.kathyivan.com**

**Follow Kathy on Facebook at**
**facebook.com/kathyivanauthor**

**Follow Kathy on Twitter at**
**twitter.com/@kathyivan**

**Follow Kathy at BookBub**
**bookbub.com/profile/kathy-ivan**

## NEWSLETTER SIGN UP

Don't want to miss out on any new books, contests, and free stuff? Sign up to get my newsletter. I promise not to spam you, and only send out notifications/e-mails whenever there's a new release or contest/giveaway. Follow the link and join today!

**http://eepurl.com/baqdRX**

# CHANCE

# CHAPTER ONE

"Honey, he called again."

Tina Nelson squeezed the bridge of her nose between her thumb and finger, and scrunched her eyes closed. She almost hadn't answered the phone when she saw her aunt's name on the caller ID. That nagging feeling she always got in the pit of her stomach, the one that always preceded bad news? Right now it was doing somersaults and Rockette-style high kicks.

"What did you tell him?"

"Nothing, I swear. I will never tell that lowlife where you are. I'm just worried he's going to find you anyway."

Tina gave an almost silent chuckle. "I'm being careful, Aunt Maxie. Covering my tracks is second nature now. Jared will stop looking for me when he gets bored." She crossed her fingers at the blatant lie she'd just told her aunt, but the woman didn't need to be consumed with worry about her. Taking care of Uncle Stanley was a full-time job, and she had her own health issues to deal with in addition to his. The doctors insisted he slow down since his heart attacks, and she still felt guilty because it was her fault. Well, hers and Jared

1

Webster's.

They made a few more minutes of small talk, avoiding the topic of Jared's search for her, and she disconnected the call, but not before reassuring her aunt that she'd be careful and would call again soon.

Tina automatically scooched lower on the bench seat without realizing she'd done it and stared at the untouched bowl of chicken and dumplings in front of her. She'd come into Daisy's Diner with her bestie, Renee O'Malley, hoping they'd get to spend a few more hours together before Tina headed for Dallas tomorrow morning. It was past time to head back to Portland and get her life back on track.

"Everything okay, hon?"

Tina looked up into Daisy's face and gave her a half-hearted shrug. "I guess." She waved the phone in her hand. "Family, you know?"

"Gotcha. Just thought I'd check and see if you need anything else." Her eyes strayed to the untouched food. "You want something different? I can get you whatever you want."

Tina picked up the spoon. "No, thanks, Daisy. This is great." She shoved the loaded spoon in her mouth, and the flavor exploded on her taste buds. She gave Daisy a thumb's up, savoring the comfort dish. Daisy gave her a quick grin and walked away as Renee slid onto the bench across from her.

"Sorry that took so long. Shiloh's still a little paranoid about me going out without a bodyguard."

"Can you blame him? Even though the Blacks are behind bars, Darius' reach might not be curtailed. At least the feds froze all his accounts, and Eileen's too. Ms. Patti told me they're never going to see the outside of a prison cell again. While I hope that's true, for your sake, I'm skeptical. One or both of them is going to roll over on somebody bigger and badder, and they'll end up with a slap on the wrist."

Renee's expression clouded for a second before she looked at Tina and grinned. "I'm not worried. The FBI has at least a hundred charges they're bringing against Darius. Eileen's got her own set of problems, including assault on a federal agent from when she head-butted the guy putting her in the back of the car when she was arrested." She fiddled with her napkin for a second before unfolding it and placing in on her lap. "I'm holding on to hope, because I refuse to spend my life hiding or running. Never again."

"I'm so happy you've found somebody like Shiloh. He's one of the good ones. All these Boudreaus seem to have a chivalrous quality that's bone deep. Wonder if it's a Texas thing?"

"I think it's more a Boudreau thing. Douglas and Ms. Patti taught their sons how to be upstanding men, despite their rocky beginnings. They're the kind of guys romance novels are written about, the kind you don't believe exist in real life."

"Lucky you." She shoved another spoonful of her chicken and dumplings into her mouth before she ended up putting her foot in there. Renee really had lucked out when Shiloh Boudreau's search brought him to Portland, and she'd found the man of her dreams. Unfortunately, the man Tina thought was her own prince turned out to be the evil black knight in disguise. Too bad she hadn't figured that out before she married him.

"I hate that you're leaving tomorrow. I'm going to miss you so much."

"Renee...do you know I'm still having trouble calling you by that name? I can't stay here forever. I've got a job. An apartment. Responsibilities. I can't turn my back on everything simply because I've fallen in love with a town." Tina took a sip of her tea, smiling at what she'd learned was called sweet tea by the local Texans.

"Only the town?" Renee teased.

Tina rolled her eyes before tossing her napkin at Renee. "Let's not go there, girlfriend. I'm not looking for a guy in my life. I'm enjoying being footloose and fancy free—isn't that how the saying goes?" And she was a big, fat liar. There was one of the Boudreaus who'd caught her attention, made her consider maybe all men weren't monsters hiding inside handsome packages.

"The whole time I've known you, I can't remember you ever dating anybody for more than a time or two. Is there something I should know?" Renee's voice took on a worried tone, and Tina knew she had to nip this train of thought in the bud, because she couldn't afford to rouse the other woman's suspicions. If she started digging into Tina's past, she might uncover the ugliness she'd buried, alongside the bones of her previous marriage.

"I'm not relationship material. I get bored too easily, so it's better if I cut my losses before anybody gets too attached. Love 'em and leave 'em, that's me."

Looking down at her barely eaten bowl, she pushed it away, appetite gone. She hated lying to her friend, one of the few she had left. After the divorce, most of her friends had sided with Jared because he'd told credible lies about everything being her fault, even insinuating she'd been the unfaithful one in their marriage. Totally fabricated, but most of them had been his colleagues and their spouses, and she hadn't been part of their upper echelon circle anyway.

"Did you know you get this tic by the side of your mouth when you lie?" Renee pointed with her spoon toward Tina's mouth. "Took me a while, but I caught it. If you don't want to tell me, fine, but don't make up some bull hockey nonsense, cause I'm not buying it."

As much as she wanted to confide in her best friend, she didn't dare. Renee had come through her own horrific past and was finally getting a chance at true happiness and peace. No way on earth was Tina allowing her idiot ex-husband to cause anyone else a moment's discomfort. Somehow, she'd figure out a way to maintain the low profile she'd been living under for the past two years and pray he didn't discover where she was; otherwise, she'd have to move again.

"Let's change the subject, okay? How was South Padre Island?"

Half-listening to her friend drone on about the trip with her brother, Tina began making plans. Though she'd secretly hoped Jared had given up on trying to find her and moved on to looking for wife number three, she should have known better. Her ex didn't believe in letting anything go that belonged to him, whether it was a possession or a person, at least until he decided it was time to seek greener pastures.

She'd finally found a place, working at the coffee shop in Portland, where she'd managed to find a little oasis of peace. The thought of bringing trouble to their doorstep, when they'd been kind enough to put up with her fumbling foolishness while she'd been learning the ropes, made her want to cry.

Leaning back into the booth, she smiled at Renee's enthusiasm about her recent getaway with her newly-rediscovered brother, Lucas. Too bad her own idyllic mini-vacation was over, and it was time Tina started making plans.

*Portland, here I come.*

Chance laid his briefcase on the desk and rubbed a hand across the back of his neck. He hated mornings like this. Most of the cases he prosecuted in Shiloh Springs County weren't major crimes. He couldn't remember the last time he'd done anything more intense than burglary with the use of a firearm, when a couple of stupid teens decided to rob Jimbo's Grocery. The evidence had been cut and dried, to the point he was surprised the guys wanted to go through with the case and not plead out. Guess everybody wanted their day in court, and they'd ended up being found guilty and got a harsher sentence than if they had simply taken the plea deal.

Which was what should have happened this morning. Today's case was cut and dry; without a shadow of a doubt Marshall Goodman was guilty of assault. Marshall had a list of priors a mile long, a repeat offender who'd been out on probation when he beat the stuffing out of his ex-girlfriend's new fella. Eyewitnesses stepped forward, and there was even video footage from multiple bystanders. He'd worked out a plea deal with defense council, hammering out every little detail, and headed into court this morning, expecting to be in and out in under an hour. Instead, he'd been blindsided when the defendant decided to toss the deal out the window, opting for a jury trial.

*Idiot.*

The rest of the afternoon had been spent arranging for the court date, then moving around another case he'd been working on, shoving it off onto the assistant district attorney. It wasn't like they had a ton of court cases every day. Usually, two days a week he'd have to show up either in front of the bench or behind the scenes in the judge's chambers dealing with the small stuff. Shiloh Springs wasn't exactly a hotbed for criminal activity. The most excitement they'd had in a long time had been when the high school had been locked down during a hostage situation. That case was pending before the county court, and he couldn't wait to sink his teeth into a nice, juicy case of gun running, multiple counts of kidnapping, and a variety of other charges. For once, he'd get to hone his skills on a meaty offense.

Shrugging off his jacket, he folded it, laid it across the back of a chair, and loosened his tie. Time to get comfortable since he didn't have to go back to court today. Opening his briefcase, he pulled out his laptop and moved around to sit at his desk. He had converted an entire bedroom in his place to a home office, and that's usually where he spent his evenings, buried in work and research. Today, his attention wasn't on work, though. Well, not in the traditional sense.

Clicking on the mouse, he opened the e-mail from Destiny, his friendly neighborhood hacker. He'd hired her off the books, because looking into Tina Nelson's background wasn't for any professional case he was prosecuting. No, this was personal. He'd read through the e-mail at least a dozen times already, and studied the attached photos, yet he found himself coming back again and again, searching for clues. Nuances and kernels of truth were contained within the dossier, he just had to weed them out one by one. Destiny had done her usual excellent job of digging out information others would have overlooked, or never found in the first place. She was just that good.

Clicking on the first photo, a pretty, smiling brunette popped up on screen. Head thrown back, she was laughing at something her companion said, her eyes shining with life. His chest tightened at the sight of her vivacious, infectious smile. She'd wormed her way into his head, haunted his thoughts from the moment he'd met her. Their first meeting had been eventful, to say the least. Darned woman attempted to brain him with the hotel ice bucket.

*Tina Nelson.*

The woman he'd been tasked with babysitting in Portland, and later brought into his parents' home here in Shiloh Springs. In a pinch, she'd watched out and protected his sister when she'd been hiding from the people hunting her. Taken a beating when a hired mercenary wanted information on how to find Renee. She'd refused to tell him where Renee was, even though it meant she'd endured physical pain. Admiration for the spunky brunette warred with the facts on the page. The ones that troubled him, made him wonder if she could be trusted.

Clicking on another picture, he studied the man seated beside Tina. He carried himself with an air of somebody who came from a privileged background. Obviously taken at a business dinner or event of some kind, the sandy-haired man sported a tux, complete with cummerbund, but Chance couldn't tear his eyes away from Tina. Her dark hair had been longer then, falling in waves past her shoulders. The royal blue gown hugged her curves in all the right places, displaying a lush body any woman would envy. Though she smiled at the camera, her eyes told the truest picture. They were haunted, filled with an anguish clearly visible to anybody looking beneath the saccharine smile. Her arm was entwined with the taller male's, his fingers resting atop hers in a possessive gesture.

Chance blew out a deep breath. Maybe he was trying to see something in the picture that wasn't there. While he had made a career of being able to read people, from their facial expressions to their mannerisms, Tina remained an enigma.

Moving the mouse to the next picture, he clicked it, and expanded it larger on his screen. Again, she was with the man from the previous photo, but there was a world of difference between the two pictures. In this one, she appeared beaten down, her vivacious spirit extinguished. Shoulders slumped, she seemed withdrawn into herself, as if trying to appear smaller, not wanting to draw anyone's attention.

Checking the metadata between the two photos, he noted they'd been taken about three months apart. Such a short period of time, yet the differences were night and day. What happened to the woman he'd spent the last few weeks with?

The final picture showed a woman almost unrecognizable. The long hair she had before was cut into a modern edgy style, buzzed on the left side close to the scalp and colored a platinum blonde, so white it almost appeared to have no color. The quirky grin he'd come to know since her days at the Big House was the most recognizable thing about her. He knew women liked to do makeovers, update their looks with new hairstyles, new makeup and clothes, but this? It almost appeared like she was trying to reinvent herself.

*Or maybe change the way she looked so she could hide in plain sight.*

Destiny provided him with a list of cities and towns Tina had lived in for the last couple of years, never seeming to stay in one place more than a few months. The longest place she'd taken root was Portland, where she'd been for the last nine months. Every place she'd moved, she'd used a different last name and variations of her first. Guess when you're trying to be inconspicuous, you go with what's familiar.

Tina's maiden name provided a plethora of information. She'd been born Christina Phillips to a working-class father and a stay-at-home mother. An only child, she'd excelled in school, always in the top of her classes, third in her high school class of over five hundred. Earned a full scholarship to Stanford. On the educational fast track, with recommendations from her professors and faculty, Tina was accepted into the medical program where she met her husband, Jared Webster. Chance had yet to look at his file, though Destiny had provided an extensive one on the man. Destiny was nothing if not thorough.

Leaning back in his chair, Chance closed his eyes, remembering his first meeting with Tina. After the long drive from Shiloh Springs to Dallas, he'd flown into Portland, and headed for the hotel Lucas booked. Of course, his brother hadn't bothered to tell him he'd be sharing the room with Renee's feisty friend. He'd allowed Shiloh to twist his arm into playing bodyguard instead of lounging on the balcony of his condo on South Padre Island, which had been his plans when he'd taken a week off work.

He'd slid the keycard into the lock and walked into the room, planning to get settled into his room, and then check in with the woman he'd been sent to babysit. Instead, he'd heard a banshee-loud yell, followed by excruciating pain in the back of his skull.

The image she'd made, standing inside the room, with a towel wrapped around her body and another atop her head, wielding the room's ice bucket in her hand made his lips curve in a rueful smile. Though at the time he hadn't been smiling, he'd been puzzled and in pain. He'd made an educated guess that's what walloped him in the head, and he raised his fingers and touched the goose egg coming up on the back of his skull. He knew where the blame lay, because Shiloh hadn't bothered telling Tina they'd be sharing a room, either. Once they'd straightened out the misunderstanding, she'd apologized profusely, before grabbing her clothing and dressing in the bathroom. A shame that, because she had the kind of body meant for sin, a woman with curves and legs that went on forever. He'd noticed the black eye and split lip, and the bruises covering her arms, which made his blood boil, but that dimmed when he'd focused on how good she looked in next to nothing. Too bad he couldn't touch her. She was most definitely off limits because she was Renee's friend.

With a shake of his head, he looked at his laptop screen. He refused to pull up the photos of Tina again; he had them memorized anyway. No, he needed something different, something he could sink his teeth into, a puzzle to solve and keep his mind off the beautiful woman who was quickly coming to mean something to him.

Moving the mouse over Jared Webster's file, he clicked open and started reading.

# CHAPTER TWO

Tina grabbed a handful of clothes out of the dresser and placed them inside the open duffle bag on the bed. The Boudreaus' hospitality extended to her having a guest room all to herself. The homey warmth of the room made her want to cuddle in the armchair beside the window, and gaze out onto the vast green pastureland beyond the barn and paddock. The enclosure held at least a horse and the family donkey, Otto. She smiled remembering little Jamie's face when she'd grabbed Tina's hand and pulled her over to introduce her to Otto. Apparently, he was one of Jamie's favorite things about visiting the Boudreau ranch.

With a sigh, she turned away, grabbed the rest of her clothes, and tossed them in with the others in the duffle. She didn't have a lot, because she'd left Portland with only the clothes on her back. A shudder skittered down her spine, thinking about that awful day when the hired mercenary followed her home from her job, intent on obtaining information about Renee. If she dwelled on it, she could remember the pain of each blow, see the fist moving in slow motion toward her face.

*Stop it. Forget about the pain. You've done it before. Shove it behind you and get on with your life.*

"Knock, knock."

Tina looked up at Ms. Patti's smiling face. The Boudreau family matriarch amazed her. She'd opened her home to a complete stranger, welcoming her like she was a member of the family. Even with a business to run, and more sons than she could shake a stick at, along with an amazing husband, the woman still managed to maintain her loving and giving personality. Though she'd only known her a few weeks, Tina hoped a bit of Ms. Patti's kindness and love rubbed off on her and she could pay it forward.

"Come in. I'm packing up my stuff, so I'll be ready to leave bright and early."

"We're going to be sorry to see you go." She walked into the room, her hand trailing across the chenille bedspread. "I know having you here made things easier for Renee. She needed a friendly face, an anchor, after being dropped smack dab into the midst of a family she didn't know, in a place she'd never been. Thank you for that."

"She'd have been fine. Our gal is resilient. Surrounded by all the love and affection you've shown her, she's thriving. And being around Lucas has made a world of difference. Honestly, I kind of envy her. She's found the love of her life along with an adoptive family who adores her. Believe me, that's something special."

Ms. Patti sat on the bed and patted the mattress beside

her. Tina shoved the duffle back and sat beside the lovely older woman. She'd told the truth; she was envious of Renee, at least a teensy bit. She was getting an amazing woman as a mother, one who'd always be there for her, no matter what. Too bad her own mother hadn't been anything like the Boudreau matriarch. She drew in a ragged breath thinking about her mother, who'd turned her back on her when she'd divorced Jared. It still stung that her parents had believed his lies and fought her when she tried to tell them the truth.

"I wanted to make sure you know you're welcome here anytime. Not just because you're Renee's friend, though that's how it started." Ms. Patti patted her hand, and Tina almost jumped at her action. She hadn't been expecting it.

"Thank you. I've loved visiting your family and Shiloh Springs. You're lucky, it's a wonderful place to live."

Ms. Patti studied her with such an intensity she fought the urge to squirm beneath it. She'd hate to think she'd been weighed and found wanting, failing to measure up to the Boudreau standards.

"I'm not going to pry into your business, Tina. It's not my place. Just know, if you ever need anything—a soft place to land, a shoulder to cry on—I'll be here for you. I've raised a passel of young'uns, each one unique and different, seen them through some of the worst things imaginable, and I hope I helped them along the way. Lost a few too, who refused to accept help."

"Ms. Patti, I—"

"Hear me out. Since you're leaving, this is the only chance we'll have to talk alone." Tina met her straightforward gaze and read a depth of understanding and affection she hadn't expected.

"Okay."

"I have the feeling you've had a few rocky times in your life."

*You have no idea.*

"Don't worry, I'm not going to ask. Between you and," she paused, pointing toward the ceiling. "Just know this—if you need help, you pick up a phone and call me. Doesn't matter what time it is, day or night, I'm here for you. Douglas too, though he's a smart man and is letting me tell you."

Tina chuckled when Ms. Patti gave her a wink. "Tell him I appreciate it. I do. I just…have to get back to my job. My apartment." *My lousy life with no real friends because I'm never sure when Jared might show up.*

Ms. Patti pulled a piece of paper from her pocket and handed it to Tina. "Take this. It's a list of phone numbers. My cell. Douglas' number, too. Also the office number, where you can leave me a message if you can't get hold of me directly. I check in with them several times a day." She gave Tina a sheepish grin. "I also included everybody else's numbers too, because hey, you never know."

Tina felt tears welling up, and blinked rapidly in a vain effort to keep them from falling. When Ms. Patti pulled her into her arms and rubbed her back softly, the waterworks started flowing. Something broke inside her, and she couldn't stop crying. Sobbing, she allowed the gentle older woman to rock her gently, while whispering soothing words.

After what seemed like an eternity, she pulled back, rubbing her hands on her cheeks. What must Ms. Patti think of her, falling apart like that?

"Good. I'm sure you needed a good cry. You've kept so much bottled up inside, it's a wonder you hadn't exploded long before now, honey."

"I—how'd you know?"

Ms. Patti gave her a sympathetic smile. "It takes a survivor to recognize another one."

"You? I can't imagine Douglas—"

Her laughter stopped Tina's words cold. "Oh, sugar, Douglas has never laid a finger on me in anger, not from the minute I met him. It happened long before we met, and it's not something I like to talk about. I just wanted you to know you're not alone anymore. You've got friends who have your back."

Tina threw her arms around Ms. Patti and squeezed her tight. "Thank you."

"You're welcome. I'll let you get back to packing. I know you're planning on leaving early." With a brief smile, she walked out, leaving Tina sitting alone with her thoughts.

Chance pulled up in front of the Big House just before six. Though Shiloh volunteered to drive Tina to the airport, Chance felt like he should be the one to take her. Since he'd been the one responsible for making sure she got safely to Texas, it was up to him to ensure the trip back went just as smoothly.

Lights shone inside the house, and he knew Tina would be waiting for his brother. Surprise, she'd get him instead. After taking a week off work, he'd been busting his backside, catching up on the backlog of cases, and hadn't been able to spend as much time with her as he'd wanted. Plus, after reading the dossier Destiny complied, he had more than a few questions he wanted to ask. Maybe he shouldn't, because she was leaving, going back to her life in Portland. He couldn't help wondering how long she'd stay there, because if she followed true to her pattern, it wouldn't be long before she'd get another hit of wanderlust and move on to newer, more exciting things.

Climbing from behind the wheel, he took the steps two at a time, and walked inside. Momma was in the kitchen, and he smelled coffee, and if he wasn't mistaken, freshly baked cinnamon rolls.

"Morning, Momma." He pulled her in for a quick hug before reaching into the cupboard and grabbing a to-go mug. Filling it to the top, he added cream and took a big swallow. The warm burn going down was what he needed, and he smiled.

"Are you here for Tina? I thought Shiloh was driving her to the airport."

"Change of plans."

His mother eyed him, and he could almost see the wheels turning in her head. If he was right, he needed to nip that train of thought in the bud before it had a chance to take root. Momma playing matchmaker was the last thing he needed. Bachelorhood had its privileges, ones he intended to enjoy for several more years, if he had his druthers.

"She'll be down in a few minutes. I'm going to miss her. It's been nice having her around to keep Renee company. She's made Renee's transition easier. It had to be hard being dumped in the midst of a bunch of strangers, not knowing anybody and having them claim a familial bond. Tina helped her overcome that hurdle simply by her presence."

"Well, at least it's safe for her to go home now. I put out feelers among some of my associates, and it looks like Bruce left the country, just like he said. Nobody using his ID or passport has reentered the country, so she shouldn't have any worries about going back to her life in Portland."

*So, why does the thought of her leaving tug at me?*

She placed a plate with a large warm cinnamon roll in front of him and handed him a fork and napkin. Digging in, he wolfed the thing down in three bites. He had a sweet tooth a mile wide, and Momma knew the way to his heart. If he didn't work out religiously every day, he'd be too big to fit through the front door, but he wasn't about to turn down one of her treats. As a kid, before he came to live with Momma and Dad, he'd rarely gotten sweets of any sort. The minute she'd heard that, Momma had immediately commenced spoiling him, until he'd become a little pudgy around the middle. It took a while, but he'd learned moderation, and working out kept him in good physical shape and allowed him to indulge from time to time.

He stood up from the table and took his empty plate over to the sink. Before he could pick up the sponge, his momma swatted his hand, and took it from him. Holding up both empty hands in surrender, he dropped a kiss on top of her head.

"Good morning."

He spun around at Tina's soft greeting. Dressed in a pale sage green shirt and dark jeans, she placed a duffle on the floor and laid a black jacket on top. The color of the blouse brought out the green hue in her hazel eyes, and he couldn't help thinking how beautiful she looked. Dark hair framed her face, the ends curling under, her porcelain complexion tinted with a barely-there blush of pink in her cheeks.

"Morning, Tina. Come on in, I've got the coffee ready."

"Perfect. I'm dying for a cup." His momma waved her toward the kitchen table, but Tina ignored her, pouring her own cup and adding cream and sugar to it. Taking a sip, her eyelids lowered, she had an almost blissful appearance on her face. His breath caught in his chest as a wave of desire coursed through him. Though he couldn't put his finger on why he was so attracted to Tina, he also didn't try and deny what he felt. It was more than her simply being a beautiful woman. He'd dated his fair share of women over the years, including a former Miss Texas. None of them made his insides shiver the way a single glimpse of Tina Nelson did.

"Chance is going to drive you to the airport."

Her gaze met his briefly before glancing away. "I thought Shiloh was taking me."

"He was. Figured since I'm the one who brought you to Texas, the least I could do is see you safely on your way." *Liar. I want to spend what time she has left with her before she heads home, out of my life for good.*

"Oh. I'm ready when you are."

"It's probably a good idea to hit the road a little early anyway. Might run into a couple of stretches of ice after the storm last night. Shiloh Springs only got a light dusting of snow, but further north they had freezing rain."

"Any chance her flight might be canceled?" Momma wrapped up four of the cinnamon buns she'd baked. Guess she thought they'd be hungry on the road. Wasn't like he was going to let Tina starve in the couple hours it took to get to Dallas Fort Worth.

"I doubt it, but it couldn't hurt to check." He turned to Tina and added, "If you'll give me your flight information, I'll go online and check the status."

Walking back to her duffle, she pulled out her printed ticket information and handed it to him with a small smile.

"Thanks."

Striding into the living room, he could hear his momma and Tina talking softly, though he couldn't hear what they talked about. Pulling out his cell phone, he logged onto the internet and went straight to the airline's website. A quick check showed the plane was scheduled for departure on time. A small part of him wished it had been cancelled, so she'd have to stay another day.

Walking back into the kitchen, he handed Tina back her flight information, before turning to his mother. "I'll give you a call when we get to the airport."

"You be careful. Now I'm gonna worry about you driving on ice."

"It'll be fine, Momma. It's never as bad as they say, and I'm taking my truck. It's got four-wheel drive, not that I'm going to need it." He pulled her in for a brief hug. "Say your goodbyes. I'll take Tina's bag out to the car."

"I love you, son."

"Love you too, Momma."

He walked out the door, leaving his momma and Tina their few moments of privacy. They'd grown close in the short time Tina had stayed at the Big House, and he wanted to give them a chance to say a proper goodbye.

Climbing behind the wheel of his truck, really a fully tricked out SUV, he turned it on and blasted the heater, hoping it would warm up before Tina got in. He didn't want her to be uncomfortable.

A blast of chilly air flashed into the truck when Tina opened the door and slid onto the passenger seat. He watched her rub her hands against her upper arms briskly a couple of times before reaching around and clicking on her seatbelt. It would have been the gentlemanly thing to do, to get out of the car and help her in, but he didn't want to get an earful about how she was a grown woman and could do it herself. His lips quirked up as he pictured an exasperated look on her face. They'd already butted heads a couple of times when he'd arrived in Portland, because he was born and raised a Texas boy, and had been taught to treat ladies with respect. That meant opening doors for 'em and paying the check.

Tina wanted no part of the good old boy attitude and his antiquated ideals of chivalry, she'd informed him frostily the first time he'd done it, or when he'd held open the taxi door when they'd left for the airport. She hadn't been thrilled when he'd been the one to open the door for the room service waiter when they'd ordered dinner in the hotel room, though she hadn't put up too much of a fight then, after what happened with the mercenary earlier that day.

"Your mom is the best."

"She is one of the most amazing women I've ever met. You're lucky. She invited you into her inner circle of friends, which makes you practically a member of the family."

"Really?" Tina sat quietly, obviously contemplating his words. "Then I'm doubly honored. It's been nice, hanging out with a real family. It's been a long time since..." Her words trailed off.

"Don't you have family?" Chance asked the question softly, already knowing the answer. Destiny's report had been thorough.

"We've been—estranged—for years."

"That's too bad. Having family makes a world of difference in everyday life. I don't know what I'd do without Ms. Patti and Douglas. Might be willing to lose a few of my brothers, though."

Tina chuckled. "I don't believe that for an instant. You love every one of them."

Chance smiled, acknowledging the truth of her words. He kept his attention on the road in front of him; he didn't want to end up in a ditch before they ever made it to I-45. Piles of white slush lined both sides of the road, but they'd encountered no ice or even slick spots since leaving Shiloh Springs.

"Yeah, they're alright, but don't tell them that. It'll go to their heads, and I'll never hear the end of it."

They drove for another thirty minutes, and Chance turned onto the service road of I-45 heading north. Traffic wasn't too heavy, though it was moving a little slower than normal due to the road conditions. Occasional chunks of slush hit the windshield, thrown up by the cars in front of them, and he flicked on his wipers, clearing off the dirt-stained mess.

Tina swiveled in her seat as far as the seatbelt allowed, watching him. She'd been quiet for the last thirty miles or so.

He'd hoped the drive would lull her into feeling calm and maybe a bit serene before he hit her with his questions. Guess time was up.

"You don't like me much, do you?"

Startled at her blunt question, he glanced at her for long seconds before looking back at the road. "I like you."

She made a harrumph sound. "Something's different, though. Yesterday you were aloof, treating me almost like a stranger. This morning, you're all moody and broody, nothing like you were in Portland or even when I first got here. What happened to make you change your mind about me?" Abruptly, she straightened, the seatbelt pulling taut against her. "You had me checked out. Paid somebody to run a background check on me, because you don't trust me. That's it, isn't it? Were you afraid if you grilled me, I'd lie?"

"Wouldn't you?"

She sighed and leaned her head back against the headrest. "Probably. Guess it doesn't matter anymore. I'm going back to Portland, you'll head back to your fancy lawyer job, and we'll never see each other again."

"Tina—"

"Tell you what, counselor. Why don't we play a little game of twenty questions? You ask one and I'll answer truthfully. But you've got to do the same. Whatever I ask, you'll answer with the whole truth. Agreed?"

Without missing a beat, he quipped, "Agreed."

Tina's light chuckle filled the truck. "This is gonna be fun."

# CHAPTER THREE

Riding beside Chance in his SUV, she'd had a lot of time to study the man. He sat relaxed and confident behind the steering wheel, hands clasped loosely around it. Driving under the speed limit because of the conditions, she had the feeling he rarely exceeded it, even when it was bright and sunny. A total Boy Scout, that was Chance Boudreau. Described him to a T.

It stung that he'd had her investigated. While they weren't best buds or anything, she hadn't realized he distrusted her enough to dig into her background. Fortunately, most of it was hidden beneath layers of false information, thanks to Nico's savvy computer skills. Coincidence was a funny thing. She hadn't realized she'd ended up using the same guy Renee found to do her fake IDs. A few weeks after landing in Portland and after a few judicious and discreet inquiries, she'd run into Nico. He'd helped her lay a false trail, obscuring her real life and creating a brand new one, with a few extra bumps along the way, to make it look legit. There was no way Chance's computer guru was clever enough to wade through the layers Nico established—not unless they were a genius. Nico was just that good.

"First question. What's your real name?"

"Wow, going straight for the jugular, counselor?" Her lips quirked and she bit the bottom one to keep from laughing, because she'd been expecting him to dive in feet first. In the courtroom, he might try to put his witnesses at ease, but she didn't expect him to treat her with kid gloves. "I was born Christina Phillips, but I've always been called Tina."

Watching his face closely, she spotted the slight upward tug of his lips, which confirmed he already knew that information. Score one for Chance.

"My turn. What was your name, before it got changed to Boudreau?"

"Well, it's always been Chance. Only the last name changed. When I turned eighteen, I legally changed it to Boudreau. It's kind of a family tradition. Before that, it was Donovan. Why'd you leave California?"

Her eyes widened at his question. "Your investigator is pretty good. My parents and I had a…falling out…and it was best for everyone if I exited the picture."

"Want to elaborate?"

"Not really."

"Where'd you go after you left your parents?"

"I stayed in California because I was attending school and lived with my aunt and uncle. They're amazing and I adore them. Things have been a little rough the last few months. Uncle Stanley's had some health issues, and Aunt Maxie's been taking care of him." Thinking about the two people who'd stood by her when her life was falling apart gave her a twinge of homesickness. They'd been her rock when her whole world exploded, lending her their support and their love.

"Your turn. What made you choose to become a lawyer?"

A tinge of pink spread across his cheeks, and she realized he was embarrassed by the question. *Oh, boy, this is gonna be good.* Internally, she was rubbing her hands gleefully together, because if he refused to answer her question, she was off the hook and wouldn't have to answer any more of his.

"Well now, that's kind of a long, mostly boring, story. You sure you wouldn't rather ask a different question?"

"Counselor, if you refuse to answer the question, our game is over. I don't mind. I'll just lean back and take a nap. Of course, you'll never know if your dossier about little old me is accurate."

She gave an exaggerated stretch and shifted in her seat, getting comfortable. Either he'd spill his secret, or she'd get some quiet time without him prying into old wounds. Win-win.

Chance breathed out a long sigh and she thought she heard him mutter a curse beneath his breath. "It was about a year after I came to live on the ranch. I guess I was thirteen, maybe fourteen. Adjusting to living with new people, and a bunch of other guys as screwed up as I was, it wasn't easy. I'd never been much of an outgoing kid, definitely shy and introverted."

"You? Somehow I can't picture it."

"Do you want to hear this or not?"

"Absolutely. Please continue." She kept her tone light-hearted, because something deep in her gut told her things could take a very serious turn if she wasn't careful with her words.

"Anyway, it was summertime, and the temperatures were scorching. One hundred plus during the daytime, and still in the low nineties in the evenings. Hot enough it felt like your skin would peel off. Add in that I was at the stage where I hated everything and everybody, well, it was a recipe for trouble. I snuck out of the house late at night. Everybody was already in bed, and they didn't hear anything. Hightailed it down to the road, and a couple of guys from school picked me up."

"Thirteen or fourteen? Not old enough to drive."

"This is Texas, darlin'. We learn to drive right after we learn to walk. Working on a ranch or a farm, we drive tractors, ATVs, three-wheelers for hauling feed. If it had an engine and tires, I could drive it."

"Gotcha. So, these friends picked you up. Where'd you go?" Tina found herself immersed in his story, despite knowing he was only answering because of their little game of twenty questions. Didn't matter, he was telling her a small piece of the puzzle that was Chance Boudreau, and she found herself eager to hear more.

"We headed into town. Specifically, the local high school. Of course, it was locked up tight, but that wasn't a problem, we just climbed the fence and snuck in. I told you it was hotter than blazes, but we weren't there to swim." He chuckled and she found herself grinning, because she had an inkling he was about to impart some of what he'd called "mischief". "Jimmy and Henry had collected our bounty that afternoon. Now, remember, I was a kid, and kids do stupid stuff and think it's cool."

"I vaguely remember what it's like to be a teenager."

Chance shot her a look, his eyes heating as then skimmed her from head to toe and back again. "You weren't a teenage boy. We don't mature the way girls do. Me and my buddies were simply playing a prank. Nobody would get hurt, and we'd laugh our butts off. Like I said, we climbed the fence at the school, and headed straight for the water. Jimmy carried a pillowcase full of snakes."

Tina jolted upright at his word. "Snakes?"

"Yep. Nothing venomous, just rat snakes and grass snakes. Harmless. We thought it would be cool to dump them in the water and see what happened. Only, before we could toss them in, a security guard with a big flashlight caught us red-handed. Yelled for us to stop. Instead, Jimmy shoved the pillowcase in my hand and he and Henry took off running, leaving me holding the bag."

Tina covered her mouth with both hands, holding back her laughter. She could picture this towheaded teenager with big baby blue eyes standing there like a deer caught in the headlights as the security guard was bearing down on him, while his buddies left him high and dry.

"Did he call the cops?"

"Worse. He called Momma."

"Oh, dear."

His shoulders shook with his own suppressed laughter, and she couldn't hold back any longer. It spilled from her, a deep belly laugh and he joined in. Wiping at her eyes, she brushed away the tears.

"Well, don't stop there. Tell me what Ms. Patti did."

"That one hour waiting for her to drive into town was the longest one of my life. I accidentally dropped the bag and all the snakes got loose anyway, slithering all over the cement, and some of 'em got into the water. Others made a mad dash for freedom through the chain-link fence. Anybody watching me and this poor security guard chasing after those little buggers would've thought they were watching an old vaudeville routine. I grabbed hold of one, lost my balance, and fell into the pool headfirst."

She jerked forward, the seatbelt stretched taut across her chest when he slammed on the brakes at the snarl of traffic, which had slowed down to a slow crawl. Red brake lights flashed in every lane, a stark highlight in the gloomy gray morning.

"Sorry. I should've paid closer attention."

"Not your fault. Blame the weather. Besides, nobody got hurt, so it's all good." She gave him a smile, letting him know everything was okay. Honestly, she was having fun hearing about his boyhood adventure. Besides killing time, it gave her a glimpse into the man Chance Boudreau was, and how he'd become the person who was liked and respected by everyone in Shiloh Springs.

"We've got a while to go yet. Do you need more coffee or anything? I can pull over and hit a drive-thru."

"I'm good. Plus, we've got the cinnamon rolls your mother sent if you get hungry. So, tell me what Ms. Patti did when she got to the pool?"

"That's just it. She didn't do anything. She spoke to the security guard for a few minutes, and then turned to me. I waited for her to explode. Anybody else would have, being called at one o'clock in the morning, yanked from their bed to come fetch their kid for breaking the law. I expected her to yell or scream or hit me. Something. Instead, she simply said let's go home and walked toward the car. There was complete silence on the drive home. I think I'd rather she yelled. I kept wondering if this would be the thing to make them send me away. In the back of my mind, I also anticipated being put back into the system. It's part of the welfare mindset. You go into a foster home, stay a couple months, end up back in the system, and the cycle repeats until you turn eighteen, then you're out on the streets on your keister."

"I can't picture Ms. Patti or Douglas doing anything of the sort. They'd never turn their backs on their kids."

"Ah, but you're looking at it through the eyes of an adult. I was a snot-nosed punk who didn't have a lot of friends. I was short, pudgy, and sullen. Nobody'd ever wanted me around, and I kept waiting for the inevitable."

Tina reached across the space dividing them and touched his arm softly. The rock-hard muscle beneath her hands didn't surprise her; she'd seen him almost naked that day in her hotel room when Bruce managed to get in. He was a hot, yummy, off-limits package she couldn't afford to get involved with. Caring about someone led to heartbreak.

"What happened?"

"She pulled up in front of the Big House and cut the engine. The entire way home, she hadn't said a word, but her disappointment was thick enough it almost choked me. She hadn't even looked in my direction once we got in the car. I thought she couldn't bear to be around me. I jumped out of the car and raced into the house, only to find Douglas waiting for me. The look of sadness on his face nearly did me in. I swear, I'd rather one of them beat on me than see how much I'd let them down. I hadn't realized until then how much I'd grown to love them, and now I'd broken their trust. It opened my eyes in a lot of ways that night."

"Did Douglas punish you?"

"No. They sent me to bed. No yelling about how I shouldn't have snuck out, or how I'd broken the law. No condemnation of hurting their standing in the community. I'd done something awful, and their silent disapproval was worse than any punishment. I laid awake all night. I thought about packing, because I'd convinced myself they'd be calling Child Protective Services in the morning, to come and get me. Except I was afraid Brody would wake up. We shared a room and I was already in enough trouble. I didn't need my brother piling on more guilt."

"Obviously they didn't call CPS, because you're still a part of their family. You're a Boudreau."

"The next morning, we drove into town, straight to the sheriff's office. Talk about scared; I was petrified. I swear I almost peed my pants. They could've thrown me into juvie, and there wasn't a thing I could do about it."

She shook her head, her soft gaze studying him. "It's impossible to imaging Ms. Patti or Douglas doing anything like that."

"Remember, I was just an arrogant jerk with an attitude and I felt like I deserved anything they threw at me."

He breathed out a long sigh, his gut clenching with the memory of that morning. Scared spitless, he'd huddled in the back seat. Shaking like a leaf, he'd wanted to pretend he was a big man, that he wasn't afraid of anything they threw his way, which couldn't be farther from the truth. Sometime during the long, sleepless night, something inside him shattered, leaving him with the realization he didn't want to leave. The Big House had become a sanctuary, a place where he finally felt at peace. And he'd tossed it all away with a stupid prank.

"Adolescence and puberty are rough, especially when you don't have an anchor, something to cling to."

He gently eased up on the accelerator as the brake lights ahead flashed on, like strobe lights in an uneven pattern. Tightening his grip on the wheel, he couldn't help wondering how their conversation had gone from a teasing game of twenty questions into a revelation of his youthful indiscretion.

"You can't leave me hanging, counselor. What happened when you got to the sheriff's office?"

"That's a story for another day. Whose turn is it now?"

"Hmm, I guess since you shared an embarrassing incident, it's mine. Hit me with your next question."

Before he could frame one, he glanced in the side mirror, some instinct pulling his attention to the cars behind him. A dark red sedan sped northbound on I-45, water from the asphalt spewing from beneath its wheels. Idiot was driving way too fast for the conditions, but then there was usually one who thought they were invincible and didn't give a thought to other people's safety. Not sure why, he moved over one lane to the right, putting a little distance between and the moron coming up fast.

"Chance?"

"Hang on, Tina. I want to let this guy—"

The sharp impact threw Chance forward, the abrupt

jarring jerking his head forward. From the side of his vision, he saw the seatbelt pull taut across Tina's chest before she slammed back against the seat. The truck skidded on the slick road, and he steered into the slide, wrestling with the wheel, his foot off the accelerator. He knew better than to slam on his brakes, that was a sure path to disaster.

Guess they weren't going to make it to the airport after all.

# CHAPTER FOUR

Chance grappled with the steering wheel, hands wrapped around it tight, trying to stay on the asphalt, reeling from the impact from the other vehicle. The jolt rocked the truck, and he grimaced as he wrestled the steering wheel, trying to keep them on the road. The outside tires skidded against the rocks and grass lining the sides of the interstate. Piles of slush and ice flew up as the truck hit a slick patch of ice and started to slide. With a jerk of the wheel to the left, he managed to get them back onto the highway, though he knew they weren't out of the woods yet. Horns honked as people sped past him, and he wondered what crackerjack box they got their driver's license from, because they'd obviously never been through an actual DMV test.

Tina jerked forward, her body stopped by the seatbelt, and she grabbed onto the handle above the passenger door, righting herself. She stared at him, her eyes wide. The breath soughed in and out of her chest, and he wished he could pull her into his arms and comfort her.

"Hang on, honey."

"Somebody hit us." Her words were colored with shock,

but overriding her voice was the sound of screeching brakes all around him. The odds of staying on the interstate were slim to none, with brake lights flaring to life ahead of him, as cars swerved around haphazardly like balls in an old-fashioned pinball machine. He struggled to keep from ramming into their fellow motorists.

Before he could answer her, a second car plowed into the rear of the truck, sending them spinning and skidding, and Chance slammed his foot on the brake, turning into the direction of the skid. Without control, they spun once, twice, before leaving the asphalt completely, tumbling down the drainage ditch on the side of the highway, before coming to a halt nose first, pointing away from the roadway.

The truck jolted to a halt, and Chance threw the gear into park before rubbing his shaking hands across his face. His heartbeat raced, his head spinning with the thought of just how close they'd come to disaster. Drawing in a deep breath, he exhaled slowly and turned to face Tina.

"Are you okay?"

Face pale, she gave a shaky nod. "That was some amazing driving, Mr. Boudreau."

"I need to get out and see how bad the damage is. Stay here, I'll be right back."

"How about I call nine-one-one while you do?" She pointed toward the front, looking through the windshield. "Looks like a couple other people spun out, too. We're going to need tow trucks and maybe ambulances."

"Good idea." Pulling out his cell phone, he handed it to her, wincing at the pulled muscles in his shoulder. He vaguely remembered hitting it against the driver's door when the first car hit them. It didn't feel like it was dislocated, but he had a feeling he was going to be bruised.

"Are you injured?" Chance's eyes moved over every inch of her, studying her intently, hoping against hope she hadn't been hurt. Luckily, she'd been wearing her seatbelt, or things might have been a whole lot worse.

"I'm good. A little shaky, because of a big old jolt of adrenaline, but other than that, I'm okay."

"Good."

His door opened easily enough, and he climbed from behind the steering wheel, groaning when he looked at the front panel. Where the other driver hit him, the frame was bent and pushed in, with a sharp jagged edge embedded into the tire, which was now flat. Walking around the truck, the passenger side seemed undamaged, but the rear of the truck had a large impact area, where the bumper hung off the right side completely, dragging along the ground. The left side of the rear door was pushed in. No opening that without a pry bar. Fortunately, the glass was intact, since it was freezing outside. In the mid-thirties when he'd left the Big House, the temps hadn't climbed much, and the sun was playing peekaboo with big, fluffy, gray-tinged clouds.

Shaking his head, he climbed back into the driver's seat, and pulled the door shut, noting a hairline crack in the glass.

He hoped it held until help came, otherwise, it was going to get cold pretty darn quick.

"Did you get through to nine-one-one?"

She nodded and handed him back the cell phone. "Yes. They're sending first responders as quick as they can, but we're not the only accident. Everyone's backed up dealing with traffic messes up and down I-45."

"Guess you're not going to make your flight."

"Looks that way. On the plus side, neither of us is hurt." She pointed toward the three other cars. "Think we should check on them, see if they need help?"

"That's what I'm fixing to do. I only came back to give you a head's up and grab my coat."

"I'll go with—"

"No, you stay here. It's too cold for you to be out there without a jacket. Sit tight, and I'll be back as quick as I can."

The look she shot him clued him in to the fact she wasn't about to stay in the warm SUV, at least not without an argument, and he didn't have time for that. He hoped nobody needed medical assistance, but he had rudimentary knowledge after living with Brody most of his life. Having a firefighter and EMT for a brother meant every member of the family ended up taking CPR and keeping their certifications current.

"I'm going with you. A little cold isn't going to hurt me. The least we can do is make sure everybody's as comfortable as possible until the first responders get here." She flung the passenger door open and climbed down, her feet hitting the grass before he made it around the truck.

"Put this on." He held out his heavy coat, and she started to shake her head. Giving her a don't-argue-with-me stare, she simply turned and slid her arms into the sleeves. He grinned when she pulled it close around her, the large garment swallowing her smaller frame. It reminded him of a little girl playing dress up in an adult's clothing, with the sleeves hanging past her hands. Grabbing the lapels, he pulled her close and pressed a quick kiss against her lips before he could stop himself.

The feel of her lips beneath his felt like being struck by lightning. A quick jolt sped through him, lighting him from the inside. The sweetness of her mouth against his was a taste of paradise. Nothing else mattered except pulling Tina into his arms and losing himself in her kiss.

The sound of screeching brakes pulled him back, and reluctantly he broke the kiss and took a step back. Tina raised a hand to her mouth, pressing her fingers against her lips, her eyes huge. And he felt like an idiot for having forgotten where he was and what he should be doing.

"Chance—"

"Let's go."

Without another word, he started toward the closest vehicle, a sedan that had landed up against the side of a pickup truck. The wailing of an infant broke through the traffic sounds, and he sprinted forward, and looked through the driver's side window. Two women sat in the front seats, appearing shaken. A trail of blood trickled down the driver's forehead. She didn't notice him, and he tapped lightly on her window. She turned toward him, and he motioned for her to lower her window, which she did. The other woman attempted to climb between the bucket seats, and he noted the passenger door was dented inward, and the car rested cattycorner against the truck. In the backseat, the baby's cries grew louder. He noted the child seat securely attached to the back seat, which was a blessing.

"Everybody okay in there?" He watched Tina attempt to open the car's back door, but it didn't budge. "Ma'am, can you unlock the doors so we can check on the little one?"

When she blinked at him without moving, he stuck his hand through the open window and hit the door locks, heard the click as they disengaged. Tina pulled the door open and motioned for the woman climbing the seat to stay where she was.

"Does anybody need medical assistance? We've already called for tow trucks and ambulances if you need help."

"I think we're okay. Somebody hit us and we skidded on the ice. Emma, is the baby okay?"

"He looks like he's fine," Tina smiled as she reassured the woman. "He's a real cutie pie. What's his name?"

"Russell, but we call him Russ."

"That's a great name." He watched Tina unbuckle the child from the child seat and scoot across the back before handing him the infant. Holding the child carefully, he did a quick cursory check, and the baby smiled at him. He found himself returning his smile, thankful the little boy appeared to have weathered the incident without injury. Easing his torso through the open window, he handed the child to the woman in the passenger seat, who clutched him to her chest, tears running down her face.

"Thank you! Bless you both." She rained kisses against Russ' cheeks. "I was so scared when I couldn't get the door open."

"We'll send somebody back to check on you. Honk if something happens. I need to check on the driver of the pickup."

Chance moved around the sedan and headed for the pickup. An older man in a tan-colored cowboy hat grimaced in the driver's seat, his lips clenched in obvious pain. Looked like he was the lone person in the cab of the truck, thank goodness, Chance thought. He watched Tina move past him, and she pointed to the SUV about fifteen feet further away. With a nod, he let her go, knowing the older man needed help.

"How badly are you hurt?"

The guy shook his head. "Think my leg's broken."

"Already called nine-one-one. EMTs and ambulances are on the way. Think you can hold out until they get here?

He nodded again, pointing a shaking hand toward the SUV. "Go, help your lady. I saw that SUV flip over once. It landed upright, but I'm not sure how bad they're hurt."

"Honk if you need me."

Chance sprinted toward Tina and watched her disappear into the back of the SUV. She left the rear door open, and he couldn't see what she was doing until he got closer. Stopping beside the driver's window, he noted the driver was out cold, but a young woman lay sprawled across the back seat. Tina kneeled at her feet, running her hand along the woman's legs, and she screamed.

"I think her hip's broken or dislocated. She's holding her arm at an odd angle, too. Could be it's broken or badly sprained."

"It's...definitely...broken. Heard it snap when it hit the window." Her face screwed up at the pain when she tried to move."

"Shh. Stay still. Ambulances and help are coming. Hang in there. Who is the driver? Do you know how badly he's hurt?"

The girl shook her head. "He's my dad. We were driving up to Fort Worth. I had a dance competition, and we were going up a day early so we could meet up with some friends. He had his seatbelt on, but he hit his chest pretty hard on the steering wheel."

The whining sound of sirens grew louder, and Chance looked up, seeing the flashing lights coming up along the side of the highway, riding the passing lane on the outside. Traffic was at a standstill, backed up as far as he could see, nobody moving aside to allow the EMTs and ambulances through, forcing them to ride the side of the road.

Within minutes, first responders were swarming all over the scene. Chance updated them on each vehicle, and the condition of each person. He wanted them to look at Tina, worried she was hurt and hiding it, helping others and not worrying about herself. Once the madness cleared, he'd insist she get checked out.

"Looks like we're not getting to the airport any time soon." Tina moved to his side and slid her hand in his, twining their fingers together. With a sigh, she leaned her head against his shoulder. Surprised, yet pleased, he gently squeezed her hand.

"Not today anyway. I should probably call one of my brothers to come and pick us up, because the truck's useless. It'll have to be towed."

"Yeah, I figured that as soon as I saw the front end. Go ahead and make the call."

When she tried to pull her hand free, he tightened his grip on her, refusing to let go. He liked having her close, feeling her hand within his. In the midst of all the chaos, holding onto her felt like a lifeline, keeping him anchored.

She handed him back his cell phone, pulling it out of the coat's voluminous pocket. Gripping the phone, he stopped, trying to decide which brother would be the closest. As much as he hated it, he'd have to call Dane, since he was at the ranch, which made him almost an hour closer than anyone else. Pressing his brother's speed dial, he waited.

"Hello."

"Hey, Dane."

"Chance, thought you were on your way to DFW."

"Change in plans. We got into a fender-bender. Somebody skidded on ice and hit us. Well, technically, two people hit us, and we ended up on the side of I-45."

He heard Dane's gasp of surprise. "Are you and Tina okay? Do I need to call nine-one-one?"

"Thanks, but that's all handled. EMTs and ambulances are already on the scene. We're both okay. But we're going to need somebody to come and get us, because the truck's not drivable. I figured you'd be the best one to call, since you're closest."

"Tell me where you are. I'm on my way."

Chance felt the tension in his shoulders immediately ease. He felt better knowing his brother wouldn't let him down. Tina needed to get out of this mess and get someplace safe and warm. Meeting her eyes, he smiled, trying to convey that everything was going to be okay. Even if part of him was secretly glad she'd have to stick around, at least for a little while.

"About an hour north of Shiloh Springs. You can't miss it; traffic's backed up at least a mile, maybe more. When you get close, you might want to exit and come up the service road. It'll probably be swamped too, but it'll be moving. I'm not sure how long it'll take to clear up this mess."

"Gotcha. Be there as soon as I can." Dane disconnected without saying goodbye, but that didn't surprise Chance. He was probably halfway to his truck already.

"Dane's leaving the ranch now. He'll be here as soon as he can. I need to call Frank's Garage, and see if they'll send the tow truck to pick up my truck. Why don't you go and sit in it, and get out of this wind? You've got to be freezing."

"I will, but only if you take your coat back." She started to shrug out of it, but he put a hand on her arm, stopping her.

"Keep it on. I'm going to make the call, then check to see if there's anything I can do to help. Then I'll come back and sit with you." Pulling her close, he dropped a kiss against the top of her head.

He watched her climb back into the truck before dialing Frank's Garage. Frank Jennings was an institution in Shiloh Springs, owning and operating the town's garage for decades. All his brothers took their cars to Frank. There wasn't anything the man didn't know about cars or trucks, all their inner workings, and he trusted his baby in Frank's hands.

"Frank's Garage, Dante speaking."

Chance grinned at the other's voice. Dante Monroe was Jill's brother, one who'd had a bit of a checkered past, but had gotten his life back on the straight and narrow. He'd worked with Lucas, telling his story about illegal gambling in Texas, because he had first-hand knowledge about how devastating falling into the twisted net of gambling could be, and how despicably far-reaching its insidious tendrils could be.

"Hey, Dante, it's Chance. Listen, I got involved in an accident on I-45, and the truck's undrivable. Think you or Frank could come and tow it back to the garage? Dane's on his way to pick me up, but I don't trust anybody else to take care of me except for Frank's."

"Hang on a second." Chance pulled the phone away from his ear when he heard Dante yelling, "Hey, Frank, Chance Boudreau needs a tow, up on I-45. His truck ain't drivable. Want me to pick him up?"

Within seconds, he was back. "Frank said he'll come pick it up. Tell me where you are."

Chance gave him directions, along with the closet mile marker. He'd got that information from the ambulance driver he'd spoken to earlier. Holding the phone to his ear with one hand, he rubbed at his forehead, grimacing at the headache pounding behind his eyes. Great. The last thing he needed to make this day perfect—a migraine.

"Alright, my man, Frank will be there as soon as he can. If he runs into any trouble, he's got your number."

"Thanks, Dante."

"No problem. Stay safe and warm."

Disconnecting the call, he walked back to his truck and climbed behind the wheel and looked at Tina. She was curled up on the seat, facing him, her eyes closed, a tiny smile turning up the corners of her lips. How was it possible every time he looked at her, she seemed even more beautiful? He didn't need nor was he looking for a woman in his life. While most of his brothers had found their soulmates and were engaged, or in Brody's case married, Chance wasn't ready for a commitment. He had plans for his life, his career, and it didn't call for getting serious about a wife for several more years.

But when he looked at Tina, he wanted to toss all his good intentions out the window. See where things would go if he decided to explore his feelings for her. Would it lead to heartbreak, leaving him gutted and alone? Or would it lead to something like his momma and dad had, a sharing of their lives and souls that surpassed romantic expectations?

"Did you talk to the garage?" The husky edge in her voice made his breath catch.

"Yeah, Frank's on the way. Dane will probably get here first. Frank will recognize the truck, and he knows what to do. We'll be back at the ranch before you know it." He started to turn toward her and felt the pulling in his shoulder. Yep, he definitely would end up bruised before the end of the day.

"I'd feel better if you'd let one of the EMTs check you out, make sure you're okay."

Tina shook her head, her lips tight in a stubborn line. "I'm fine, but I don't think you can say the same. I've noticed you favoring your left side. Did you hurt your shoulder?"

"It's nothing." She made a scoffing sound, and he chuckled. For a second, she sounded just like his baby sister, Nica. "I promise, I'm fine. Maybe a couple of bruises, that's all."

"Right, counselor." She sighed and leaned her head against the headrest. "Everything's been so crazy. This is like the cherry on top my crazy sundae."

"Want to talk about it?"

"Nope." She gave him a cheeky grin. "Gotta have some secrets, counselor. Otherwise, where's the fun?"

"You do realize you're making me want to dig deeper, find out what makes you so unique?"

"Dig all you want to. There's nothing to find. I'm pretty much an open book."

He quirked a brow and she laughed, the joyous sound filling the truck's interior. The happy sound brightened his mood, making him almost forget he needed to figure out all the intriguing secrets that made Tina Nelson tick. He doubted she was dangerous, at least not intentionally. But some instinct, that inner warrior who awoke whenever he sensed something wasn't quite right, stirred deep within, and he knew there was more to the quirky brunette than just a coffee shop java slinger.

Good thing she'd be sticking around for a little while longer, because he felt an overwhelming need to keep her close. There was a lot more he needed to know, to not only satisfy his curiosity but to keep those he loved safe. Even if it broke his heart.

# CHAPTER FIVE

Tina smiled when Dane pulled up at the medical clinic and parked his truck. Chance sat beside her, his muscular arms crossed over his chest, the perpetual scowl decorating his face. She wanted to laugh when Dane refused to take them to the ranch, instead bypassing it and heading into town.

"I don't need to see a doctor. My shoulder's fine."

"And I'll believe that when Doc Jennings gives you a once over and takes x-rays. Stubborn goat."

"Jackass," Chance shot back.

"Sissy." Dane grinned when his brother tossed the insult back at him. He looked at Tina. "You see the thanks I get? It took me two hours to reach y'all, and does he appreciate it? Nope. Idiot thinks he's the boss of me."

"I'll show you who's boss—"

"Yeah, yeah. You're not the one who'd have to answer to Momma if I brought you home hurt. Why don't I give her a call and let you talk to her?"

Chance leaned his head back and banged it against the headrest several times. "Fine, you win. I'll let Doc Jennings take a look, but I'm telling you there's nothing wrong except some bruising."

"And if that's the case, we'll be in and out and on our way back to the ranch in no time. Look, bro, you know as well as I do, sometimes you get caught up in the middle of all the excitement and the adrenaline rush, and you're hurt worse than you think. I'd rather not take the chance, if it's all the same to you."

"Please, Chance, let the doctor make sure you haven't injured your shoulder." Tina reached over and laid her hand on his thigh. She'd ended up in the middle of the truck's cab between the two larger men, and had listened to their light banter all the way back to Shiloh Springs. It was obvious the two brothers not only cared for each other, but they were charming, keeping her entertained all through the hour plus drive back to Shiloh Springs.

The ambulances had loaded their patients and left the scene of the accident by the time Dane had shown up to rescue them. Frank's tow truck pulled up behind Dane's truck within minutes of his arrival, and she'd stood by watching as the truck was hooked up to the big red tow truck and rolled away.

It hadn't taken Dane long to notice Chance favoring his left shoulder. She'd shifted to sit far enough away she didn't keep bumping into him with every jolt, but she'd watched Chance's face, the clenched jaw doing nothing to mask the fact he was in pain.

Dane parked the car in front of the clinic, and Chance stepped out and turned, holding his hand out to Tina. She hesitated, thinking maybe she'd sit in Dane's truck and wait while he got checked out. There was something about visiting a doctor with somebody else that felt so…intimate.

"Come on, sugar, if I've gotta let Doc Jennings poke and prod, the least you can do is hold my hand."

Placing her hand within his, she climbed out of the truck and they headed inside. Dane jogged past them and opened the clinic's front door, and they stepped through. A wash of heat spread across her skin and Tina sighed. She hadn't realized how chilled she'd gotten. Dane had run the heat inside the cab of the truck, but it wasn't the same as walking into a warm building.

"Hey, Julie, is Doc Jennings around? Chance banged up his shoulder and needs to get it looked at."

A pretty thirty-something blonde smiled at Dane, her brown eyes giving him that all-over look that a woman gives a man she finds attractive. She couldn't blame her. Dane Boudreau was a handsome man, with rugged good lucks and a muscular build that his Carhartt jacket did nothing to hide. Julie obviously liked what she saw, because she gave him a come-hither smile and sat a little bit straighter, displaying her not-inconsiderable assets to their best advantage.

"Hi, Dane. Doc Jennings isn't in today. Doctor Stevens is covering. Why don't y'all have a seat in the waiting area, and I'll let him know you're here."

"Thanks." Giving her a flirtatious wink, Dane turned and motioned toward the row of chairs to the right of the reception desk. Within minutes a tall, dark-haired man came from the back, an air of confidence and competence surrounding him like a cloak. In his early to mid-thirties, he carried himself with an aura of strength and self-assurance that made Tina immediately trust him.

"Chance, Julie said you injured your shoulder. What happened?"

"Car accident. I banged it on the door. It's nothing."

Doctor Stevens grinned. "Let me be the judge of that. Come with me and let's get an x-ray, so we've got a better idea of what we're dealing with."

Chance turned to her. "I'll be right back. If you need anything, Dane will take care of you."

"No problem, bro. Go get your shoulder fixed."

Chance followed Doctor Stevens into the back, and Tina took a deep breath, letting it out slowly. "Is he always this stubborn?"

Dane chuckled. "You have no idea."

They sat quietly for a few minutes, and Tina nibbled on her index fingernail, hoping Chance's shoulder issue wasn't serious. She felt guilty, because if he hadn't been driving her to the airport, he wouldn't have gotten hurt.

"Stop it."

"What?" Looking at Dane, she watched his disapproving stare morph into sympathy.

0

"You've got nothing to feel guilty about. You didn't cause the cold snap that moved through. Happens at least once each winter, we get some snow, maybe some ice. It's here and gone in a day or two. Chance volunteered to drive you to the airport. You ask me, he wanted to spend more time with you before you went back to Portland."

Tina shook her head, the soft locks brushing against her chin. She knew she was due for a haircut, but with everything happening, first with Renee and then with her attack, personal fashion choices took a back seat.

"You're wrong. Chance probably thinks I'm his responsibility since he's the one who brought me to Shiloh Springs. I bet he can't wait to see my plane heading west."

"You're a smart cookie, Tina. That's one of the things I like about you. But it seems like when it comes to Chance, you're blind. If he didn't care about you, he'd have let me drive you to the airport. I offered, and he shot me down almost before the words came out of my mouth."

"Like I said, he feels responsible for me."

She looked up when she saw Julie sit down behind the reception desk. Worry about Chance had her antsy and she barely refrained from getting up and pacing in the waiting room. Ah, to heck with it. Standing, she walked over to the desk.

"Julie, how's Chance?"

The other woman looked at her, narrowing her eyes before answering. "I'm sorry, miss, but I'm afraid I can't give you any information unless you're family." Her smirk clearly indicated she knew Tina wasn't, and her hand itched to smack that smirk right off her overly-peroxided head.

"No, but you can tell me, Julie. I *am* family." Dane's deep voice sounded from behind her, his tone indicating he wasn't about to take any nonsense from the snippy woman.

She heaved a put-upon sigh, shooting Tina one of those girl-you're-getting-on-my-last-nerve looks before answering Dane. "Doctor Stevens is with him in the exam room right now. The x-rays didn't show anything broken. That's all I know. You'll have to wait to speak with the doc."

Dane's hand on her elbow steered Tina back to her chair, his grip tight enough she knew he wasn't brooking any protest. Flinging herself down on the hard plastic, she bit back a complaint about how uncomfortable it was. She wasn't really upset about the clinic's furniture; she'd just be venting because she hated feeling useless. She wanted to march into the exam room and demand to see the x-ray for herself. Reading an x-ray would be like riding a bike; she'd seen hundreds of them before Jared ruined her life and her career.

"It's good news. He didn't break anything."

"I know." She smiled at Dane. "I'm afraid I'm not a patient person. I'm all about instant gratification."

"Well, hang in there. They're probably almost done, and then we can head back to the ranch. Momma's going to go nuts when she finds out one of her chicks is hurt. She's a big mother hen, wanting—no—needing her babies hale and healthy. Don't be surprised if she spoils him rotten. And don't take it personally, because she's likely going to pamper him and baby him, because that's what she does. She'll fuss at him for getting in the accident, even if it wasn't his fault. Next, she'll blame herself. Yeah, I know it's ridiculous, but she's Momma. Then she'll cook. It's what she does whenever any of my brothers gets a booboo."

"It's a mother's job to take care of her child when they're sick or hurt. I'd do the same." Biting back a sigh, Tina sat back and settled in to wait for Chance.

"Sweetheart, has there been any word?"

Jared's jaw tightened at the saccharine-sweet voice of his mother on the other end of the cell phone. More and more she'd taken to calling, inquiring about Christina. Closing his eyes, he counted to ten before answering her.

"Nothing yet, Mother. I talked with her aunt again, and she claims she hasn't heard from Christina. Of course, I don't believe her. I contacted my man at the assistant district attorney's office, and he's going to have her phone calls monitored."

"Is it possible Christina hasn't been in touch with her family? She always seemed so close to her aunt and uncle."

"Trust me, there's no way my wife hasn't been in touch

with her aunt and uncle. They know where she is, or at least how to get in touch with her. I'm not giving up. I know she left California several months ago, headed north. Knowing her, she'll head for a big city. It's easy to hide and get lost where there are lots of people. Strangers in small towns attract too much attention."

"Of course, honey, you're right. I want her brought back home. She needs to admit to all those lies she told about you. Of course, I'm not surprised nobody believed her. Who would believe you'd raise a hand to your wife? You adored Christina, worshipped the ground she walked on. You are a saint to want to take her back after all the trouble she caused."

"Mother, we've been over this. Christina has problems. She needs professional help. Her psychiatrist is worried because he doesn't believe she's taking her medication. If she's not, she could become manic—"

"She's dangerous and she's a liar. It's a good thing she's not a very good liar, or people might actually have believed her falsehoods about you abusing her."

A wash of rage surged through Jared at the reminder. Christina had a lot to answer for once he caught up with her, including having the insane idea of divorcing him. Unforgivable, and he'd make sure she learned the folly of her actions. His hand squeezed his cell phone tighter.

"It's part of her illness, Mother. When I find her, I'll make sure she gets the help she needs. She'll realize her delusions are simply that—delusions. Getting back on her meds will make things right."

Jared almost laughed at the whopper he told his mother. He'd embellished it over the months since Christina skuttled away in the dark of night, disappearing without a trace. The year and a half before she left him had been a nightmare, trying to diffuse all the ugliness she'd spewed to her attorney, who'd found a sympathetic judge willing to grant her a divorce. Another strike against her that she'd pay for when he brought her back home. His hands itched to administer the discipline Christina desperately needed to turn her back into a dutiful and loving wife.

"How are your sessions going, darling? All this nonsense about you having anger issues. Poppycock. There's never been a more even-tempered and loving child than you. I cannot believe the courts mandated counseling. Your father hasn't been able to get in touch with Congressman Rayburn yet, but once he does, he'll rain down a world of hurt on those idiots who've listened to your wife's lies."

"I've been going to the mandated sessions. The courts need to see that I'm doing everything they've asked. It'll make things easier when I have to prove that Christina's accusations were inventions of a fevered imagination and she's the one in need of professional help. Have patience, Mother, this won't last long. Christina will be back, tell everyone she made all her allegations up, that they were fabricated, and things will go back to normal."

*Another thing my loving wife will pay for. Idiot judge, thinking I need counseling for anger issues.*

"How are things at the hospital, dear?"

"Returning to normal. I've had all privileges reinstated and my record expunged. All Christina's falsehoods and lies were erased after a thorough investigation proved her allegations false. No one believes I'd ever raise a hand to my wife. The gossip has died down, although it's hard to believe the rumors swirled throughout the hospital for so long. Of course, the people Christina worked with refuse to believe she lied. Misguided loyalty from a few of her diehard friends, but Human Resources quashed it."

"Excellent. You're an excellent surgeon, the best that hospital has ever seen. I cannot believe they'd allow the ravings of a lunatic to ruin your career."

"Mother! Do not call Christina by that offensive label. She's got a disease that causes her mental issues. I love her and I'll do whatever it takes to get her back."

"I know, dear. She's a lucky woman to have someone as special as you love her. Sometimes I think you're too forgiving."

"She's special, Mother. She owns my heart and always will. I just need to make sure she understands her place, and everything will be fine."

"Well, keep me posted, and let me know if you need anything. Your father and I will support you with whatever you need. Anything you need, consider it done."

"Thank you, Mother. I'll talk to you soon."

Disconnecting the call, he placed the cell phone on his desk and leaned back in his big leather chair. The sounds of the hustle and bustle of the hospital activity drifted through the open door of his office, and he studied the shining placard affixed to it. Jared Webster, MD, Chief of Surgery. He'd clawed his way through the ranks at med school, forgoing a social life to maintain his grades, though it had been a struggle. While he was a magician with a scalpel, doing the class work wasn't his strong suit, and meeting Christina Nelson had been like a light shining down from the heavens. She'd been better than a tutor, doing his homework, drilling him until the facts and figures stuck in his brain, and helping him ace his tests. The intellect shining in her eyes was the first thing that made him fall for her. Fall hard. And he'd won her, too.

Balling his hands into fists, he contemplated what he'd do when he finally found her again, stood across from her face to face. Images of his revenge played through his mind, and he smiled.

He couldn't wait.

# CHAPTER SIX

C hance winced when Dane's pickup hit a rut in the drive. Doc Stevens assured him neither his shoulder nor his arm was broken, but that didn't mean they didn't hurt. Discoloration had already started. Probably by this time tomorrow, he'd look like a kid's birthday pinata. One that had already been pounded a few too many times.

He barely stifled a groan when he spotted not only his mother's white Cadillac Escalade parked in front of the Big House, but also his dad's truck. And if he wasn't mistaken, Antonio's brand-new Lexus was parked right beside it. Great, he'd have an audience to his misery.

"What's Antonio doing here?"

"No clue. Wasn't here when I left to come get you." Dane expertly pulled up beside his mother's car and shifted into park. At the clinic, Tina had peppered Doc Stevens with a hundred questions, everything from his x-ray results to his aftercare instructions and the name of the painkiller he'd prescribed. Once he got over the shock of hearing 'doc speak' coming from her, she hadn't said much the rest of the way home.

Before he opened his door, his father was already on the porch, feet spread apart, arms crossed over his chest. Shadows obscured his face, but Chance had a pretty good idea why his father was home and not at the job site. He shot a frustrated glare at Dane, who simply shrugged, and climbed from behind the wheel, a smirk on his lips.

"Big mouth."

"Well, somebody's gotta take care of you, and it's not going to be me. You're always a grouch when you're sick."

"Am not," Chance shot back.

"Are too."

"Boys, play nice." Tina slid across the bench seat and climbed out of the truck before Chance could help her down. It would've been one-handed help, but still, he'd been raised a gentleman.

Walking toward the porch, he tried to keep his shoulder still, because every little movement shot pain through the joint. All things considered, it could've been worse, but for the next few days he knew he was in for a world of hurt.

"Honey, are you alright?" Ms. Patti pushed right past her husband, elbowing him out of the way and racing down the steps. "Dane called me from the clinic, said you and Tina were in an accident."

Chance pulled his mother into a one-armed hug on his uninjured side. "We're fine. The truck slid on some ice when I tried to avoid another car. A few of us ended up in a ditch off the shoulder of the interstate." He shot another aggravated glare at his brother. "Dane's a worrywart, and insisted Doc Stevens take a look at me because I hit my shoulder against the door."

"What did he say?" His momma continued patting his arm softly, the movements almost timid, as if afraid if she patted too hard, he'd keel over in excruciating pain. During this whole interlude, Tina stood off to the side, isolated and alone, and something about her posture, or maybe it was the closed off, almost distant expression on her face, made him realize once again she'd barely spoken since they'd left town.

Leaning down, he whispered in his mother's ear, "Momma, do me a favor? Take care of Tina. I think this whole thing has rattled her a smidge, though she hasn't said anything."

Ms. Patti stood on her tiptoes and pressed a kiss against his cheek. "Honey, you head inside and get settled in the living room. Leave Tina to me, I'll take good care of her."

"Thanks, Momma."

His momma walked over to Tina and pulled her close. For a brief moment, she held herself stiff, but finally her rigid posture eased, and she relaxed into his mother's arms.

"Tina, sugar, are you doing okay? What a horrible way for your trip to end. Although, on a positive note, you get to stick around for at least another day or two."

"Don't worry about me, Ms. Patti. Chance is the one who got injured. I simply held on tight while we did an imitation of a carnival ride. Remind me never to get on a roller coaster again."

Chance watched his father slowly climb down the front porch steps and stop in front of him. His perusal felt like it covered every inch of him, hat to boots, before he gave him a sharp nod, and continued past him toward his wife. Chance breathed a sigh of relief, because with that single nod he knew his dad would rein in his mother's overexuberant maternal instincts. All the Boudreaus knew Ms. Patti could become a tad overdramatic in her care and feeding of sick or injured family. Though his mother was a good cook, he wasn't looking forward to bowl after bowl of chicken soup.

Doc Stevens hadn't insisted he wear a sling, for which he was grateful. He'd ended up in one a long time ago, after falling out of the huge live oak down by the creek and dislocated his elbow. It hadn't taken more than a day before he'd developed a deep and abiding hatred of that sling.

Dane followed him into the house and headed for the kitchen. He heard water running, and within a minute he handed Chance a glass of water and a couple of ibuprofens. Doc Stevens had called in a prescription for pain medication, but he hadn't wanted to hang around town until it was ready to be picked up. If he needed it, he'd pick it up later, or have one of his brothers drop it off at the Big House.

Tina walked through the front door, his mother's arm wrapped around her shoulders as she pointed her in the direction of the kitchen. He smiled, knowing his momma was about to expend some of her maternal instinct on poor, unsuspecting Tina.

"Want to tell me what happened?" His father lowered his massive frame onto the ottoman across from him, his expression filled with concern. "Dane called Liam right after he left to fetch you and Tina. Liam called me, because—well, because he knew how your momma would react. Plus, the job site I was at today was closer to home than his."

Chance leaned back against the cushion, forcing himself to relax and hoping the ibuprofen would kick in soon. During all the commotion after the accident and helping others, he hadn't really hurt much. Now the adrenaline had worn off, his body let him know it wasn't happy. Not much he could do about it, except deal with the pain until the bruising subsided.

"Pretty much what I said. I hit a patch of ice and spun, sliding off the interstate into a ditch past the shoulder. A couple other cars spun out. One rolled. Frank brought the tow truck out and picked up the truck. Dane was closest, so I called him to come get us."

"Why do I think there's probably more to it than what you're telling?"

Chance placed his right hand over his heart. "I swear, that's all. Except for Dane going all overprotective and driving straight to the clinic, even though I told him nothing's broken."

Douglas huffed out a laugh. "I'd have done the same thing."

"Dad, you should have heard Tina talking with Doc Stevens. Before he'd said more than a couple of words, she was asking him all kinds of medical questions. Wanted details about the x-rays, and specific muscles, strains versus sprains, and she used a whole bunch of anatomical and physiological words."

"Could be she's worked with doctors in the past."

"I wanted Tina to get checked out by Doc Stevens too, but she refused. She swore she wasn't hurt, so I gave her a break and didn't insist."

Chance remembered Tina's response when Doc Stevens came along with him to update Dane and Tina. He'd been surprised with her extensive knowledge of medicine. Destiny's report mentioned she'd been taking classes required for premed students, but she hadn't stayed in school long enough to study medicine. Tina had the brains and the grades, and she would have made a great doctor, but she'd never finished. Then he remembered she'd been married to a doctor. Thinking about her ex made him want to hit something—or somebody. It was none of his business, beyond the cursory report Destiny had done, and he didn't have the right to dig any deeper into Tina's background. But he was doing it anyway. If she wanted to change her name every time she changed cities, that was her business, as long as she wasn't doing anything illegal. Thus far, that seemed to be the case.

"Your momma's grown fond of Tina. Knowing she

helped Renee simply endeared her more in your mother's eyes." His dad stared at him for a second, opened his mouth like he wanted to ask something, then stopped and shook his head.

"What? You've got a question, Dad, ask."

Douglas shook his head, a tiny smile playing along his lips. "I know you, son. Pretty sure the minute you brought Tina into Shiloh Springs, you had a full background done on her. You probably know more about her than even she does. Is there anything I need to be concerned about? Because I won't have your momma being hurt."

"You're right, Dad. I had Destiny do a background report on her. Tina has a bit of a mysterious past, but I didn't see any red flags that she's done anything illegal or immoral. I think she got caught up in a situation that proved tenuous at best and downright dangerous at worst. She was born Christina Phillips. Moved around a bit over the last couple of years. Married once, ended in divorce."

"If you wanted to know about me, Douglas, all you had to do was ask. Of course, Chance knows most of this, after our game of twenty questions in the car, along with the dossier he had his hacker dig up."

Tina stood highlighted in the entryway, his momma standing at her side, a scowl on her usually placid face. Uh oh, he was in trouble. His father stood, proud and unapologetic.

"Nothing personal, but I'd have done the same thing

Chance did. It's my job to protect this family, and while I like you, Tina, I don't know much about you, other than you helped a family member. For that alone, you've earned my sincerest thanks. And I owe you. If you're in trouble, we'll help."

"Yes, we will," Ms. Patti echoed, reaching out and squeezing her hand.

"I understand. I give you my word, it isn't my intention to bring any trouble to your doorstep. My issues are—personal. Now that Renee is settled and happy, I can move on with a clear conscience, and head back to Portland."

"Why don't you stay? You like it here. You've got friends in Shiloh Springs now, and you've got us."

Chance wasn't surprised his mother wanted Tina to stay. He'd watched them growing closer with each passing day, and he'd watched his mother's face this morning when they'd headed for the front door. Though she'd maintained her composure for Tina's sake, he could see the anguish in her eyes at letting her leave.

"I can't stay. I have a life in Portland. A job." He wondered who she was trying to convince, his mother or herself.

"I know. I guess I'm being selfish, wanting you to stay."

"I'll add my two cents to my wife's. If you want to stay, we can make it happen." Douglas moved over to stand in front of Tina, blocking her from Chance's view. When he tried to lean to the left to see her better, his shoulder's scream of pain stopped his movement in its tracks. Not a good idea.

"Thank you. I appreciate the offer. Trust me, I wish I could stay, but I—" Tina cut off when her cell phone rang. "Excuse me, I'd probably better get that."

Reaching into her purse, she pulled out her phone and swiped her finger across the screen.

"Hello."

The next few seconds were a blur, because all of a sudden, his mother was yelling for his father, who stepped forward and grabbed Tina when her knees buckled. As he struggled to push past his father, his dad gently placed Tina on the sofa beside him, giving him a "stay put" glare. Ms. Patti picked up the phone, and Chance could hear an anxious sounding woman's voice, incessantly calling Tina's name. Holding out his hand, he waved his mother over, and snatched the phone from her hand.

"Hello? Who's this?"

"Where's Tina? Did something happen to her? One second I was talking to her, and the next—"

"Ma'am, slow down. Who are you, and why were you calling Tina?"

"I'm not telling you anything until you assure me Tina's alright. I want to talk to her right now."

"Can't do that, ma'am. How about we start over? My name's Chance Boudreau—"

"Boudreau? Any relation to Shiloh Boudreau?" The sudden shift from angry and anxious to warm and friendly had Chance's mind reeling like a ping-pong ball, but he'd play along until he got answers.

"Yes, ma'am, Shiloh's my brother." Chance saw his mother startle at the mention of Shiloh's name.

"He's such a nice man. I'm Gertie. I own the Roaster's Roost in Portland. Now, how's about you tell me what happened to Tina, because I'm getting more than a bit concerned she hasn't gotten back on the phone."

Chance paused and took a deep breath, his eyes glued to Tina. His father sat beside her on the sofa, gently patting her hand and urging her to take deep breaths. Her eyes met his, and he read the panic in their deep blue depths, along with a hint of fear. Whatever put it there, he planned to make sure it got taken care of, because he never wanted to see that look in her eyes again.

"Gertie, Tina's fine. She got a bit...lightheaded when you were talking and needed to sit down for a second. I'm going to hand the phone to her now, okay?" Chance hit the speaker button, and handed the phone to Tina, biting back his chuckle at the glower she shot him.

"I'm here, Gertie."

"Tina! I'm so sorry, I didn't mean to upset up. Ain't it just like me to jump right in with both feet without even a hi, how are ya?"

The corners of Tina's lips curved up at the other woman's words. "All part of your charm. Gertie, you said someone called asking for me? Tell me again exactly what he said. Word for word."

"Well, it's been a crazy busy morning, since we've got a cold snap and I'm short my best waitress." Gertie chuckled, before continuing. "Carlos answered the phone, but you know how he gets. Unless its family calling because somebody lopped off an arm, he doesn't have time to deal with it. So, I took the call. It was a male voice, very cultured. Extremely polite. Kind of like you hear in the movies, all upper crust type, where they've got all the money in the world and everybody else is beneath them."

If Chance hadn't been watching her closely, he wouldn't have noticed the blood drain from her cheeks, making her normally porcelain skin appear translucent. The slight shaking of the hand holding the phone was another dead giveaway that Gertie's words hit like a hammer blow.

"What did he say, Gertie?"

There was a prolonged pause on the line before Gertie's voice came back. "He said he's your husband, and he wants you to come home."

# CHAPTER SEVEN

"Ex-husband." The finality in Chance's voice shook Tina. While she'd known Chance had looked into her past, he almost sounded angry at the thought she'd been married before.

"I'm sorry, what?" They'd gathered around the kitchen table after Tina disconnected the call, and Ms. Patti poured them all coffee. Wrapping her hands around the cup, she felt the warmth seep into her palms. Maybe if she held it long enough, it might permeate her whole body, because the icy chill encasing her froze her to the core.

"I said he's your ex-husband. At least, that's what my records show."

"You're right. Jared is my ex-husband. I divorced him a long time ago. He's having trouble letting go."

A bit of an understatement, but she didn't want them to know about her past. It was sordid and ugly, and she'd walked away from that part of her life without ever looking back. At least, she'd tried to. Too bad Jared wouldn't let her go. Now, she had no choice but to leave Shiloh Springs. She'd have to get out of Portland too, because if he'd found out where she worked, chances were good he also knew where she lived.

"I'd say there's a bit more to the story, otherwise you wouldn't have passed out when Gertie mentioned him." Douglas took a sip of his coffee, and smiled at Ms. Patti over the rim of the mug. "We're good listeners. Maybe we can help."

"You don't seem surprised Chance had me investigated."

"I'm not." Ms. Patti moved around to stand behind Douglas and placed her hands on his shoulders. "First off, and don't be offended, but we didn't know anything about you except you were friends with Renee and helped her when she was in trouble. While that was a point in your favor, it didn't tell us much about you. Secondly, our family looks out for each other. If Chance hadn't had you checked out, I guarantee one of the other boys would have. Probably Ridge, since he's got the best computer expert." She smiled dotingly at Chance, and he nodded, confirming her guess.

"I'd already contacted an old army buddy, had him looking into your background." Douglas reached up, placing his hand on his wife's resting on his shoulder."

"You did?" Surprise colored Chance's voice.

Douglas nodded. "Gizmo owed me a favor, so I had him do a little digging."

"So, you already knew about Tina's ex?"

"I'm sure Destiny's report was a lot more comprehensive than Gizmo's, but yes, I had the facts."

"Of course, it was obvious from the start we had nothing to worry about once we met you." Ms. Patti's eyes met Tina's across the table, a wealth of understanding written in their depths. The warmth in her small smile filled Tina with hope that everything might be alright.

Tina sighed, realizing she owed them the truth. They'd been nothing but kind to her from the moment she'd met them. How could she blame them for doing something she'd have done herself if she had the time and the wherewithal to pay for it? Honestly, she kind of envied the Boudreaus, because they were unlike anybody she'd ever met. Ms. Patti and Douglas welcomed her into their home and for the first time in years, she'd gotten a taste of what a true family looked like. As hard as her aunt and uncle tried, they'd been older, and had problems of their own. Taking on a young woman loaded down with baggage hadn't helped.

"I got married when I was young." She almost choked on the words. "Young and stupid. Jared and I didn't have an amicable divorce. Truth is, he didn't want the divorce at all. As far as he is concerned, marriage is for life. Funny, I always believed that, too. I took my vows seriously, meant every word. I was head over heels in love with Jared, adored him from the day we met."

She glanced at Chance through half-lowered lids, noted his scowling face, the way his jaw clenched. Anger radiated off him, and she wasn't sure if it was directed at her or her absent ex. It wasn't like she'd hidden the truth from him.

Her lousy marriage and its turmoil really wasn't his business. They'd been having such fun on the drive toward Dallas up until the accident, joking and laughing. He'd been friendly and jovial, and she'd gradually loosened up under his gentle teasing. Now, that smiling, pleasant man was gone, like he never existed, leaving in his wake this stoic, somber stranger.

"Jared Webster. He's a doctor. A surgeon, if I recall."

Voice frozen in her throat, all she could do was nod. Talking about Jared brought all the horrible memories rushing forward, things she'd fought long and hard to quash. Forget. When her eyes met Ms. Patti's, their earlier conversation replayed through her mind. She'd found a kindred spirit in the wonderful woman, who'd intimated she'd endured some of the same experiences Tina had, and she'd come through it healthy and whole and loving.

*Wonder if I'll ever be able to put my past behind me, and have a happy, healthy relationship? A life filled with people I love and who love me? Who am I kidding, that's a pipe dream that'll never happen.*

"Jared is an excellent surgeon. I've seen him do some amazing work."

"Funny, from what I read, he didn't have great grades in medical school. He was on the fast track to failing out when he suddenly turned things around. Right about the time he met a premed student who aced all her courses—you." Chance's steely-eyed gaze bored into her, and her stomach clenched. Guess he wasn't going to let things slide. She doubted he'd pull his punches, either. The lawyer part of him, the prosecutor, would go straight for the jugular. Hadn't she bled enough covering for her ex?

"Jared had the skills to be one of the finest surgeons in the country. But he had trouble taking tests. Studying, retaining classroom-style lessons and facts didn't come easy. I—helped him, taught him some tricks for retaining information. Studied with him, tutored him in some instances, and he turned things around."

"And lost your own scholarship in the process, right, Tina? Saving Jared's chances to be a doctor caused you to lose your own shot."

"It was my choice." Her voice was barely above a whisper, remembering how devastated she'd been when she'd found out she couldn't continue her studies to become a doctor. Practicing medicine had been her dream, almost her entire life focused on becoming a neurosurgeon.

"We were crazy about each other, and it only made sense to get married. Once Jared got his practice established, we'd planned for me to go back to school and make up my classes." It was hard disguising the bitterness in her words. Even now, she felt like an idiot for believing his promises. It hadn't taken long to realize Jared had no intention of letting her go back to school. In Jared's eyes, his wife needed to be at home, creating the perfect family, being the perfect physician's wife.

"Did you? Go back?" Ms. Patti's softly voiced question

didn't surprise her.

She shook her head, biting her bottom lip to keep from screaming. Talking about this was hard—harder than she'd imagined. There were few people who knew the truth of her failed marriage, and she wanted to keep it that way. Shame flooded through her, not for the first time, at how young and gullible she'd been. Never again, she swore.

"Were you happy?" Chance's casual question surprised her, especially given his previous veiled hostility.

"In the beginning. I guess it was part of the honeymoon phase, where everything is champagne and roses. We didn't care, because Jared's practice was thriving. I worked part time and managed our home. Jared comes from a wealthy family and was used to the finer things. It was an…adjustment for me. While my family wasn't dirt poor, there wasn't a lot left over for luxuries. Scholarships meant I could attend college; otherwise, I'd have gone straight from high school into the work force."

Tina stopped talking when her phone's text alert sounded, startling her into silence. She'd almost forgotten she'd laid it on the table when she picked up her coffee cup. Hand shaking, she slid her finger across the screen and looked at the message. The words seemed to blur together, and she felt her breathing speed up until she couldn't catch her breath.

Within seconds, she felt a hand on her back, forcing her forward.

"Take a deep breath, honey. That's good. Let it out

slowly. Alright, do it again. Breathe in. Now let it out. Good girl." Ms. Patti's hand rubbed small circles between her shoulder blades, and while she still felt lightheaded, the wave of panic receded.

Chance eased the phone from her shaking hand, and she let him, feeling numb. She'd finally felt like she had her life together, that Jared had gotten the message she wasn't coming back. None of the reasons she left had changed, yet he refused to allow her to be free.

"Son of a—"

"Chance Elliott Boudreau, watch your language in this house."

Tina watched the flush spread across Chance's cheeks at his mother's rebuke. His expression reminded her of a little boy with his hand in the cookie jar who'd been caught red-handed.

"Sorry, Momma. Tina, who's Gustavo Herrera?"

"My landlord." She was proud of the fact her voice didn't break on the words, because inside she was trembling, jittery as an aspen in the wind.

Chance handed the phone to his father, and she watched his eyes widen slightly at the message. A muscle in his jaw tightened, but that was the only outward change she noted in the big man.

"You're not going back."

Tina's eyes widened at the almost monotone statement from the Boudreau patriarch. His voice contained no anger, no censure about bringing trouble to his front door. But his eyes—there was a fire burning in their depths she was glad wasn't directed at her. If it had been, she'd have found the deepest, darkest hole, climbed in and pulled the dirt over herself, to save him the trouble.

"What does it say, Douglas?"

"Her landlord texted her apartment was ransacked. The police determined it was not a random break-in, since there was a message written on the wall." He turned his gaze to Tina. "Though he didn't sign it, we can assume it's from your ex." It wasn't a question.

She pulled in another deep breath and felt Ms. Patti's hands tighten on her shoulders. How had things deteriorated so quickly? More importantly, why had Jared tracked her down again? She'd gone back to using her maiden name after the divorce, which infuriated him. When she'd moved from place to place, she'd decided changing her last name only made sense, since the whole point was to avoid him at all costs. Of course, he always found her, faster than she counted on most of the time.

"Jared has an issue with anger management. Douglas, I must go back. You read the message. The police have questions…"

"Call them. Answer their questions on the phone. You can Skype or Zoom if they need a face-to-face confirmation. I'll be with you, act as counsel to protect your rights." Chance reached across the table and grabbed her hand, squeezing it gently. "The police need to know the extent of harassment by your ex, and that it's escalating. That it's a situation of habitual and continual abuse."

She winced at his words because she didn't want to admit her weakness. Abuse was an ugly word and an even uglier act. Shame flooded her, remembering how long she'd lied to herself about Jared's actions, to the point where she believed she deserved his punishments.

"Honey, Chance is right. If you go back, you'll have to see him. Which is exactly what he wants, to draw you out, make you come to him. My guess is he's done this before, hasn't he?

Tina nodded again, beginning to feel like one of those bobblehead dolls. When Ms. Patti squatted down beside her chair, she placed her hand beneath Tina's chin and lifted her head up until they locked eyes. Ms. Patti's gaze was firm and direct, filled with compassion and a wealth of understanding only another survivor would comprehend.

"Let us help." The other woman's eyes darted over at Chance and Douglas before meeting Tina's again. "Even if it's simply holding your hand and helping you deal with the police questions, you're not alone.

"I thought he'd finally given up." Her words were barely above a whisper. "I felt like I finally got the fresh start I wanted in Portland. Now it's all falling apart."

"We'll fix this, Tina. I promise."

With his words ringing like an oath, Chance stood and

walked out of the kitchen, his hand reaching into his pocket for his cell phone. Tina watched him stride into the living room and felt a wash of abandonment flood her, which was ridiculous. She had no right to expect Chance to stand by her side, holding her hand. He'd help her because it was his job as a protector. It made total sense, since he worked as a prosecutor, helping victims and punishing those who preyed on them. Viewing it as anything personal, because he cared about her, would be courting disaster. Even if deep down she wished she were more than another helpless woman, waiting for a white knight to ride to the rescue. And Chance Boudreau definitely filled the role of crusader to a T.

Ms. Patti refilled her coffee mug, and then slid onto the chair Chance had evacuated moments earlier. Douglas sat silently, but Tina knew he followed every word, every movement, and probably could repeat verbatim every word she'd spoken since they'd entered the kitchen.

Chance strode back through the opening, his expression grim. Stopping beside her chair, he squatted beside her, one hand on the back of her chair, and the other he placed gently atop hers.

"I need to go into town for a little while. You'll be safe here. Momma and Dad are here, and Dane's going to keep an eye on things, make sure nobody gets onto the property without his knowing about it. Okay?"

"Of course. Go do whatever you need. I need to call Gertie back, and let her know what's going on. I'll get online, contact the airline and get my ticket handled."

"Don't worry, son, we'll take care of Tina." Douglas stood and walked over to where Chance was and placed his large hand on his shoulder. "Lemme know whatever you need, and I'll make it happen."

"Thanks, Dad."

When he stood and released her hand, Tina felt bereft. Her whole world turned topsy-turvy, yet somehow it felt different this time. Probably because she was used to dealing with Jared's threats alone, his none-too-subtle attacks, but she'd come to expect them. Prepared herself for him finding her and having to pick up and run, but this time enough time had passed he'd blindsided her.

"Walk me out?" Chance extended his hand, and Tina stared at it, trying not to read more into the simple gesture than what it was—an offer of support and friendship. With a tentative smile, she slid her hand into his and stood, following him out the front door and onto the oversized front porch.

"I've called Ridge and he's going to figure out exactly where your ex is, so we can get eyes on him. I'm not going to let him get anywhere near you." When he ran his fingers through her hair, she found herself leaning into his touch. "Do you have a restraining order against him?"

"I did, but I agreed to drop it if he'd sign the divorce papers."

"Well, we're going to make sure another one gets put

into place ASAP. Might take some work, since he resides in California and you live in Oregon, but if he's causing problems in Portland, we'll need to get it in place in their jurisdiction."

Tina's shoulders slumped, and she felt like a balloon slowly deflating. Kind of the story of her life the last couple of years. Things would finally start feeling right, and then like a slow leak, her world would begin closing in until Jared forced her to leave everything behind, all because he couldn't accept she didn't love him anymore.

"If you want to know where Jared is, tell Ridge all he has to do is check with his mother. Jared rarely makes a move that Mommy dearest doesn't know about, and most times instigates. While Jared makes a decent amount from his career, his mother holds the purse strings, and she's uses them to control him."

"Interesting. I'll let him know."

Leaning forward, he placed his forehead against hers, and she closed her eyes, simply letting the moment be. Chance made her feel things she hadn't felt in...forever. Like somebody cared about her for more than what she could do for them. First, it had been her family, riding her coattails when she got into Stanford, with scholarships and student loans. Then Jared using her to help him pass his classes and get his residency off the ground. Somebody always wanted something from her. Everyone except Chance.

"I have to go. I shouldn't be long, but you'll be fine.

Momma and Dad will be close by if you need anything. You've got my number. We'll figure out our next step when I get back."

"Our?"

The corner of his mouth ticked up, and the sparkle in his eyes should have warned her. With a finger beneath her chin, he tilted it up until her eyes met his.

"Definitely ours."

With that, he swooped in, capturing her lips with his in a searing kiss. She hadn't expected it, and the touch of his mouth on hers was an unexpected delight. Instinctively, her arms slid around his neck and she moved closer, lips parting beneath his. He took her silent invitation, deepening the kiss, and Tina allowed herself to get lost in the sensations rocketing through her. All clear thought disappeared after that, and she responded, allowing Chance to lead the delicate dance of lips and tongues.

Far too soon, he drew back, the breath soughing in and out of his chest like he'd run a marathon. She wasn't in any better shape, and she raised her fingers to her lips, still feeling an echo of Chance's mouth against hers. Wow, the man could *kiss*.

He tucked a lock of hair behind her ear, his fingertips skimming across her cheek, and she felt a subtle hum everywhere he touched.

*This man is dangerous. If I'm not careful, I could find myself falling hard.*

"I've gotta go. Behave while I'm gone."

She chuckled. "Now why'd you want to go and spoil things, counselor?"

With a swift move, he leaned in and brushed his lips against hers again, and then sighed. Without another word, he took the porch steps two at a time, and headed for his father's truck. She stayed on the porch until he'd disappeared from sight.

"I'm in so much trouble."

# CHAPTER EIGHT

Chance wasn't sure how he made it back to Shiloh Springs. He'd driven on autopilot almost the whole way, unable to think about anything but *the* kiss. Tina's lips beneath his felt like he'd found paradise. While he wasn't a hound dog and had more than his fair share of relationships over the years, nothing had ever felt as right as holding Tina in his arms. Kissing her? Pure magic.

The small ache from his shoulder didn't bother him too much. The doctor had given him an injection for the pain. Fortunately, it was one that didn't make him drowsy, or he'd never have gotten behind the wheel of the truck. He wasn't an idiot, and he'd prosecuted enough driving under the influence cases to know better. Plus, his dad would've plucked the keys right out of his hand before letting him leave the ranch if he'd thought Chance wasn't firing on all cylinders.

Pulling into the parking space for his condo, he pulled the keys out of the ignition and swapped them for the ones in his pocket. With a ragged sigh, he started up the stairs for the second floor. He'd lived here for the past couple of years, but it had never felt like home. Shaking his head, he wondered if any place would ever feel like it belonged to him the way the Big House did. Man, he loved the ranch. Too bad he hadn't gotten the ranching bug the way Dane had, but while he didn't mind helping out, dealing with smelly cattle and cantankerous cowhands every day? Not even for a million bucks.

This day had gone from him vacillating between wanting to get Tina to the airport and headed back to Portland, and not wanting her to leave. Why did that confuse the heck out of him? Between the accident, the doctor's office, and going back to the Big House, most of the day was shot.

Climbing the last stair, he turned toward his condo, pausing when he noted two men standing beside his doorstep. Great. He wasn't surprised to see Brody standing there. Dane probably called him the minute they got back to the ranch, if not sooner. Brody was the worrier, the caretaker, who couldn't stand to see somebody hurting or in pain. He'd anticipated seeing Brody before nightfall.

What did surprise him was the other man standing beside him, talking quietly to his brother. He hadn't seen Joshua in months. More and more lately, he'd been away from Shiloh Springs. When he'd asked his dad, he'd merely said Joshua had things he needed to work out for himself, and to give him time and space. Since he trusted his father's judgment when it came to his sons, Chance backed off, though it took a lot of effort, knowing Joshua was suffering in silence. Maybe, since he was home now, he'd let him know there wasn't anything he couldn't talk to Chance about, with no judgment and no questions.

"What are you guys doing here?" He inserted the key into the deadbolt and flung open the front door, waving his hand to invite them in.

"Dane said you'd been in an accident on your way to Dallas."

Chance chuckled softly, not surprised he'd guessed right.

"I'm fine. Banged my shoulder, and Doc Stevens looked at it. Other than a little bruising, he gave me a clean bill of health, so I don't need a babysitter or a nursemaid."

"Wow, somebody whacked you with the snarky stick." Brody sank down onto the dark leather sofa, stretching his arm along the back. "Beth wanted me to come over and make sure you were really okay. Think I'll tell her you injured your sense of humor, bent it outta shape."

Chance waved his middle finger at his grinning brother, who quickly returned the gesture. Joshua glanced between them before sitting on the other end of the sofa. Taking a second, Chance studied his taciturn brother, noting the dark circles beneath his eyes and several days of scruff covering his cheeks. He looked tired, and there was an air of weariness Chance suspected had nothing to do with lack of sleep. Something felt off about his brother, and a grim determination filled him to not only figure out what was wrong, but to do everything within his power to fix the problem. Didn't matter what said problem was, either. That's what brothers did, especially Boudreau brothers.

"I'll be happy when this lousy weather clears up. The drive up I-45 turned into a nightmare. Tina missed her flight, and my truck's sitting at Frank's Garage."

"And you're heartbroken she's having to stick around?"

Chance resisted the urge to wipe the smirk off Brody's lips. Barely. Instead, he turned and walked into the kitchen, pulled three bottles of water from the fridge, and handed one to each man before sinking deep into the armchair that matched the sofa.

"There's a lot going on y'all don't know. Tina's got a lot of…baggage…from her past."

Joshua's sudden burst of laughter startled Chance, and his gaze swung to meet his brother's.

"Dude, there isn't a single Boudreau male who has been attracted to or fallen in love with any female who could be described as Little Susie Sunshine. We tend to fall for complicated women with complicated histories. If Tina has a 'checkered past', well then, she'll fit in well with the rest of the Boudreau women."

Chance couldn't help noting Joshua's use of present tense when talking about falling hard for a woman. Was he involved with somebody? If he was, it was news to him. He doubted anybody else in the family had heard a peep about Joshua's love life; otherwise, his momma wouldn't have been able to resist spreading the word to the family. She wanted all her boys to be settled and happy.

"Renee thinks Tina pretty much walks on water. Tessa invited her to come back for the wedding. And don't get me started on how much Nica likes her." After taking a long drink of his water, Chance asked Joshua, "Have you met Renee yet?"

Joshua shook his head. "I'm having dinner with her and Shiloh tomorrow night. I talked to her on the phone, and she seems to be adjusting well to having a whole new family. I ran into Lucas earlier this morning at Jill's bakery. I swear, he's practically glowing. I can't believe he actually found Renee after all these years."

"Poor kid. She had it rough, but she's strong, and the family's helping her realize she's loved and part of a group who pull together when one of their own is in trouble. The threat to her has been eliminated now that Darius and Eileen Black are behind bars. They are up to their eyeballs with enough charges to keep them in and out of court for the next decade. Best chance they've got is to make a deal with the government and plead out, because the feds have Renee willing to testify against them. And she's ready to bury them."

"What if they try to hire a hitman from prison to take her out?" Brody leaned forward, hands clasped between his spread knees.

Chance grinned at his brother's serious expression. "You've been watching too much television, bro. They aren't wandering around in general population, interacting with burglars and drug dealers. They're in federal custody, with no access to the outside except through their attorneys. Renee's gonna be fine."

*No need to tell them I've got my own feelers in place to make sure she stays that way.*

Joshua set his bottle on the coffee table in front of the sofa and leaned forward. "You said Tina's got some baggage. Anything the family needs to worry about?"

"I just left the Big House. Momma, Dad, and I sat down with Tina and had a long chat. Her ex-husband—ugly divorce—is causing her some problems. Their split definitely wasn't amicable. Though she never came out and said it, my gut's telling me he was abusive."

He wasn't surprised when Brody sprang to his feet, a curse on his lips. Of all his brothers, Brody had the softest heart. It was part of why he'd become a firefighter and EMT. Knowing someone was hurting, whether physically or otherwise, he'd want to help. It was his nature.

"Is he a threat?"

"I don't know. She got a call from her employer in Portland, who said her ex was trying to find her. She's moved a couple of times in the past, going so far as to change her name in an effort to stay away from him. Guess he didn't get the message she wants him to leave her alone."

"Can't she get a restraining order against the jerk?" Brody paced as he talked, clearly upset.

"That's what I'm planning to look into. I think there's a lot Tina hasn't told me yet."

Joshua's inelegant snort drew Chance's attention back to his brother. "You got something to add?"

"Brody might buy your act, bro, but you're not fooling me." Reaching into his back pocket, Joshua took out his wallet and began pulling out twenties. "I've got…a hundred and eighty bucks that says you had Destiny or Ridge already run a background check on little Miss Tina five minutes after you met her."

Chance sighed, not surprised his brother guessed his actions. "Wish I could take your money, but I can't. Destiny ran a full background check on her before I boarded the plane to Portland."

Joshua chuckled before putting the money back in his wallet. "Everybody thinks Rafe's the guard dog for the Boudreaus, but he ain't got nothing on you. You'll never let anybody hurt a member of this family. You're simply more subtle about your methods."

A wave of shock rolled through Chance at his brother's words. Not that he was wrong, because he'd protect every single one of the Boudreaus with his last breath. But he didn't realize anybody knew him that well, especially since Joshua had been gone more than he'd been home the past year or so.

"He's right." Brody moved to Chance's side and squeezed his shoulder. "You've always been the protector, the fire-breathing dragon who never lets anybody threaten what you hold close. It's ingrained deep inside you, what makes you so good at what you do. Being a prosecutor is a pretty thankless job, but you are the voice for the underdogs, the victims. The old Texas Ranger saying 'one riot, one ranger' always reminded me of you."

Chance's throat tightened at his brother's words of praise. He'd never thought of himself in that way. All he'd ever wanted to do was give a voice to those who didn't have one. Growing up with ten brothers who'd all gotten rotten deals in their early years, without anybody to stand up for them before Momma and Dad, he'd needed to make sure others got a chance for justice.

"Guys, I—"

Brody cut him off. "What did Destiny find? I know Momma likes Tina, which counts for a lot in my books. So whatever her problem is, I'm guessing we'll be circling the wagons soon enough."

He loved that phrase because it's what he always called it in his head. Momma had called it that once, and somehow it stuck. Any time there was trouble, the Boudreaus gathered, ready and willing to fight for those they loved.

"Hang on a second." Getting up, he walked to his office and grabbed the file he'd printed out from Destiny's e-mails and carried it back, handing it to Joshua. There wasn't anything in there that couldn't be found on a good internet search, so he wasn't breaking confidentiality. Destiny had yet to get him her results from the deeper dive she was currently running on Tina.

There was quiet for several minutes as Joshua flipped through the pages. Chance watched his brows raise a couple of times, the muscles around his mouth tightening. Taking a deep breath, he handed the folder to Brody.

"What can we do?"

"Right now, be there for her. Make sure her ex stays in California. If he shows up in Texas, I've got legal avenues, actions I can take."

Brody nodded once and laid the folder on the coffee table without reading it. Straightening to his full height, he turned toward Joshua.

"You ready? I need to get back to Beth and Jamie. Need to assure her Chance is okay, then get some work done."

Before Joshua could answer, Chance interrupted. "Do you mind sticking around for a few minutes, Joshua? I'll give you a ride if you need one, but I'd like to talk to you."

Joshua's expression didn't reveal anything, he simply shrugged. "Sure."

Brody's eyes darted between his brothers before he walked to the door. "I'm serious, Chance, you need any help with Tina or her ex, you call me."

"I will."

There was a beat or two of silence after Brody left, and Chance wondered if his brother would confide in him whatever his problem might be. He wasn't above prodding and poking to get the answer, because if he didn't, Momma would.

"Everything okay with you? Haven't seen you around much lately."

Joshua shrugged and a long lock of hair fell across his forehead. Almost absently, he brushed it aside. The lines around his mouth were deeper than Chance remembered, and the haunted look in his gaze made him appear older than his years.

"It's been a rough few months."

"Talk to me."

"Nothing to tell, bro."

Chance crossed his arms over his chest and stared at Joshua, not saying a word, wondering how long his brother would be able to hold out. When they'd been younger, Joshua had always been the one to fold under the silent stare. When he simply leaned his shoulders back against the sofa back and crossed his arms over his own chest, his expression mulish, Chance almost chuckled.

*Darn, he's gotten stubborn in his old age.*

"You know you can talk to me, right?"

Joshua rubbed a hand across his face, and Chance wondered if he'd give him a clue what was eating at him. Instead, Joshua simply shook his head, and blew out a long breath.

"Just let it go, bro."

"I can't. What if it was me, acting distant and unapproachable? Would you simply sit back and do nothing?

Lemme put it this way, you can talk to me and I'll head Momma off, or you can deal with her on your own. You know she's not going to simply stand by while you're hurting and not find out what's happening."

Joshua rolled his eyes and barked out a short laugh. "I'm surprised she hasn't hunted me down long before now." He paused for a long moment, as if debating what or maybe how much to say.

"Whatever you tell me, I won't say a word. Not unless you tell me to."

"Chance, if there's one thing I know about you, it's that you can keep a secret. The only problem is—it's not my secret to tell."

"Answer me this…is this other person in trouble?"

Joshua shook his head and leaned forward, picking up the file on Tina again. "Not this kind of trouble. It's personal, not legal."

"At least tell me she's pretty." When Joshua's body jerked at his words, Chance knew he'd guessed right. Whoever it was, Joshua cared about her a lot. He'd give him a break—for now. But if he got even a hint his brother was getting in over his head, he'd have no problem sticking his nose in his business.

"Chance, just let it go."

Studying his brother's rigid posture, the subtle tightening in his jaw, Chance decided to take a step back. Didn't mean he would keep his eyes and ears open, because nobody deserved to be alone without somebody watching their back.

"Alright, I'll drop it."

*For now.*

"You have plans tonight?" At Joshua's head shake, he continued, "Feel like heading over to Juanita's? I'm starving."

"Only if I'm driving."

Chance chuckled. "Deal."

# CHAPTER NINE

Jared pulled open the door to Roaster's Retreat, his nose wrinkling at the overwhelming smell of coffee. It never made sense, how people would crowd into little coffee shops to drink the swill available over the counter. As far as he was concerned, if it wasn't the specialized blend he bought from Kona, it wasn't worth drinking. He shuddered, remembering some of the swill he'd be forced to drink from vending machines and the cafeteria when he'd been working his residency and internship.

Shaking his head, he made his way past the throng of bodies two and three deep, clustered into small groups, guzzling their lattes and mochas and other frou-frou coffee drinks. Standing in line, he studied the people waiting to place their orders, wishing again he wasn't wasting his time chasing a ghost. Except, he'd gotten the impression from the woman he'd talked to on the phone that Tina did, indeed, work in this—he wasn't quite sure what to call the enterprise. Oh, well, people needed work, and this was as good a place as any for those poor minimum wage workers.

Finally, he stood face-to-face with a cute blonde taking

orders. "One French vanilla iced coffee."

*Hopefully they can't screw that up too badly.*

The smiling girl handed him his receipt. "We'll have that ready in just a second."

With a nod, he stepped to the side, grimacing as another wave of coffee-scented air hit him square in the face. As much as he wanted to turn and walk out the door, he couldn't. He needed to find the woman he'd talked with, the one who'd lied to him about Tina.

A murmur of voices close to him made him wince, and he glanced toward the women. Three women stood, coffee cups in their hands. Two of them appeared in their late twenties or early thirties, dressed in business casual outfits. The third woman was much older, and he immediately straightened when he heard her speak.

*It is the woman from the phone call.*

"Still short staffed, Gertie?" That was from the brunette.

"Yeah. Tina's taken some personal time. Remember Elizabeth, the other gal who worked here?"

Jared turned his head slightly, catching the two women nodding at Gertie's question.

"Turns out Elizabeth had family who was looking for her. This sweet guy came looking for her, and she ended up falling head over heels for him. Lucky girl, because he was quite a catch."

"I wondered why she hadn't been around lately."

"Elizabeth and Shiloh—he's the man who came and

found her—went back to Texas."

*Texas?*

"And Tina went to Texas with them? I know they were friends, but that seems a little…I don't know…odd." Again the brunette, who seemed to be the more inquisitive of the two women Gertie spoke with. Trying to appear inconspicuous, he eased a little closer, not wanting to miss a single word.

"You know I don't like to gossip," Gertie chuckled at her own joke before adding, "but Tina ended up meeting Shiloh's brother, and he apparently talked her into going to Texas, too. Can't say I blame her, if he's anything like Shiloh Boudreau, because he was something else."

*Boudreau? Not a name I'm familiar with, but then I've never set foot inside Texas. But if Tina's there, looks like I'll be headed there.*

"Tina said Elizabeth is deliriously happy, because she's been reunited with the brother she hadn't seen since she was a little girl. Apparently, the whole family welcomed her with open arms and she's planning on staying there. Tina said she'd be back soon. Personally, I can't wait. She brings so much life to the place, and the customers have missed her like crazy."

Jared's brow raised at the praise for his ex-wife. Gertie's description of the outgoing, friendly woman didn't sound anything like the woman he knew. Had she changed that much since she'd run away with her tail tucked between her legs?

"Thanks, Gertie. We've gotta go, or we'll be late."

The perky blonde who'd taken his order walked from behind the counter and handed him his iced coffee, and he took a sip, surprised at the deep, rich flavor. While it wasn't his favorite Kona blend, it wasn't half bad.

He headed for the front door, deciding not to speak with Gertie. The information he'd gotten from eavesdropping on the conversation had provided him with a wealth of information, more than he'd expected when he'd walked through the doors.

Slipping outside, he pulled his cell phone out of his jacket pocket and dialed the one person who supported and encouraged his search for Tina.

His mother.

Tina placed her e-reader on the arm of the chair, and leaned her head back, closing her eyes. As much as she loved Jana Deleon's books, not even the slapstick antics of the crazy old ladies held her attention today. Her mind kept replaying her conversation with Chance before the accident. Their not-so-subtle flirting in the midst of answering personal questions had been a combination of fun and insightful. Opening up to someone for the first time in a long time had felt almost cathartic in a weird way.

The Big House was eerily quiet, though she wasn't afraid. If she'd been a betting woman, she'd wager somebody was close by, keeping an eye on things. Ms. Patti had driven into Shiloh Springs to deal with her job. After having spent a few weeks with the woman, she understood why she was one of the best realtors in the county. She'd never met anyone who could multitask the way the Boudreau matriarch did. Douglas had headed out to meet up with Liam at one of the construction sites.

The hard rap on the front door startled her enough, she knocked the e-reader onto the floor. Leaning down and picking it up, she walked over and pulled the door open, finding a dark-haired pixie standing on the other side. She was dressed from head to toe in black jeans, a black tank, with a large canvas messenger bag hung across her body. Sparkling blue eyes shone with intelligence and a hint of mischief, and Tina recognized a kindred spirit within the petite package. She spotted a tattoo peeking out from the top of the tank, bright vivid colors, though whatever the design was couldn't be interpreted easily. Except maybe she spotted...wings?

"Hi. I'm Destiny."

"Tina. Can I help you? I'm afraid Ms. Patti and Douglas aren't around."

"That's okay, I'm actually here looking for you."

That took her aback for a second. Why would somebody be looking for her—wait, Destiny? Where had she heard that name before?

"Why are you looking for me?"

Destiny tugged on the crossbody messenger bag, the action looking like habit more than discomfort. Blowing her bangs out of her face, she gave a delicate shrug.

"Could I come in? This might take a few minutes to explain. Or, if you're not comfortable with that, we can sit out here on the porch. I work for Ridge Boudreau, if that helps."

Of course, that's where she'd heard Destiny's name before. Chance had mentioned her when they'd talked with his parents. She was the hacker who'd done a deep dive into Tina's background, giving Chance the info about her past.

"Come in. I'm going to grab something to drink, so why don't we head into the kitchen. Would you like something?"

"Sweet tea if you've got any." Destiny followed her into the kitchen, and Tina noticed the woman appeared quite at home in the Boudreau house. For some reason, that made her feel a little better. If she tried anything weird, she could always yell. She was sure Dane was around somewhere close.

"There's always sweet tea around here. I think I've gained five pounds since I've been here, just from drinking it."

Pulling two glasses from the cupboard, Tina filled them with ice and poured the tea from the pitcher in the refrigerator that always seemed ready and waiting. It was like one of those mystery spots, where no matter how much you took, the next time you looked it was filled again.

Passing one of the glasses to Destiny, she slid onto the chair across from her, curious about what the hacker wanted from her.

"You're wondering why I showed up on your doorstep, right?"

"I'll admit, I'm curious."

Destiny's grin was infectious, lighting her gamine face and turning her from being cute to stunning. Her dark hair was cut into a pixie style, with bits and pieces pulled around her face. It was an attractive style, but Tina had the feeling it fell that way naturally and wasn't something Destiny put a lot of effort into.

"This is a bit awkward, so I'm just going to plunge in instead of pussyfooting around. Honestly, that's not my style anyway." Reaching around behind her, she stuck her hand into the messenger bag she'd hung on the chair back, and pulled out a tattered file folder, and slid it across the table.

"What's this?"

"A few weeks ago, when they found out about Renee being in Portland and her involvement with you, I was asked to do a file on you. Look into your background, basically find out everything I could about you, and whether you were a danger to Renee."

Tina stared at the file folder, eyeing it like a coiled rattler sitting in front of her. The contents held details about her life, the good, the bad, and the ugly. Probably way too much ugly stuff she didn't want to have to confront a second time.

If only she could grab matches and burn it, never open it and relive her moments of shame and humiliation. But that was the coward's way out, and she'd never go back to being a meek, timid doormat. Never again.

"I'd never hurt Renee. She's my friend."

"I know. Which is exactly what I told—"

"Chance. Yes, I know he's the one who had you looking into my life, dissecting everything under a microscope. He told me."

Surprise colored Destiny's expression. Guess she hadn't expected that.

"You're right. I gave him everything I had. Well, everything I had at the time."

The bottom dropped out of Tina's stomach as her words settled over her like a weighted blanket, only they provided no comfort, no sense of safety and security like the cover would. Instead, an overwhelming feeling of dread coursed through her, an eerie premonition of something bad coalescing in her gut.

"Everything's in here, isn't it?" Her fingertips skimmed across the folder.

Destiny nodded, her gaze filled with sympathy. "Yeah. I haven't told Chance what I found. I'm not sure that it's any of his business, to be honest."

Tina picked up her glass, amazed that her hand wasn't spilling the tea all over the tabletop. Lifting it, she guzzled down half before wiping the cool glass against her forehead.

"He knows most of it already. I talked with Douglas and Ms. Patti, too. Ms. Patti had already figured out most of it."

"I haven't had the pleasure of meeting Mrs. Boudreau yet, although Ridge talks about her all the time. Sounds like she's quite a character."

"You have no idea."

When her hand reached to flip open the folder, Destiny's hand landed lightly on top of it, and Tina lifted her gaze to meet the other woman's.

"Before you open that, you should know if you don't want anybody else finding this information, I can bury it deep enough nobody will find it. It's nobody's business but yours."

"I don't care if Chance finds out, but…thank you."

"By the way, whoever did your documents in Portland, he's good. Really good. Like they would've passed more than a cursory inspection. But he's got a few holes in your background info, but a couple of hours work can fix that."

*Good to know Nico hasn't totally lost his touch.*

Taking a deep breath, she opened the folder and looked at the detailed report Destiny had prepared. She had to admit, the woman had serious skills. Flipping page after page, looking at her life outlined in black and white, it didn't paint a pretty picture. She'd been foolish and stupid, and she'd been paying the price for her idealistic naivety and the horrible choices she'd made because she'd thought she loved Jared. Seeing the results of her actions, she realized she'd been an idiot.

"There's more." Destiny's voice was almost a whisper.

"More than this?" Tina gestured toward the folder. "You seemed to have found everything." She wished she could keep the bitterness from her voice, but it bled through.

"Look, I was just doing my job, what I'd been hired to do. Add in the fact I like the Boudreaus, and didn't want anybody scamming them, or putting them in somebody's crosshairs—"

"I'm sorry. You're right, and I shouldn't take my frustrations out on you. I've made a lot of mistakes and bad choices I'm not proud of, and seeing them like this," she gestured toward the pages, "it's hard."

Destiny blew out another huffed breath, her bangs again moving slightly. "I wasn't sure I was going to show you this, but I like you. After reading that," she nodded toward the file, "I think you deserve to know what's happening. Honestly, girl, how could you stay with that...I want to call him some really nasty names, but I'll refrain."

"You can't possibly call him anything I haven't more than once."

"Yeah, but you're still blaming yourself for something that wasn't your fault."

Tina blinked, her eyes awash with tears. Most of the time, she liked to think she was strong, that she'd grown and become a capable woman. Then the past would rear its ugly head, and she'd be back to being the passive milquetoast she'd been when she lived with Jared.

"You said you've got more? Might as well hit me with it."

Twisting around in her chair, Destiny reached into her bag, and Tina spotted another tattoo on her left shoulder, mostly hidden by the black tank. Looked like Destiny liked decorating her body with pretty ink.

Another folder hit the table, smaller than the first, but still making Tina feel physically ill. Whatever was in that second folder had the little hairs on her neck standing at attention, and not in a good way.

"Did you know your ex-husband is in Portland?"

"No. I knew he called my work, talked to my boss, because she called and told me. I thought he was still in California. He usually has private investigators trying to find me. He only shows up once they've told him where I'm at."

"He flew to Portland late last night. Guess he thinks that's where you're at. Will your boss tell him where you're at?"

Tina shook her head. "Absolutely not."

"Good. Next question, what can you tell me about Randolph Webster?

"He's my father-in-law, I mean my ex-father-in-law. Why?"

Destiny hesitated for a fraction of a second before she spoke. "Because I think he's dead."

# CHAPTER TEN

Tina knew her mouth hung wide open after Destiny's outrageous remark. Slamming it shut, she stared at the woman sitting across from her, trying to gauge if this was a joke or whether she'd lost her mind.

"Dead? Did you say you think Randolph is dead?"

"Bear with me, let me explain."

"Better be good. That's a serious accusation."

Destiny held up both hands in front of her. "I'm not accusing anybody. Well, I have my suspicions, but nothing to base them on except my gut."

Tina scrubbed her hands over her face, trying to wrap her mind around what had started out as a vivisection of her own life, and apparently had degenerated into a murder mystery. Was she supposed to guess whodunnit?

"Start at the beginning, so I can make heads or tails of what you're alleging."

Destiny reached into what seemed to be a bottomless bag and pulled out a large yellow legal pad with writing across several pages. Girlfriend had been busy, Tina mused.

"When I started digging," Destiny shrugged, "I also

looked into those closest to you. Your Aunt Maxie, Uncle Stanley, who seem like they're good people. Your parents—"

"I get it. They aren't Ward and June Cleaver."

"Who?"

Tina blinked a couple of times. "Guess you didn't watch a lot of old TV shows growing up, did you? The Cleavers were part of an old TV show. They were the perfect family, with kids who got into mischief and the parents were forgiving and willing to pass along life lessons. The antithesis of my own little nuclear family."

"Ah, got it. Guess that's another thing we have in common." Destiny's look of sympathy said without further explanation she'd had a similar home life. Which was a shame, because she seemed like a really nice woman.

"Anyway, I noticed whenever you were together with the ex's family, you seemed to spend more time with Randolph than anybody else."

Tina nodded. "He wasn't half bad. Not like Liliana. She was a monster-in-law from the very beginning. If she'd had her way, Jared and I would never have married. I never measured up to her lofty expectations. I wasn't rich enough or cultured enough. I didn't come from a prestigious family. I wasn't smart enough or pretty enough for her standards." She laughed, hearing how ugly it sounded. "I was the one thing she couldn't convince Jared to stay away from. In every other thing, he kowtowed to her every wish and whim. Honestly, I'm surprised he bucked her wishes and married me."

"From what I saw, you probably wish he'd listened to Mommy dearest."

"Let's get back to Randolph." Tina pictured the older man in her mind, seeing his salt and pepper hair, his sparkling blue eyes filled with intelligence. He'd stood a full head taller than her, his body honed from hours spent on the golf and tennis courts when he wasn't in his high-rise office building, making deals and adding to the family's already overflowing coffers. Yet, he'd always had a kind word or a smile for her. He'd been the one bright light in her disastrous marriage.

"I shouldn't have said anything." Destiny started to shove the legal pad back into her messenger bag, and Tina jumped to her feet, reaching across the table and slamming her hand down on top of it.

"No way, Destiny. You can't drop a bombshell like that and then leave me hanging. Maybe you don't have proof, but you found enough to make you think something's wrong. Tell me."

Destiny blew out a heavy sigh. "Randolph Webster hasn't been seen in the office in weeks. His administrative assistant isn't exactly the chatty type, but I managed to get her talking and she said Liliana Webster keeps saying he's out of town, taking a little time off. Except he was negotiating some big takeover of another company, and his assistant said he'd never leave things hanging like this. When she pressed Liliana, she claimed he was under the weather, and his doctor didn't want him coming into the office."

"Randolph would never go out of town in the middle of negotiations. He's known as a savvy shark when it comes to money matters. It's like a game, a competition to him, where he always wants to come out on top. This doesn't sound right."

"That's the impression I got about the guy. I talked to a few more people at the main office. Word of advice; never go straight to the top, they'll never tell you anything. Always talk to the people really in the know, like admins. Catch them at the right time, chat them up like you're their best friend, and you'll be amazed at how much info you'll glean."

"Good to know. What else?" The gnawing in Tina's gut wouldn't quit. Of all the Websters, the only one who'd treated her with any kind of respect was Randolph. The thought that something might have happened to him seemed inconceivable.

"Nobody at their home is talking. I mean nobody. Gardener, maid, cook, nobody. Which raises a few more questions. I know, I know, that in and of itself doesn't mean a thing. So, I did something I wouldn't normally do. I caught a flight to California and did a little snooping. I went all old school, hitting the bricks." Destiny grinned and it lit her face with an inner beauty that was hard to disguise.

"Okay, I'll bite. What did you find, Sherlock?"

"Liliana Webster hasn't left her house in several weeks,

right around the time Randolph went missing. Sound like her?"

Tina shook her head. Liliana was a social butterfly, on a number of committees and charity fund raisers. Always featured in the social pages, though rarely in the gossip rags, because they'd quickly discovered she didn't mind siccing one of her coterie of lawyers on them.

"She'd never be out of the spotlight for that long, not without a good reason."

"That's what I thought. Now Jared, he's been going about his usual routine. Performing surgeries, heading his department at the hospital, dealing with patients at his office. Nothing out of the ordinary."

"Except making my life a living nightmare."

Destiny nodded. "Yeah, there is that."

"This still doesn't explain why you think Randolph is dead."

"I looked into his finances, specifically his credit cards. If he was supposedly out of town, he'd have used either personal or business cards, right? Well, there has been no activity on any of his cards for months. Even the joint cards he has with Liliana, the only activity has been hers."

"Maybe he used cash?"

"It's possible, but was that normal for him? Especially if he was out of the city or out of the country? It didn't fit the pattern of behavior from his previous trips. Everything is charged, especially in business, where there needs to be a paper trail for taxes and expenses."

"But..."

"Like I said, this is only my gut feeling. Enough time has passed to arouse suspicion in my books. He's somebody who's a well-known businessman, energetic and fairly athletic if his country club records are correct. Yet he suddenly disappears off the face of the earth with nobody's suspicions being aroused? Somebody's covering up something. Either he's sick enough to be incapacitated, he's been institutionalized—though I can't find any record of that, but it might be under a fake name—or he's not around to raise a ruckus."

Tina's mind was awhirl with everything Destiny said. Jared wouldn't be hunting her so diligently if his father fell ill. Her ex was a control freak, and needed structure and discipline in every aspect of his life, including his ties to his family. If his father was sick, he'd have taken him to the most prestigious hospital in the world, no matter the cost. Destiny was right: something was wrong, but she wouldn't go so far as to say Randolph was dead.

"Okay, I agree something seems fishy, but I don't see where it adds up to him being dead. It seems like a stretch."

"You know the family better than me, Tina. I probably shouldn't have said anything, but it's been picking at me. Like an itch you can't scratch. Anyway, you've got the full file of what I found. I know I should have given it to Chance, since he's the one who hired me, but I'm not going to. If you want to share with him, that's your business."

"Thank you." Tina laid her hand atop the file folder containing every aspect of her life. Every secret, everything she'd done. The good, the bad, and the ugly. And she had to admit, there'd been some ugly times. Ones she wanted to forget, but it seemed like the past always caught up to her eventually.

"A word of advice?"

"Sure."

"The few times I've talked to Chance about you, it seemed like he really cared about you. Oh, he never came out and said those words, but I could read between the lines. If you care about him, tell him what's in there. As much or as little as you feel he needs to know, but don't start any kind of relationship by hiding the truth. It never works the way you think it will. Speaking from experience, it'll only hurt you in the end."

Destiny stood and pulled her bag off the back of the chair, then reached and grabbed her glass of tea, swallowing down the rest until the remaining ice clinked against the sides.

"I appreciate you coming all the way out here and giving me the choice about talking to Chance. And the info about Randolph and Liliana. I'm completely out of the loop with them, deliberately, but I hope your gut instinct is wrong."

"Me, too."

Tina rested her chin on her hand and studied Destiny,

again catching the peekaboo tattoo above the edge of her black tank.

"Can I ask you something?"

"Sure."

"Your tattoo. I couldn't help noticing it, because the colors are so bright and vivid. What is it?"

Destiny set down her bag on the chair, and pulled down the top edge of her tank, exposing the tattoo in its entirety. It wasn't big, maybe three or four inches tall, but it was exquisite. A blooming rose in shades of crimson, the petals looking like velvet, and so realistic and lifelike, it almost looked like it had just been plucked from the garden. On the edge of the flower sat a fairy, kicking her legs, with her wings half-furled behind her. Long dark hair spilled over the fairy's shoulders onto the brilliant sapphire pixie dress covering the fairy's torso. While the scene might appear whimsical, the artist's ability made the piquant scene come alive with movement. A shiny drop of dew glistened on one of the rose petals, appearing to hang from its edge, like it would drip off any moment.

"That's beautiful."

"Thanks. A friend of mine did it," Destiny smiled.

"Well, he or she is an extraordinary artist. I've seen a lot of ink work, and this is topnotch."

"I'll let her know. She works in a shop in Austin. She did this one, and the one on my shoulder."

Tina moved a little closer, looking closely at the fairy.

There was a mischievous expression on her face, and if she wasn't mistaken, she was winking. Before she could straighten, she heard the back door open followed by a masculine gasp. She knew before she even looked up that Dane had walked in and immediately gotten the wrong impression. Typical male reaction, their mind always headed straight for the gutter.

"What's wrong, Dane? Haven't you ever seen one girl looking at another girl's boobs?"

"What?"

Tina shot Destiny a quick look, noticing the woman's eyes widen. She was staring at Dane like a chocaholic standing in front of an all-you-can-eat dessert buffet. Hmmm, interesting.

"I was looking at Destiny's tattoo. Want a peek?"

"Um, that's okay. I came in for a drink, but I can come back." He shifted from foot to foot, but Tina noticed he hadn't taken his eyes off Destiny, who still had the top of her tank top pulled down, like she was frozen in place.

"Let me grab you some tea." She hip-checked Destiny as she walked past. Couldn't leave her new friend standing there like a fish on a hook. Dane hadn't moved an inch since he'd stepped into the kitchen, the back door still standing open.

She made quick work of pouring him a big glass of sweet tea from the pitcher and handed it to him. Leaning toward him, she whispered, "Dane, you're staring."

That seemed to shake him out of his stupor, and he lifted the glass, drinking down half of it in one swallow.

"I've got to hit the road before the boss starts looking for me." Sliding the messenger bag across her body, Destiny headed for the front door, and Tina followed close behind.

"That's Dane Boudreau?" Destiny's eyes darted back toward the kitchen.

"Yep."

"Ridge has mentioned him. He runs the ranch, right?"

Tina's lips curled up, aware that Destiny was fishing for information. Guess she'd liked what she saw. Not that she blamed her; Dane Boudreau was worth a second look.

"He does. Want an introduction?"

With one final glance toward the kitchen, Destiny simply shook her head. "Not a good idea."

"Well, if you change your mind, let me know. By the way, can you send the info about your tattoo artist friend? I might want to check her out, if I'm going to be around for a while longer. I could use some new ink."

"New ink? You have tats?"

"One on my right hip, and one on my right shoulder."

Destiny's grin suddenly filled with mischief. "Chance see them yet?"

Laughter burst from Tina at her not-so-subtle question. "No, he hasn't."

"Maybe you should consider showing them to him. He's a nice guy and sexy as sin."

Silently Tina agreed with Destiny's assessment. Chance was a walking, talking advertisement for the perfect guy. But she'd fallen for that before, and once burned…

"Thanks again." She hesitated for a moment before adding, "If you hear anything else about Randolph, would you let me know?"

"You got it."

Tina stood on the porch and watched Destiny drive away. After several moments, she heard footsteps behind her, and Dane joined her on the porch. His gaze followed the beat-up sedan until it was out of sight, not saying a word.

"Her name's Destiny. She works for your brother."

"The hacker?" His voice deepened with the question.

"Yep. Seems to know her stuff. Brought me a file on everything she'd dug up on me."

"In other words, some light reading."

She gave an inelegant snort. "If you want to call it that. She's cute, isn't she?"

"What?"

"I can introduce you properly, if you want."

A wistful expression crossed his face before he shook his head.

"You sure? She seemed to like you, too." She couldn't understand why he'd turn down her offer. His eyes had practically eaten the other woman alive in the kitchen.

"I need to get back to work. You need anything?"

"I'm good."

Without another word, he walked down the front porch steps and headed around the side of the house. She couldn't help wondering about his reaction to the pretty computer expert and his refusal to get to know her better. Seemed like there might be something going on with Dane. If she was sticking around, she'd probably stick her nose into his business, but she wasn't. She had to head back to Portland.

No matter how much she wanted to stay.

# CHAPTER ELEVEN

C hance made arrangements with his office to have the assistant district attorney handle things for the next couple of days, citing family issues as well as his shoulder. Might as well use the minor injury to his advantage, since he needed to make sure things with Tina didn't escalate. He was still concerned about Jared Webster being in Portland. He was escalating his hunt for Tina and getting much too close to finding her. Thank goodness she was in Shiloh Springs. And she wasn't alone.

He pulled his car into a parking spot in front of Gracie's Grounds, because there wasn't any parking in front of Daisy's. Earlier that morning, he'd called a family meeting with a few of his brothers, wanting to figure out his next move. He trusted his brothers' opinions, especially since Rafe and Antonio both had experience dealing with men like Jared Webster.

Walking past Jill's bakery, he smiled when he noted several people milling around the display case at the front. Looked like business was booming for his brother's fiancée, and he couldn't be happier. Being with Jill had changed

Lucas, making him happier than he'd seen his brother in a long time. They both deserved each other, and though their path back together had been rough, they'd made it through to the other side, and he couldn't be happier.

He strode past the sheriff's station, noting his brother's car parked out front, and kept walking. Within minutes, he glanced through the big picture window at Daisy's Diner and stuttered to a halt. Several tables had been pulled together, and he spotted Rafe, Antonio, Liam, and Ridge. Not surprising, since he'd called them and asked for this brunch-time meeting. What did surprise him? Tessa, Serena and Maggie occupied seats around the table.

Chuckling, he walked through the front door, calling out hellos to a few friends seated in the booths. He loved his hometown, and the people he worked to serve. The community was a family, and he liked and respected each and every one of them.

"Morning, bro. You're late." Rafe had an arm slung around Tessa's shoulder, her chair pulled up close beside his. He couldn't believe how much of a difference the pretty redhead made in his brother. The taciturn sheriff of the county smiled more, and the love he felt for his fiancée shone through like a lighthouse beacon in the darkness.

"I'm right on time. You're early."

Chance pulled out the one empty chair and slid onto it, smiling at Daisy, who'd walked over with the coffee pot and a fresh cup.

"Morning, Chance."

"Good morning, Daisy."

"Y'all ready to order, or do you need a couple minutes?" She poured Chance's coffee and topped off the other cups. "Ike's got some stuffed French toast this morning that's to die for, if you're interested. Fresh blueberries with cream cheese, brioche bread, and powdered sugar. It's amazing."

"Sounds good. I'll have that."

"Make that two," Liam added. "I missed dinner last night, and I'm starving."

"Add a side of bacon, and I'll have the same." Rafe's smiled after Tessa elbowed him in the stomach.

"Heathen. It's not fair, you get to eat anything you want. I'm still trying to lose another five pounds before the wedding." Tessa looked at Daisy, giving her puppy dog eyes. "Can I get a small bowl of fruit?"

"Sure thing, sugar. How about you, Maggie?"

"I should have the same, but you've tempted me with the French toast. I'll have that."

"Get the fruit too, honey, and we'll share." Ridge pressed a kiss to her cheek, and she laid her head on his shoulder.

Once all the orders had been placed, Chance let his eyes stray to the people seated around the table. His family. The people he loved and respected above all others. It might have taken him a while when he first moved in with the Boudreaus to adjust to changing his entire life, but he'd never again take for granted the blessing he'd been given.

"So, Chance, what's with the nine-one-one?" Liam took a long sip of his coffee, eyeing him over the rim. "How can I help?"

"How can we help, bonehead." Ridge popped Liam's shoulder with the back of his hand, and Liam simply rolled his eyes, like it happened every day.

"I wanted to talk to y'all about Tina."

"Told you," Tessa whispered to Rafe.

Chance chose to ignore them, plunging ahead. "I'm actually glad you brought the ladies along, because I'd like to ask a favor."

"Of course. Whatever you need." Serena smiled at Chance, and he remembered everything she'd been through since coming to Shiloh Springs. Of course, all of the women seated at the table had been through their own tough times, and they'd come out stronger at the end. Just like Joshua had said, the Boudreau men seemed to be attracted to women who weren't doormats. They were complicated, complex women, and he adored each and every one of them. He'd never understood how each of his brothers had changed, grown and matured after meeting the love of their lives. Until he met Tina.

"I think Tina needs to stay in Shiloh Springs—"

"That's awesome!" Serena's grin spread across her face and she high fived Antonio.

"Yay! I knew you'd come to your senses," Tessa jumped from her chair and raced around, hugging Chance's neck.

"She's perfect for you!"

"Wait, wait! I think you misunderstood. Let's backtrack for a second."

"Too late, bro. You might as well surrender now, because they've got you halfway to the altar already. Right, Red?"

"You hush." Tessa pointed at Chance. "Explain, please. Why do you want Tina to stay?"

Chance sighed, realizing he'd stuck his foot in his mouth. Fortunately, everybody seemed to be handling his faux pas okay, though he had a feeling the women were about to start conspiring behind his back, playing matchmakers.

"Destiny found out Tina's ex-husband showed up in Portland yesterday. I'm sure Gertie won't tell him anything, but that doesn't mean he won't figure out she's no longer there. He's not going to give up until he's standing in front of her. He's obsessed with her. I'm afraid if she heads back to Oregon, he'll find her."

"Didn't he already break into her apartment?"

"Not him personally, Rafe. Probably one of his hired help. Left a nasty message scrawled on her living room wall." Chance's blood ran cold, remembering the text message Tina had received from her landlord. While the message hadn't contained the kind of threat law enforcement could act upon, the inherent threat beneath the words was evident. It was precisely why he'd filed for restraining orders for Tina in Oregon, and if he got her to stay in Shiloh Springs, he'd get one here, too.

"You're right, she stays here. What can we do?" Maggie shifted in her chair, leaning forward and putting her forearms on the table. "If you need, she can stay at my place. I've got state of the art security. Nobody's getting anywhere close without me or Ridge knowing about it."

"She's not kidding, dude. Plus, she's practically got her own armory locked up tight there."

"Appreciate it, Ridge. Thanks for offering, Maggie. If things get rough, I might take you up on it. Right now, I want her to stay because she wants to. The last thing she needs is to feel like she's a prisoner. I have the feeling she got enough of that when she was married to her ex."

The expressions on his brothers' faces were mirror images of each other and echoed how he felt. He had his suspicions that wasn't the only abuse she suffered at Webster's hands, but he didn't have solid proof. Tina hadn't admitted such, though through her actions, he suspected. Working with victims every day, he'd gotten adept at reading the signs.

"Chance, tell me what I can do. I want to help any way I can." Serena reached across the table, placing her hand atop his, a sad smile touching her lips. "We all want to help."

He swallowed past the lump in his throat. "Thanks. I don't think Webster's figured out she's in Texas. Like I mentioned, I don't think Tina's boss will tell him where she is, and her landlord definitely agreed not to say anything without contacting me first. But I don't want her to feel like she's a prisoner at the Big House, either. Maybe you can spend some time with her. Bring her into town, go shopping. Make her feel a part of things, not isolated and alone."

Serena nodded. "We can do that. The biggest thing is to make sure she's never alone, right?"

"Right." He wasn't surprised she'd picked up on his thoughts. Maybe he was being too controlling, but better safe than sorry. The thought of Tina being harmed in any way made him want to punch something—or somebody.

"Not like it's a hardship to spend time with somebody we already like. I can include her in some of the wedding planning."

A collective groan went up around the table.

"What?" Though she acted offended, Change saw the laughter in Tessa's gaze, and she winked at him.

"I think she'd like that, Tessa."

"Alright, I'll contact the rest of the womenfolk, and we'll make sure Tina's never vulnerable. Beth will definitely want to help, and I'll bet Renee will drop everything to help. Tina's her friend."

"You said Destiny found out Webster was in Portland? What else did she find out?"

Rafe's question didn't surprise Chance. As the county's elected sheriff, he was darned good at his job. Sharp and intuitive, Rafe had a knack for getting to the heart of a problem, and looking at a situation from an angle and perspective others missed.

"She's still looking into Webster and his associates. I'll let you know when I have all the information." Chance was sure his brothers would read between the lines and realize he didn't want to talk about Tina's business in public.

Daisy walked up before he had to add more and started unloading the tray holding their food. Another waitress held a second tray. She was the new girl Daisy had hired, somebody who'd moved to Shiloh Springs recently, though he couldn't remember her name.

Once all the plates of food and glasses of juice were handed around, he dug into his French toast, closing his eyes at the first bite. Daisy hadn't exaggerated; Ike had a winner with this dish. The taste of fresh blueberries burst across his tongue, with a hint of cream cheese, along with the custardy goodness of the eggy bread. Without a doubt, this was going to become one of his favorites, even if it meant an extra hour or two on the treadmill.

The conversation turned to mundane topics, though if he knew his brothers—and he did—the discussion wasn't finished, it would simply be continued later.

He could hardly wait.

Jared Webster leaned back against the upholstered leather of the town car. He'd hired a driver for the day to pick him up at the airport and take him to his mother's house. After he finished here, he'd have the driver take him home, to the house he shared with Tina during their marriage. He hadn't sold it after the divorce. Why would he? The house was a wedding present from his parents, and Tina had made it into a home.

The driver pulled up onto the large circular drive that fronted his parents' home, the house where he'd grown up. A beautiful three-story mansion in Pacific Heights, his grandfather had purchased the home when he'd made his fortune years earlier. His father had inherited the home when Jared was a toddler, and he'd spent his formative years running around on the polished marble floors and racing through the gardens.

Climbing from the car, he didn't bother knocking, simply walking into the grand foyer. The ornate double staircase provided an extravagant backdrop for the lush décor. His mother had brought in some swanky, high priced designer a couple of years ago, and had redone the entire mansion in understated elegance. While it was precisely her taste, he preferred the more personal touches Tina left on their home.

Shaking his head, he called out for his mother.

"I'm here, dear. Did you just get back?" He spotted her just inside the opening of the formal parlor.

"Yes, I came straight from the airport." Leaning forward, he brushed a kiss against her cheek. As always, his mother was dressed exquisitely, from the top of her coiffed blonde head to the tips of her Christian Louboutin heels.

"Well, don't keep me waiting. Did you find her?"

Sliding his hand on her elbow, he steered her back into the front parlor, and helped her onto the velvet tufted chaise. Moving to an adjacent chair, he stretched his legs in front of him and steepled his fingers, drawing out the moment.

"Jared…"

"Not this time, Mother."

"I don't understand. How is she able to stay one step ahead of us? We're paying for the best investigators, and yet she's still slipping between our fingers."

A small smile curved Jared's mouth. At least this time he hadn't come home empty handed. He had viable information, more than he'd had when he'd headed to Portland.

"She's in Texas."

"What! How do you know?"

"Serendipity, my dear. I happened to be in the right place at the right time."

His mother smoothed a lock of hair behind her ear and huffed out a sigh. Jared bit the inside of his cheek to keep from chuckling. While she tried, she couldn't quite hide her frustration that he didn't immediately spill his guts. Too bad. He was enjoying drawing out the moment, since there hadn't been many since Tina vanished.

"Well? Tell me."

"I went to the place where Tina works. Of course, she wasn't there, but I planned to interrogate her boss. Work my charm on the old biddy and have her eating out of my hand by the time I asked about Tina. Turns out, I didn't need to.

I overheard her talking to some customers, and who do you think they were talking about?"

His mother sat up straighter on the chaise. "Tina?"

"Precisely. Her boss mentioned Tina was in Texas, though she was supposed to come back soon. She also mentioned a name, some friend of Tina's." He gritted his teeth, jaw tight, at the thought of Tina with another man. "Someone named Shiloh Boudreau. I have the team looking into him now. Before you know it, we'll have a location. I can't wait to have my wife in my arms again."

"Of course, darling boy. But don't forget the end goal. We need Tina happy and willing to return home. Once we've brought her back into the fold, you'll have your happily ever after."

"First things first, Mother. As soon as the investigators get us the information on where Tina is in Texas, I'll head down there, and—"

"You'll do nothing of the kind." The vehemence in her voice startled Jared, had him shifting in the chair, straightening at the command in her tone.

"But—"

"You have to carry on with your life. Everything needs to appear normal and above board. You'll go to the office. You'll tend to your patients, perform your surgeries, and deal with your duties at the hospital. When it comes to bringing Tina home, leave that to me."

A shiver skittered down his spine at the eerie calmness in

her voice. The gleam in her eyes threw him back into memories from his childhood, evoking feelings he kept deeply buried.

"I think I should be the one to bring her home."

She stood and closed the distance between them. "You just leave everything to Mother. Before you know it, everything will be as it should be, and everyone will be happy."

Leaning down, she kissed him on the cheek and strode from the room, back ramrod stiff, her heels barely making a sound on the polished marble floors. Jared closed his eyes, wondering if his life would ever be the same again.

# CHAPTER TWELVE

Two days later, Tina stood on the front porch of the Big House, surrounded by women. Over the last fifteen minutes, cars had pulled up and parked in front. Serena arrived first, bounding up the steps with an energy Tina envied.

Next, Tessa showed up. She climbed from her car, opened the back door, and filled her arms with canvas bags, boxes, and what looked like white binders. Within a few minutes, Beth and Jamie arrived with Renee. Jamie immediately ran to Tina, throwing her arms around her waist, talking a mile a minute, telling Tina that since it was Saturday, she didn't have school, and her mother promised her ice cream if she was good, and wanting to know if she could go see Otto, the Boudreaus' donkey. At her mother's nod, she raced through the house, and Tina heard the back door slam as Jamie went to visit her equine best friend.

"I swear, some days I think I'm going to collapse before noon trying to keep up with all her energy." Beth leaned against the pillar of the front porch and blew out a long breath. "She woke up this morning before six, and she's been going nonstop ever since."

"And you offered her ice cream? I doubt that will calm her down, all that sugar."

Beth smirked before answering. "I'm gonna stuff my baby girl full of ice cream, and then hand her off to her daddy, and then I'm going to take a long-deserved nap."

Tina chuckled at the evil gleam in Beth's eyes. "Sounds like an excellent plan. Now, would anybody care to tell me why you're here? I have the feeling you're not here to visit with Ms. Patti, because she's in town."

Serena looped her arm through Tina's and led her through the front door. "Nope, we're here to see you. Figured since you were still in Shiloh Springs, we'd come out and keep you company. Plus, we have wedding stuff to go over with Tessa, and thought since you're here and don't have anything else to do, you can help us. A new, fresher set of eyes, so to speak."

"I thought Tessa had all the wedding stuff already handled," Tina protested as Serena guided her to the Big House's living room, where Tessa had spread out a plethora of stuff on the coffee table. So...much...stuff.

"We're in the final stretch," Tessa answered without looking up, pulling something else from her seemingly bottomless bag and adding it to the wavering stack. "There's only two months until the wedding, and I have to make sure I have everything taken care of, because it has to be perfect."

Tina slid onto the sofa beside Tessa and grabbed her

hands before they could dive back into the bag and pull out even more stuff. "Slow down. I'm sure you've got everything handled. Let me give you a word of advice. I worked as a wedding planner for almost a year, and I can assure you that no matter how much planning and scheduling, double and triple checking everything, something always gets skipped or forgotten. The only thing that matters is having your friends and family around you, standing up before God and the people you love, and pledging your heart and life to Rafe. Everything else is just stuff."

Tessa's eyes filled with tears, and she shot forward and flung her arms around Tina, hugging her tight. Over Tessa's shoulder, she saw Beth with her hand over her heart. When she met Tina's gaze, she mouthed the words, "thank you."

Tessa pulled back slowly and wiped at her eyes. "You're right. I guess I'm obsessing over all the small things that might go wrong, instead of focusing on the fact I'm marrying the man of my dreams."

"It's perfectly normal to want everything to be perfect. This is your wedding, the thing every girl looks forward to from the time they pin a pillowcase to their hair and parade down an imaginary aisle. And I know you've planned everything exactly the way you want it, and it will be beautiful. Just don't let it get in the way of you living."

"I bet you were an amazing wedding planner." Beth perched on the arm of the chair, and Serena took up space on the ottoman, nodding at Beth's words.

"You'd be wrong. I was awful at it. You might not have noticed, but I'm not the most patient person in the world, and brides tend to be a tad overexcitable. Especially over the small stuff. I dealt with one too many bridezillas, and decided I needed a different profession."

"I find that hard to believe. Not about the bridezillas, because that seems to be the norm nowadays. But the part about you not being patient." Beth waved her hand in Tina's direction. "I see how you are with Jamie, and she can be a handful."

"And I worked with you, remember? I've seen you handle the most belligerent customers and never break a sweat." Renee walked in from the kitchen, carrying glasses and the pitcher of tea from the fridge. "The coffee shop could be crowded, I mean wall-to-wall people, and Tina never lost her cool. By the time she got them all served, they were laughing and smiling and happy to be there."

"Okay, sheesh. Let's just say it wasn't my favorite job. Weddings are beautiful, but they are a lot of work." She pointed to the mound of wedding paraphernalia on the coffee table. "Now, anybody want to tell me why you're really here? Oh, wait, let me guess. You're my new babysitters!"

She almost laughed at the guilty expressions crossing each woman's face. Yep, she'd guessed right. Chance was definitely working to earn his Boy Scout badge for being overprotective.

"It's not like that," Beth protested. "We all want to spend time with you."

"I get it." Tina let her smile grow, because she couldn't be mad at these women. They'd become friends since her time in Shiloh Springs, and she'd have missed them all terribly when she went back to Portland. Or she would, when she actually left.

"Okay, I'm gonna lay all the cards out on the table," Tessa leaned forward, catching Tina's eye.

"Where are you going to put them?" Tina joked, point to the mound of things already decorating the coffee table. "I think you're out of room."

"Hardy har har, Miss Jokester. Laugh it up. Seriously, our guys told us what's going on with your ex-husband. That he has been looking for you, and he actually found out where you live in Portland."

"Tessa's right." Renee narrowed her eyes at Tina. "We're friends. I stayed at your place in Portland. I worked beside you every day. How did I not now you'd been married?"

Tina drew in a shaky breath, a rush of memories flooding her. Other than her Aunt Maxie and Uncle Stanley, nobody knew the true facts of her life with Jared. And even they didn't know everything.

"It's not something I like to talk about. It wasn't a happy marriage, and the divorce was less than amicable. Jared can't seem to accept the fact that I didn't want to be married anymore."

"Men. Pfft. Can't live with 'em, can't bash 'em in the head with a shovel." Serena lifted her glass and drained it in one long swallow. "Tina honey, all of us," she waved the hand holding the glass around, pointing at each of the women, "could tell you about our personal nightmares with the men in our lives—pre-Boudreau. We've all had moments where our lives have been threatened or put in danger, right down to and including Jamie. Just know this, with us you're in a safe place. You can tell us as much or as little as you're comfortable with, and we'll keep your confidence."

Tina scanned the faces of the women assembled in the living room of the Big House and read the truth of Serena's words. Each woman there had been through their own personal nightmare, and come out the other side whole and able to move forward and find love again.

Her thoughts turned to Chance, the sweet, stubborn man who both tormented and titillated her alternatively. Even from the moment they'd met, there'd been a spark there, unlike anything she'd experienced before. Now, sitting here amidst these strong, self-sufficient women, she wondered if she'd found the sisters she'd always craved.

Bracing herself mentally, she sat up straighter, and made her decision.

"Alright. I'd like to tell you about my life." And she did, not leaving out any details, knowing they'd keep silent about what she told them. These women had formed their own family, the Boudreau women, and she trusted them.

And secretly wondered if maybe she'd be part of them. She hoped so.

Chance pulled into the parking lot of the emergency clinic. He'd promised to come back for a follow up visit, though he didn't feel like he needed to. The shoulder hadn't given him any problems, other than the unsightly black and blue bruises that had now turned to an ugly yellow-green.

The waiting room contained a bunch of sniffly, snot-nosed kids who were hacking and coughing, and he hoped he didn't catch anything contagious. He had far too much to do, and getting sick wasn't on his agenda. He checked in with the front desk and took a seat in one of the plastic chairs, nodding at Felicity Warren. He'd gone to school with her, though she'd been a year ahead of him. The minute she'd graduated, she'd married her high school sweetheart and started popping out kids. At last count, if he remembered right, she had six young'uns.

"How are you, Felicity?"

"We're getting along, Chance. The twins haven't been doing good the last couple of days, so I brought them in for a quick check up. I haven't seen you in ages. Hope everything's okay. How's your momma and daddy?"

"They're fine. I just need the doctor to give me a clean bill of health. Banged up my shoulder, that's all."

"That's good. There's a nasty bug going around, which is why I wanted to make sure the twins haven't caught it. The last thing I need is them spreading it to the rest of their brothers and sisters. Ugh. You might as well commit me if all six of them come down with a flu bug at the same time."

Before he could come up with a response to the thought of six puking, screaming kids, his name was called and he was escorted to a room. He didn't have to wait long before Dr. Shaw strode through the door, looking a little disheveled, his hair mussed and the stethoscope around his neck hanging at an angle.

"Afternoon, Chance. Looks like you're here to follow up a shoulder injury."

He nodded. "It wasn't much, just banged it on the truck door when I had an accident. It's fine."

"Let me be the judge of that." His words were followed with a tired smile. "I looked at the x-rays from your last visit, and they looked good. Lose the shirt and let me get a gander at the bruising."

He turned his back, and Chance unbuttoned and shrugged out of his shirt. Dr. Shaw slid on a pair of gloves, and gently examined his left shoulder, having him move it several times, and reach over his head.

"I'm not seeing any swelling. Any pain or discomfort with reaching out to the side or overhead."

Chance shook his head. "It's fine."

"Alright. You've got an all clear for full use. Anything

else you're having problems with?"

"Not physically. Can I pick your brain with a couple medical questions?"

"Sure." Dr. Shaw pulled off the plastic gloves and tossed them into the trash can beside the tiny sink. "As long as it doesn't have anything to do with patient confidentiality."

"Nothing like that. It's more of a physician thing."

Dr. Shaw's lips quirked up into a full-blown smile. "A physician thing? Now I'm curious what you consider a physician thing."

Chance shrugged back into his shirt, doing up the buttons and tucking it into his jeans. "I guess that wasn't the best turn of phrase. I'm wondering about ethical behavior with regards to a physician. Someone who is in a position of authority. Let's say for the sake of this discussion, chief of a department at a major hospital."

"What type of ethical situation are we talking about?"

"What kind of action could be taken against, let's say a surgeon, who was accused of spousal abuse? Would he lose his job at the hospital? Lose his standing as the chief of the department but still have privileges to treat patients? What about his private practice, how would an accusation affect it?"

Dr. Shaw leaned against the doorframe, arms crossed over his chest, a contemplative expression on his face. "I'm assuming this hypothetical question has something to do with a case you're working on?"

Chance debated whether let him believe that, or to tell him the truth. The man had been in Shiloh Springs a little over a year now, having relocated from out of state. It had been something of a coup for a small town like Shiloh Springs to snag a big city doctor who was willing to relocate. Of course, the last year had been overflowing with one drama after the next within his family, and he hadn't taken the time to get to know him well. He had testified at one deposition regarding a fraudulent disability case, confirming the guy claiming to be incapacitated with a debilitating back injury was lying through his teeth. Trusting his gut, he decided to give him the truth.

"Dr. Shaw—"

"If we're going to talk off the record, you might as well call me Gabe." He accompanied the statement with another smile.

"Gabe. This isn't for a case. It's personal. I'm helping somebody whose ex-husband is threatening her. He has no convictions or arrests for abuse, because she divorced the jerk."

"Good. I hate to see people staying in relationships where they're basically punching bags for their spouses, and too scared to leave."

"Then we're on the same page. Anyway, she hasn't come right out and said he physically abused her, but there was definitely emotional and verbal abuse. I suspect there was physical too, but she will not confirm or deny."

"How big a hospital are we talking about? Big city, prestigious, or a smaller place with an insular population?" Gabe's stance had shifted, becoming more relaxed, as if he'd weighed Chance's worth and found him acceptable.

"California. Large, prestigious. Family comes from old money and lots of it."

"Hmm. I'll say that makes things trickier. I'd say he'd be removed from the chief position immediately, pending an investigation. And the wheels turn slowly when it's an accusation without definitive proof. As for his practice, he might lose patients but this isn't an instance of malpractice, which would be the biggest reason he'd lose his practice."

Chance bit back the curse that rose to his lips. "Pretty much what I suspected. Appreciate your feedback."

Gabe straightened from the wall. "If you feel like you could use the assist and can trust me with the name, I'd be happy to put out any feelers. I know quite a few people in the medical field in California."

"Would this be considered patient confidentiality?" Chance was only partly joking.

"In our case, yes." He held out his hand and Chance shook it.

"The physician I'm referring to is Dr. Jared Webster. Graduated from Stanford. He's chief of surgery at their teaching hospital and has a thriving private practice."

The lines around Gabe's mouth tightened and Chance noted his hands fist at his sides.

"Jared Webster. Are you talking about Tina? You think he *hit* Tina?"

Uh oh. What were the odds a doctor in the middle of small-town Texas would know not only the physician he was talking about, but his wife?

"How do you know Tina?" Chance heard the hardness in his voice and didn't care. He hoped he hadn't made a mistake in confiding in Gabe.

"I went to medical school at Stanford. While I didn't associate with them a lot, I know them. Tina is one of the smartest women I've ever met. Sharper than Webster, that's for sure. She was on the fast track. Professors loved her. Then Webster got his hooks into her and charmed her, seduced her into helping him. It started out as private tutoring after class. In my opinion, he was stupid as a stump, at least about learning and following instruction. Man's a brilliant surgeon, don't get me wrong. I watched him do things most veteran surgeons wouldn't be capable of, and saved lives. But he was rotten inside, if you know what I mean."

"Never met the man personally, and he'd better pray I never do."

Gabe moved over and stood beside Chance, until they were basically shoulder to shoulder, and stayed quiet for a minute before asking, "Is Tina alright? Tell me she isn't still with that SOB."

"She's doing fine, other than her ex stalking her."

"Wish I could say I'm surprised, but he's one of those

OCD-type people, where everything has to be exactly the way he wants. He got that from his mother. Talk about a piece of work. I only met her once and trust me, once was one time too many. Cold woman, the kind that freezes your blood in your veins. I can't imagine how Tina dealt with having Liliana Webster for a mother-in-law. Definitely the monster-in-law type."

"The more I find out about Tina's ex-husband, the more I'm glad she's out of his reach. He has no idea she's in Texas—"

"Texas? Wait—is she in Shiloh Springs?" Gabe's surprise was evident, and he spun to face Chance.

"Yeah, she's staying at the Big House."

"I don't know her all that well because she kind of dropped out of sight after she got involved with Webster. Tossed aside her intention of getting her medical degree for that—"

He cut off his words, but Chance got the gist. He felt pretty much the same.

"I have somebody with her all the time, so she's never alone. Momma and Dad know what's up, and they're in agreement she stays here until we neutralize Webster's threat."

"Do me a favor? Let Tina know I'm here, if she wants to talk with an old friend."

"I will."

"I'm going to make a couple of calls, see if I can find out

anything from a couple of colleagues who work at the teaching hospital. I'll let you know what I find out."

Chance held out his hand and Gabe shook it, his grip firm and steady.

"Appreciate it."

"Now get outta here. I've got a room full of snot-nosed kids waiting for their lollipops."

"Can't have that. I know how important a good sucker is." With a quick wave, Chance headed to the front desk and checked out.

Time to head to the Big House and to Tina.

# CHAPTER THIRTEEN

Tina leaned against the pillar on the front porch, watching the truck driving toward the Big House. She recognized Douglas' truck, the one Chance had borrowed earlier. Her heartbeat sped up at the thought Chance was home. Funny how she'd come to think about the Big House as home, yet there it was. Even though Chance had his own place in town, since she'd been in Shiloh Springs, he'd spent a lot of his time here. He'd even taken off the past several days following the accident to give his shoulder time to heal, but she suspected it was also because he wanted to spend more time with her.

The thought that he might care for her sent a tingle through her, because she knew she more than cared for him. As much as she'd thought she loved her ex-husband, those feelings faded into oblivion with the attraction she felt for Chance. He was smart. He was funny. When she was with him, he made her laugh and smile, and almost forget that she had problems. Problems that wouldn't disappear simply because she wasn't in Portland.

The pickup pulled to a stop and he climbed out, and she

couldn't hide her smile when she noted the definite spring in his step. Guess the doctor gave him a clean bill of health.

"Afternoon, Sunshine. You staying out of trouble?"

She shook her head, fluttering her lashes at him. "Trouble, Counselor? Why would you assume I court trouble?"

"Sweetheart, I'm beginning to think trouble is your middle name."

"Actually, it's Fiona, but I've been known to answer to anything."

"Feel like taking a walk with me? Doctor gave me the all clear, no restrictions." He held out his hand, and she placed hers in his, and he guided her down the front steps. Taking her hand, he curled it into the crook of his arm, and she fell into step with him as he guided her toward the side of the house.

She loved the Big House. It was a gorgeous two-story house, the large white pillars on the front porch supporting both the front porch and a second porch on the upper level. Dark green shutters highlighted the windows on the front, with a curved arch over the front door. The whole house was painted white, and there was a brick cobblestone walkway from the parking area all the way to the front porch.

Huge live oaks sat on either side of the front yard, wispy drapes of Spanish moss hanging from them, reminding her she was in the South. Being from Northern California, this was a whole different way of life, and she'd discovered she loved everything about it.

Chance led her around the extension that had been added to the Big House, a massive master suite Douglas had built for Ms. Patti, with an extended patio she could access through double French doors. She loved the splashes of color on the patio, both from the throw pillows on the furniture as well as the cascade of blooms and flowers filling decorative pots. It was a glorious, relaxing sight, and she knew if it were hers, she could spend hours sitting in there, enjoying the tranquility.

"I'd like to show you something."

"Why, Counselor, I'm not that kind of girl."

He chuckled, letting her know he'd gotten her double entendre. "Nothing like that, Sunshine, get your mind out of the gutter. Momma has a special place here on the ranch. Most folks don't know about it; we only show it to people we…care about."

A subtle fluttering in her stomach started at his pronouncement. Knowing that he included her in the people he considered important, special, made her realize how important Chance's feelings for her were. Good thing she felt the same about him.

"It's not far. I will admit it's one of my favorite places on the ranch. When I'm having a horrible day in court, thinking about Momma's hideaway makes things, I don't know, easier."

"I can't wait to see it."

While they'd been talking, Chance had continued guiding her farther away from the Big House. There were huge pine trees reaching toward the skies, with a manicured lawn surrounding the Big House, and when they stepped between the pines, her breath caught in her throat.

"It's beautiful."

Before her appeared a wonderland. A circular white gazebo sat in a clearing, the tall pines surrounding it, their branches spreading in a canopy high above the enchanted structure. It wasn't tiny, but actually big enough to hold several people, with room to spare.

"Dad helped clear the area not long after they were married. He felt she deserved her own special place, where she could escape when she needed, something that strictly belonged to her alone."

Tina smiled, her fingertips trailing across the wooden pillars, with ivy and flowers climbing along the sides. The fragrance of the flora wasn't overwhelming, but it added another layer to the whimsy and wonder of the space.

"Your father is a very smart man."

"So he's been told."

Chance leaned into the opening and flicked a switch, and the whole interior of the gazebo lit with tiny white fairy lights. The golden glow added to the ambience, like a vision from a bygone age.

"Ms. Patti's done an amazing amount of work to get all these plants to grow. I wish I could claim to have a green thumb. I do okay with a few plants on my windowsill, but they're probably all dead now."

"I'm sorry we had to hustle you away from your home."

Tina grinned and touched his hand. "I'm not. I'd never have come to Shiloh Springs. Never met your amazing family. In case you haven't noticed, Counselor, I'm pretty spontaneous. I've learned to grab and go. You don't know how lucky you are to have stability, a sense of place. To have a family who adores you. Don't get me wrong. I love my Aunt Maxie and Uncle Stanley, but I haven't been able to go and see them. Talking with them on the phone is sporadic because of my ex."

"What would you do if your life were normal? I know you were in medical school before you married your ex."

She leaned against the pillar, her fingers running along the petals of a rose, thinking about his question. "I wanted to be a surgeon. Probably would have specialized in neurosurgery, because the brain fascinated me. Everything we are, the building blocks of what makes us individuals, tie into the brain. The intricacies of each connection, they're fascinating."

He mirrored her stance, leaning against the gazebo, with his knee bent, his whole posture relaxed yet confident. The sunlight glistening through the pines cast dappled sunshine onto his hair, lending it blond highlights and creating a halo effect. She wondered how he'd react if she called him angel.

"What stopped you? You had excellent grades, your professors lauded your knowledge and your ability to learn things almost by osmosis. You'd have been an excellent surgeon."

*How do I tell him Jared's jealousy put an end to my dreams?*

"I had an accident." She held up her hand, showing him the faint spiderwebbing of scars. "The surgery to repair the damage gave me limitation of motion of my fingers. It's not bad, I can do pretty much everything, but the fine motor skills I'd need for neurosurgery?" She shrugged.

"That stinks. But couldn't you still be a doctor? I know it's not the specialty you'd chosen, but you'd still make a wonderful physician."

"Maybe. I've thought about going back, but it's hard when I'm constantly moving every six months. Turns out, Jared's costing me my career all over again."

Fortunately, he didn't catch her faux pas, instead stepping inside the gazebo and holding out his hand. Taking his, she stepped inside, her eyes caught on the structure in the middle.

"Is that a well?"

"Sure is. When I was growing up, all of us boys called it our wishing well. I can't tell you how many coins I've tossed in there."

Reaching into his pocket, he pulled out a quarter and handed it to her. "Want to take a chance?"

"Only if you make a wish, too."

"All my wishes have already come true, Sunshine." When he smiled, she felt all fluttery and tingly inside. How had she gone from finding him obnoxiously arrogant to the man who made her insides spark?

"Well, I've got lots of wishes. Hmm, what do I wish for?"

"What's your heart's desire?"

She gave him a wink and tossed her quarter into the well, making her secret wish. At his self-confident smirk, she decided a change of topic might be prudent.

"I know all about your little foray to the pool and the snakes, but I've never heard how you wound up living with the Boudreaus. Care to share? Or if it's to personal—"

"It's fine. It's not a secret, or at least not to most people who live in Shiloh Springs. Small towns are notorious for knowing everything about everybody who lives there. The Boudreaus and the Big House tend to be the subject of conversation more often than not, especially when we were growing up. With new boys showing up all the time, we tended to be excellent fodder for gossip."

Tina walked to the bench encircling the inside of the gazebo and eased onto it, patting the seat beside her. She smiled at Chance, knowing the story he intended to share was personal and intimate, and she was truly honored he felt willing to share with her.

Chance was enchanted with the genuine joy Tina exuded, both with his momma's secret garden, and with being with him. She fascinated him in a way no other woman had before, and he wondered if she always would or would it fade with familiarity.

Telling her about his family, his past? So far, he'd found her to be open-minded and fair. In all their dealings, other than their first meeting in the hotel in Portland, when he'd surprised her coming out of the shower and she'd beaned him with the hotel ice bucket, their time together had been unique. Her sense of humor and her intelligence enticed him, making him want to know more about her, and he hoped she'd eventually open up, too.

"Unlike some of my brothers, my parents were great. I was an only child, and I admit they spoiled me. They made sure I had everything I wanted. Except the BB gun I asked for on my seventh birthday. My dad was all for it; Mom threatened to rip his arms off if he bought one. Needless to say, I never got that BB gun."

"So, no chance of shooting your eye out, like in that Christmas movie?"

He joined in her laughter, remembering the scene she mentioned. It was a cute movie and one he tried to watch every holiday season.

"I probably would have. My mom worried. I was their surprise baby. They'd tried for years, and finally decided they'd never have kids. As soon as they quit trying, voila, baby boy Chance came along. Fast forward eleven years. I was spending the night at a friend's house. It was a Friday night, and we were going to the Saturday morning movies the next morning. His mom was going to drop us off at the drug store, which was across the street from the theater. I had plenty of money to buy enough candy to induce a diabetic coma, and we were heading over to watch *Chicken Little*. That's what we told his mom."

"But?"

He put on an innocent expression, and slapped his open palm against his heart.

"You don't believe me?"

"I'm sure it was a great movie, but I can't see two eleven-year-old boys wanting to see an animated kid's story. What were you really going to see?"

He grinned. "We were going to sneak in to watch *King Kong*. All the guys at school were talking about it, but there's no way my parents would have allowed me to see a monster movie."

"Thus the sneaking in?"

"We never got that far. Tate's mom woke us up, and I knew something was wrong. I could tell she'd been crying. Her eyes were red and her face was all blotchy. She sat beside me on the bottom bunk, and I knew. Like some sixth sense, intuition, whatever you want to call it. I knew my parents were gone."

The look of sympathy on Tina's face was the last thing he wanted to see. He wasn't telling her because he wanted her to feel sorry for him. Far from it. He simply wanted her to understand one of the defining moments that shaped him into who he was, the good, the bad, and the ugly.

"I'm sorry, Chance."

"Thank you. You know I was one of the lucky ones, though I almost screwed things up with the whole snakes in the pool incident. If anybody deserves credit for keeping me from ruining my life, its Douglas and Patricia Boudreau."

"They are amazing. I haven't known them long, but I think Ms. Patti is psychic. She always has her pulse on everything going on, and she had my life story out of me before I even realized I gave it to her."

Chance grinned and patted her hand. "That's my momma."

Tina shifted on the bench until she was facing him head on. "What happened to your parents?"

"The police said it was a home invasion robbery. They think my parents came home and caught them in the act. They were both shot."

"Oh, no!"

"It took several months, but the police finally caught them. They ended up in Huntsville, both serving life without parole. I didn't have any other family, so I ended up with Child Protective Services. Floated from home to home, never sticking in any one place. Entirely my fault, because I was hurt and angry and too darn bullheaded to listen to anybody who was trying to help me. Then I ended up with the Boudreaus."

A vision of the first time he'd met Douglas Boudreau flashed through his head. The latest in a long line of social workers drove him to Shiloh Springs. He'd been sullen and pouted the entire trip, determined not to like his new situation. It would never be home, because he longer had a home. Looking back, he couldn't believe how wrong he'd been.

"I imagine going from child welfare to the Big House was a bit like culture shock. When I was in medical school, I interacted with a lot of kids who came into the emergency room from foster homes. Sometimes," Tina paused, closing her eyes, "I felt helpless. There are so many kids out there who are shoved into the system because they have no one to care about them. Help them. And far too often, the home they are placed in are worse than the situations they were removed from. Being placed with the Boudreaus? You were one of the lucky ones."

"I didn't think so at the time. If they'd given me a choice, I'd have turned them down flat. I did not want to be in the middle of nowhere. Stuck on a ranch with a bunch of other foster kids, doing chores, shoveling out stalls. I was a city kid, and this was like being dropped into my worst nightmare."

Tina grinned at his description, chuckling at his expression. Now, he could see the humor, but when you're an eleven-year-old, prepubescent boy whose entire life had been uprooted, it was a nightmare. He'd expected monsters around every corner. It was "the country", which meant rattlesnakes and coyotes, cattle rustlers and shootouts. And he was stuck, because he didn't have any place else to go.

"Guess you found out it wasn't as bad as you thought."

"Not at first. I didn't fit in with the others. I shared a room with Brody. He snored and he was a tattletale."

Tina's laughter was a panacea to his soul. Her sunny disposition gave her an inner light that warmed him, which was why he'd taken to calling her Sunshine.

"Brody, the Boy Scout, a tattletale? Hard to picture that with the man I've met."

"He grew out of that phase, thank goodness, because if he hadn't, I'd have had to beat it out of him."

"You love your family, don't deny it."

"Every last one of them. When my parents were killed, I never thought I'd find a new family. Especially one filled with love and respect and values. It didn't happen overnight. And I fought caring about them. It somehow felt like a betrayal of what I felt for my biological parents."

"I get it. My situation was pretty much the reverse. I didn't have the best parents. They weren't abusive, more like inattentive. As long as I went to school and got passable grades and didn't get into trouble, they pretty much ignored me. Until Jared started showing an interest in me. Then they were Johnny-On-The-Spot, portraying our home life as the best family since the Brady Bunch. What a joke. My Aunt Maxie and Uncle Stanley were more actual parents to me than my biological family."

"Working in the district attorney's office, I've found nobody has the perfect family. Even the Boudreaus have had their issues. We've had boys who didn't make it living here. I can think of a couple right off the top of my head. Sometimes, no matter how much love you give a person, you can't change the path they're on. You can only hope they make different choices."

"Well, I'm glad things worked out for you, because you belong here. With this family. In this town. I've watched you around the citizenry, interacting with people in Shiloh Springs. You care about every single one of them, and they care about you. I can't imagine you anyplace else."

"Me either. I went to SMU to study law. Dallas is a huge city, even though it's a sprawling metropolis. I was there long enough to realize there's no place like home. And Shiloh Springs, the Boudreaus, for me that's home."

Tina stared over his shoulder, her gaze distant, like she was lost in her thoughts. Was he boring her with his life story? She'd asked, but maybe she was simply being polite.

"Do you realize how lucky you are?" Her words were said softly, almost a whisper. "I've never felt that. I wasn't settled after I graduated high school. I went into college not knowing what I wanted, and then I found medicine. I loved it, everything about it called to me. Then it was taken away from me, stolen away a little at a time, until it was gone and I felt cast adrift. When I left Jared, I didn't have any idea where I'd land, and ended up moving, trying to stay one step ahead of him. I'm still like that, never settling, never finding...*home*."

It felt like a fist punched him in the middle of his chest. He wanted that for her, to find the place where she belonged. To find the sense of peace he'd found when he'd moved back to Shiloh Springs. But more, he wanted her to find her home in him. With him. Because he knew with a certainty that was unshakable, she'd stolen his heart, and he'd never get it back.

He raised his hand, and brushed a lock of hair that had blown across her cheek behind her ear. Her eyes widened at his touch, the moment seeming to stretch out, as their gazes locked. Moving slowly, giving her time to say no, he leaned forward and brushed his lips against hers.

The sweetness of the kiss felt perfect when she responded. Her lips moved beneath his, and his breath caught. Within seconds, he deepened the kiss, his teeth tugging softly on her bottom lip until hers parted. This felt right. Everything around him disappeared except the feel of her lips beneath his, and he never wanted it to end.

Tina's arms snaked around his neck, pressing her lips harder against his, and he knew he was lost. He continued to kiss her, trailing his lips along her jawline and her cheek before returning to her mouth. Never had a kiss felt right, perfect, and he never wanted to stop.

Finally, he pulled back, watching Tina's fingertips touch

her lips, her cheeks flushed.

"We'd better get back to the house."

"Okay." She took his offered hand. "Thank you for this afternoon. I love your mother's garden, and I'm touched you'd share it with me."

How could he tell her he wanted to share everything with her? He wanted to, desperately. But until she was free from the danger stalking her, she needed time and space, and he'd give it to her. Even if it killed him.

One of the things he'd discovered after moving to the Big House and living with a passel of brothers—he had a wealth of patience, and he'd wait until she was ready. But he wasn't going away, and he wasn't going to lose her.

Ever.

# CHAPTER FOURTEEN

The scene at the Big House was controlled chaos. Everybody seemed to want to talk at once, trying to add details about Tina's disappearance. Only half-listening, Chance felt an emptiness inside. Part of him was missing, a part he'd never realized Tina had filled from the moment he'd met her. She brought a sense of lightness and joy to his life and without her, it suddenly seemed bleak and cold and empty.

A large hand clamped on his shoulder, squeezing gently. He looked up into his father's face, which was a picture of determination mixed with concern. This man was his hero, his rock, the foundation of his life, and here he stood, loaning him his support without saying a word.

"I have to find her, Dad. She can't have just disappeared. I know she wouldn't have run off without a word."

"Of course she didn't, son. There's a reason she disappeared, and we'll figure it out and bring her home."

Chance drew in a ragged deep breath, wanting with every fiber of his being to believe his father's words. Unfortunately, the reality of the situation was they might not find Tina before something bad happened to her. The only consolation he had was the fact Destiny had confirmed Jared Webster was in California, at the hospital where he worked.

"Pipe down, everyone. I want to know what y'all remember, but one at a time. You," his momma pointed to Beth, "grab a pencil and paper and take notes, so we keep track of the facts. "You," she pointed toward Tessa, "get everybody something to drink. And you," she stared at Maggie, "since you've kept a level head since we got here, you start talking. Clear, concise, and to the point. Give me the facts, hon."

Maggie stared at Ms. Patti, and Chance almost chuckled at the look of a deer-caught-in-the-headlights expression. Level-headed, take no prisoners Maggie White looked like a guilty kid caught with her hand in the cookie jar when Ms. Patti turned on her momma bear voice. It didn't take her long to get her composure back.

"Right. Tessa, Beth, and I brought Tina into town for lunch and shopping. We headed to Daisy's Diner. We all had the same thing, chicken and dumplings, because that's the Thursday special."

His momma made a keep going motion with her hands, smiling thanks as Tessa passed her a glass of tea.

"We'd almost finished, and decided we'd start over at Golden Oldies shop. Tina hadn't been there yet. She excused herself to go to the restroom."

"Nobody went with her?" Chance posed the question,

since he knew enough about the women he'd dated in the past to know they tended to go to the ladies' room in packs. He'd never understood it.

Maggie shook her head. "No, she said she'd only be a second, and I didn't have to go." A flush colored her cheeks. "We waited a few minutes, but we were talking about something." Chance didn't miss the side eye she shot at Beth, who shook her head ever so slightly. If he hadn't been watching her closely, he'd have missed it.

"What?" He barked out the question and Beth jumped. Guess he'd been a little louder than he'd intended.

"It's nothing. It has nothing to do with Tina being missing."

"Beth, please."

"Okay, fine. We weren't going to stay anything yet, but Maggie guessed." She broke into a huge grin. "Brody and I are going to have a baby."

Everyone started speaking at once, voices blending with one another in their excitement.

"Beth, that's wonderful!"

"Oh, honey, that's amazing news!"

With all the congratulations going on around them, with hugs and laughter, Chance watched his mother closely. Her eyes filled with unshed tears, and he watched her blink rapidly to keep them from falling. While she adored Jamie and loved her like she was one of their own, this baby would be the first Boudreau child born from one of her sons. One hand lay against her heart, and her eyes met his dad's, whose eyes were filled with a shocked expression. Chance couldn't remember ever seeing his dad rocked back on his heels—until now.

"Oh, Beth."

"Ms. Patti, we were planning to tell you and Douglas this weekend. We had this whole celebration planned with a whole big announcement and everything. I didn't mean to spring this on you like this. Brody and I didn't want to say anything until we knew everything was okay with the baby."

Beth walked straight into his momma's open arms, and did this whole laughing and crying thing, and his mother placed a kiss against Beth's cheek.

"Honey, I don't care how you tell me, I'm simply over the moon with happiness and joy. My baby is having a baby. Jamie's going to have a little brother or a little sister."

"We haven't told her, either. She's been pestering us about having a baby, ever since one of the teachers at her school got pregnant."

Douglas walked over, took Beth into his arms and leaned forward, whispering something in her shoulder that Chance couldn't hear, though he could pretty much figure out. His father was a man with a big heart, and enough love to share with a whole passel of boys, not counting Nica, and he knew his dad would spoil this upcoming grandchild rotten.

Ms. Patti clapped her hands, grabbing everybody's attention. "This is wonderful news, and we'll celebrate later. Right now, we've got to get back to the subject at hand and get Tina back. Maggie?"

"Um, Tina went to the ladies' room and we waited. After I guess ten minutes, Tessa went to check on her. She wasn't there. I checked with Daisy to see if she'd seen her, and she hadn't. The place isn't that big, and one of us would have spotted her if she'd come out the front, so she must have gone out the back, though Daisy swears that door is locked during business hours, except when she goes on break."

"Thank you, Maggie. Beth, Tessa, you have anything you can add to what Maggie told us?" Ms. Patti's toe was tapping on the floor, something she always did when she was thinking, and Chance knew his momma's brain was firing on all cylinders. Which was a good thing, because he personally wasn't thinking clearly at all.

"This might sound stupid," Tessa darted a glance at Chance, and he nodded. "When I checked out the restroom, I noticed the sink was dry, and there weren't any used paper towels in the wastebasket. Most women who use the facilities wash their hands after, especially if they are eating. I don't think Tina was ever in the restroom."

All the women in the room nodded, looking like bobble-head dolls and Chance bit the inside of his cheek to keep from smiling. Tessa's comments made an odd sort of sense. He agreed; he didn't think Tina ever made it to the re-stroom.

Easing out of the living room so he didn't interrupt his

mother's information gathering session, he pulled his cell phone out of his pocket, and he hit the speed dial for his brother. Rafe was at Daisy's, trying to get a lead on Tina's disappearance. Guilt ate at him, that insidious inner voice saying she'd never have gone missing if he'd been there. It didn't matter that it didn't make a lick of sense, because he couldn't have gone to the restroom with her, and she'd still be missing, but who said that guilt was logical. He didn't care what it took, how far he had to take things, he'd move heaven and earth to get her back.

"Hello."

"Find out anything?"

"Geez, Chance, gimme a break. I'm working on it." The strain in Rafe's voice was the only thing that kept Chance from chewing out his brother. The pounding of blood in his head beat a rapid *boom, boom, boom* in his temples.

"Momma's grilling the girls about what happened at Daisy's. They all ate the same meal, so we can probably exclude tampering with Tina's food."

"Already found that out. Maggie picked up the tab, so they were getting ready to leave, according to Daisy."

Chance paced across the kitchen, eight steps in one direction, turn, eight steps back. Pacing helped him think, at least that's what he told himself. It had nothing to do with the anxiety gripping his gut, turning it into a convoluted pretzel.

"Tina got up to go to the ladies' room. Went alone. According to Maggie, she was gone about ten minutes when

Tessa went to check on her."

"That's my girl," Rafe added.

Chance ignored the interruption. "She remarked on the fact the sink was dry and there wasn't a used towel in the trash. Thought it might be significant, since apparently women always wash their hands."

"Actually, that's a good catch. Go on."

"Another thing they noted was Tina didn't leave through the front, obviously. When they asked Daisy about her going out the back, Daisy said that door is always locked, unless she's on break."

"Yeah, that's what she told me, too. When I checked it, it was locked. We took prints, but since it's a public restaurant, I'm not holding out a lot of hope of getting anything useful."

"I checked with Destiny. Jared Webster's still in California."

He literally heard Rafe's sigh of relief. "That's good news, at least."

"Doesn't mean he didn't hire somebody to take her."

"He doesn't know she's in Texas though, does he? There's no paper trail leading here. Unless…"

Chance's stopped pacing, his body taut. "Unless what?"

"We know he tracked her to Portland, under the Tina Nelson name. Shiloh purchased the plane tickets bringing her here. Were her plane ticket and reservation going back under that name, do you know?"

"I got her ticket, paid with my credit card. I used Tina Nelson for the reservation."

"Okay, so he might not have been able to track her through the airline. While it's a possibility, we can't confirm that he knows she's in Texas, much less a small place like Shiloh Springs." He heard Rafe pull the phone away while he talked to somebody, before he came back on. "The only other person who knows she's in Texas is her boss."

"Gertie promised she wouldn't tell anybody where Tina was. When Jared started snooping around, he called Gertie and she refused to tell him anything. But let me give her a call, see if anything's changed in Portland. I'll let you know if she's got any info."

"Good. Gotta go." Rafe disconnected and Chance scrolled through his phone, looking for Gertie's number. Though he'd spoke with the older woman a couple of times, it had always been on Tina's phone and—Tina's phone!

He dialed the number quickly, listening to it ring and ring. When it dumped to voice mail, he left a message, knowing it was fruitless, but doing it anyway, and dialed Rafe back.

"Quick question, bro," he said when Rafe picked up. "What about Tina's phone? I just called and nobody answered, but could you track it? I can get a search warrant."

"Already called Judge Willis' office, and I'm waiting to hear back. It's harder, because we don't have evidence there's been any foul play, even though you and I *know* she didn't leave willingly. I have to wait for—"

"Forget it. I'll have somebody else work on pinging the towers."

"Chance, don't be an idiot."

"I—"

Rafe's voice was barely above a whisper. "I already called you know who, and she's already working on it." Raising his voice, he added, "You know we have to do everything by the books. The warrant will come through and I'll get the records we need."

Chance had been around long enough to read between the lines. Somebody stood close by, and Rafe couldn't afford to be working outside the letter of the law. While that was usually Chance's modus operandi, all bets were off when it came to Tina and her safety.

"I understand. Thanks."

"No problem. I'll keep you posted if I find anything."

Everyone in the living room spoke softly, the atmosphere subdued and a little somber. Walking to the ottoman, he sat beside his momma and laid his head on her shoulder. She tilted hers until it rested against his.

"Tell me we're going to find her."

"We're going to find her, son. I promise, we'll find her."

Tina's head pounded, and the inside of her mouth felt like

she'd been sucking on a dirty sock. She slid her tongue over the teeth, trying to obliterate the awful taste, her brain foggy. Everything felt fuzzy and disjointed, her memories unclear and muddled, like she'd been out on an all-night bender. Except she hadn't done anything like that in years, since she'd been in college.

Squeezing her eyes tight, she fought the wave of nausea threatening to spew the contents of her stomach, the awful taste of bile rising in the back of her throat. Once the urge passed, she opened her eyes to near darkness. Slight light permeated the edges of her vision, and she realized a blindfold obscured her vision. Hardpacked ground lay beneath her body, adding to the beginnings of panic.

Flashes of being at Daisy's Diner came flooding back. She'd headed to the restroom, edging past a man standing in the hall talking on his cell phone. A sharp prick to the side of her neck and then nothing.

She froze at the sound of a door opening, terror shooting through her. Where was she? The footsteps moved closer, and she held herself still, barely allowing herself to breathe. When a foot jostled against her, she stayed still, trying to keep her muscles loose. Playing possum, hoping they'd think she was unconscious.

"She still out. What do you want me to do?"

When she didn't hear any answering voice, Tina figured he must be on a cell phone. A moment of silence stretched into two, before she heard any sound other than the man's breathing. She also had no clue how much time had passed since she'd been unconscious. Oh yeah, and no idea where she was. Things were rapidly accelerating from bad to worse by the second.

"I understand. We'll be here when you arrive."

Since there was no further conversation, she guessed he'd hung up. The footsteps resumed in a measured pattern, and if she didn't know any better, she'd think the dude was pacing. Nothing about any of this made any sense. Afraid to move in case her mysterious friend caught her, she let her muscles relax even further.

"You might as well sit up. I know you're awake."

Crud. Guess she'd somehow given herself away. Her tongue slid between her dry lips, and she realized she wasn't gagged. Pulling in a deep breath, she scooted on her backside, struggling to pull herself into an upright position. A hand shoved under her elbow, helping her sit straight.

"What's happening?"

She heard a snort. "Lady, you've pissed somebody off. Paid me a buttload of money to snatch you and hang onto you until they get here."

"Who?" Gah, she hated that she couldn't see his face.

"Don't know. Don't care. I do the job. I get my money. They get you." She could almost hear the nonchalant shrug accompanying his words.

"I have money," she lied through her teeth. "You can let me go and I'll give you everything I've got, I swear."

"Sorry, lady. If I reneged on a contract, I'd never get another job. My reputation wouldn't be worth a thing. Besides, you're lucky I took the job and not my competition. You are a commodity, and as such I'll treat you with kid gloves. You won't come to any harm—at least not while you're in my care. Trust me, you wouldn't fare so well in different circumstances."

Most of the fuzziness in her head had dissipated, though there was still a bit of a floating feeling, but she'd deal. She couldn't help wondering what he'd dosed her with. The pinch in her neck made her conclude injection, probably ketamine, since it had gotten increasingly popular and readily available on the streets. She wracked her brain trying to remember the side effects and symptoms of ketamine, swallowing when she thought about possible low blood pressure, stomach cramping, and other nasty stuff, including impaired breathing issues that could end in ceased respirations. Yikes!

"Can you at least take off this blindfold? I'm feeling really dizzy, and I'm afraid I'm gonna pass out again."

"Sorry, lady, but I can't do that. We're both safer if you don't see my face."

"Oh, I hadn't thought about that."

Her body jerked when she felt solid arms slide beneath her and lift her from the hard floor. Within seconds, she was carefully moved into a seated position against what felt like a wall. Leaning against it, she pulled in a shaky breath and felt her stomach roil, protesting the sudden action.

"How long was I out?"

"Couple of hours. You're a little bit of a lady, so I didn't give you that much." The sound of a match strike, followed by the scent of tobacco immediately had her stomach protesting the scent, and she gagged.

"Please put that out, unless you want me losing my lunch." Her stomach clenched, cramping sharply, and she leaned forward, pulling her knees up, wishing her hands weren't secured behind her back. Moving her wrists, she made a guess her abductor used zip ties, since she didn't feel metal, which would have indicated handcuffs. Her ankles were secured together too, making running an impossible choice, even if she'd been able to get away from her kidnapper.

"People are going to look for me. You'll get caught."

"I'll be long gone before anybody even gets close, sweetheart. As soon as the funds are transferred into my account, I hand you over, and I'm out of the country. I'm sorry. You seem like a nice woman, but business is business."

"Well, I hate to tell you this, but your business ethics suck rocks. I promise when I get out of this—and I will—I'm going to make sure you regret ever messing with me."

Only silence greeted her words. Leaning her head back against the wall, she closed her eyes and waited, praying that Chance would find her before it was too late.

# CHAPTER FIFTEEN

Tina wasn't sure how much time passed. Since she couldn't see anything but a sliver of light from the bottom of whatever was tied over her eyes, she couldn't tell if it was daylight or lamp light. Every thought imaginable raced through her mind, but she clung to one.

*Chance will find me.*

She repeated it like a mantra, over and over. Whenever panic edged closer, she'd imagine his face. That cocky grin he wore when he teased her. The cocksure way he took charge, refusing to take no for an answer when he helped others. The little boy eagerness when he was around his mom. Each endeared him to her, because there was nothing fake or artificial about the man. He was an enigma wrapped in a gorgeous package. One she'd wanted to unwrap, layer by layer, to uncover the complex, but totally lovable man.

He'd managed to do the one thing she'd sworn would never happen again: Capture her heart. In the privacy of her room, when she curled up in her bed at the Big House, she'd admitted the truth, because she couldn't hide it from herself anymore.

She loved Chance Boudreau.

Finally admitting it, letting the truth soak into her, had a freeing effect. She was in love with the aggravating, hard-headed, wonderful man. When she was with him, he made her feel alive, blossoming awake like Sleeping Beauty awakening after being oblivious to everything, her emotions buried beneath a mountain of self-doubt and fear.

Deep inside, warmth built inside her, a feeling like everything was going to work out, because she believed deep in her gut Chance would find her and bring her home. Because Shiloh Springs, the whole Boudreau family, had become her home.

Her captor, because what else could she call him, hadn't spoken another word after their earlier conversation, though she'd heard him texting a couple of times. Either that or he was playing games on his phone.

*Guess as a hostage I'm boring. Too bad, so sad.*

"Hey, what time is it? I really need to use the bathroom."

Silence answered her.

"Come on, Mr. Kidnapper, I promise I'm not lying. I've didn't get to go at the restaurant, and now I really can't hold it."

An aggrieved sigh, followed by footsteps, was the only response she got. A strong arm slid beneath her backside, another cushioning her back, and she found herself lifted in the air. She bit back her startled scream. He walked several steps, and then she was unceremoniously deposited on her feet. It took a second to get her equilibrium, and then she felt the coolness of a knife against her wrist, before a quick flick freed them.

"Five minutes. You try anything, and next time I'll let you piss yourself."

"What about my legs? Aren't you cutting them loose, too? How am I supposed to—"

"Figure it out, they stay tied. Take off the blindfold once you're in the bathroom. Put it back on when you're ready to come out. Got it?"

"Yes, sir, boss." Darn her and her sarcastic mouth. It was going to get her in trouble one of these days. Like today.

The hand in the center of her back gave her a light shove, and she stumbled forward, hands outstretched, and felt a doorjamb. One shuffling step and then another brought her deep enough into what she assumed was the bathroom, and the closing of a door behind her got her moving. Grabbing onto the edge of the blindfold, she yanked it down below her chin, and looked around the darkened room. There wasn't a window, which meant no avenue of escape there.

Because her feet were bound together, her movements were hindered. But she carefully turned around, finally spying a light switch on the wall. Clicking it on revealed a single bare lightbulb in the ceiling, shedding barely enough light to see her hands in front of her face. Thankfully there was a toilet and a small sink sitting side-by-side, because she really had to go.

Hobbling over, she managed to maneuver her jeans down to her knees and hover over the seat. No way was she plopping her backside down on it. Who knew how long it had been since it had been cleaned? Definitely a yuck moment, but it was this or squatting in the corner.

Business handled, she washed her hands and looked around, searching for anything she might use as a weapon. No sense sitting quietly like a meek victim. If the opportunity presented itself, she'd pretend to be Wonder Woman, because she was never going to be helpless again. She might be down, but she wasn't out. Too bad there wasn't anything she could find to help her. Nothing under the pedestal sink, Nothing behind the toilet, not even a plunger.

"You done in there?"

"Just a second." Taking one last look around, she spotted a rusty nail poking halfway out of the wood above the toilet, crooked and bent, like something had been hung on it that had since been removed. Grabbing hold, she pulled and tugged, wiggling it back and forth, and hallelujah, it finally popped free in her hand.

"Get out here or I'm coming in and getting you, and you don't want me coming in there."

"I'm coming, I'm coming."

With a sigh, she pulled the blindfold up past her chin, covering her eyes, and fisting the nail in her hand, she opened the door. Mr. Bad Dude clasped her arm above the elbow, his grip fiercely tight, and he started walking her across the room. After the first step, her feet tripped against one another, her bound ankles unable to keep up with his larger stride. His tight grip was the only thing that kept her upright, but she knew she'd have fingerprint-shaped bruises when she got out of here.

"Hey, big fella, shuffling gait here. Still tied up, remember?"

"Move it. This is what I get for being polite."

"Well, excuse me. I'm not up on all the latest kidnapping etiquette. Especially since it's my first time. I'll try to do better."

She felt a wall at her back, and he pulled her hands forward. Holding onto the nail took a bit of maneuvering, because he'd notice if she held out clenched fists. Positioning the nail lengthwise between her middle finger and her ring finger, she kept those two pressed tight against each other as he slid another zip-tie around her wrists and pulled it taut. The pressure of his hand on her shoulder pushing down had her scooting down the wall until her backside hit the floor.

"This whole job is turning into a gigantic mess. Stay there, and don't screw with me. I'm not in the mood."

Figuring now might not be the best time for another sarcastic comeback, Tina pressed her lips together, biting back her instinct to shoot off her mouth. Things might be turning out bad on his end, but his preoccupation had proved to be a bit of a blessing for her. Mr. Bad Dude had been careless and made a mistake. He'd tied her hands in front of her this time, instead of behind her back. The nail between her fingers, in all its rusted glory, slid into the palm of her hand and she clenched her fist around it.

Now all she could do was wait for the moment she could make her big break.

Chance braked his dad's truck in front of the sheriff's office and sprinted for the door, the engine barely having time to shut off. Everyone else stayed at the Big House, setting up their own command center and waiting to hear from the various feelers they'd put out, calling in every single favor they were owed.

He couldn't sit back and wait. This was too important. Tina had been missing for hours, and he couldn't handle it. Not knowing who had taken her, because he knew deep in his gut she hadn't just walked away. Just because Jared Webster was in California, it didn't mean he hadn't somehow arranged to have Tina snatched while providing himself with the perfect alibi. Right now, he was sitting in a board meeting at the hospital, surrounded by his peers.

He stormed through the front door, stalking past Sally Anne's desk without a word, seeing her stand as he stalked past her. Nothing was going to stop him from talking to Rafe. He'd apologize to her later, but right now, nothing mattered except Tina's safe return.

Rafe sat behind his desk, phone between his shoulder and his ear, while he shuffled through some papers in his hands. He hadn't noticed Chance in the doorway as far as Chance could tell, and from the scowl on his brother's face, he wasn't in a good mood. Did that mean he didn't have any news on Tina—or was it all bad news?

He must have made a sound or moved, because Rafe's gaze rocketed to the doorway, and he motioned Chance in with one hand, while listening to whoever chattered away on the other end.

"I don't care. I want the warrant signed by Judge Willis in my hand in the next thirty minutes, or I'm coming over there personally, and believe me, he doesn't want to have me show up on his doorstep today. You tell him he still owes me, and I'm calling in that chip. If he's got a problem with signing the warrant, he can find a new sheriff."

Slamming the phone down on its cradle, Rafe ran his hand through his dark hair, and then pressed the heels of his hands against his eyes.

"Bro?"

"I'm sorry. There's nothing new since I talked to you an hour ago."

Chance flung himself into one of the chairs across from Rafe's desk, feeling like a deflated balloon, limp and helpless.

"I can't believe somebody didn't see anything. Daisy's was busy, not packed, but it wasn't empty, either. She went out the back; there's no other explanation. Why? I'm telling you, Rafe, she wouldn't just walk away without a word. I know it."

"I've got Dusty and Jeb at Daisy's interviewing everyone. Nobody saw anything. I doubt anybody would lie about it. Unfortunately, there were several folks in there today who stopped on their way headed north, so they're unknowns." Rafe gave him a sympathetic smile. "I'm working on Judge Willis to get warrants for Tina's phone, even though I don't need it. Also getting one for Jared Webster's phone, though it's a longshot."

"I told you, I can get whatever you need."

"And I told you I want to do this strictly by the book, no favors."

Chance quirked his brow, though he didn't say anything.

"Okay, no favors called in by anybody but me. Willis owes me because I didn't arrest his grandson for drunk driving. Blood alcohol level double the legal limit, along with other questionable…things in his car."

"I've called Tina's number at least a dozen times. It keeps going straight to voice mail."

Rafe leaned back in his chair and ran hands over his face. "Yeah, Destiny's pinged the cell towers in the area, and it's not registering. I hate to say it, but it's probably been smashed and tossed, or the battery's been pulled out."

Chance mirrored his brother's action, scrubbing his hand over his face, trying to calm his racing heartbeat. Adrenaline coursed through him, and it took every ounce of discipline he had to stay seated, when all he wanted to do run as far and as fast as he could to find Tina. His gut told him she was in danger, though he refused to allow the worst-case scenario into his thoughts. She was out there, alive and scared, waiting for him to find her. There was no other option as far as he was concerned. And he would find her, no matter how long it took. He would never give up—never.

Rafe's phone trilled, and he grabbed it before it had a chance to ring a second time. He hit the speaker button, letting Chance hear the other end of the conversation.

"Boudreau."

"Boss, it's Dusty. You need to get down to Daisy's. We've got a possible witness."

"I'm on my way."

Chance rocketed to his feet and headed for the door before Rafe even got the phone back in its cradle.

"Hold up. We go together."

"Then you'd better hurry, because I'm leaving."

Rafe grabbed the jacket hanging over the back of his chair and his hat, and shoved his way past Chance, bumping his shoulder against his. "Let's go."

# CHAPTER SIXTEEN

Every minute passed like an eternity, though Tina knew it hadn't been that long since she'd come back from the bathroom. Mr. Bad Dude had given her some bottled water, and she guided it to her lips, taking small sips. She wasn't worried about it being poisoned. If he'd wanted her dead, she'd already be lying somewhere six feet deep.

Jared was behind this, she knew it. Somehow, he'd found out she was in Texas and tracked her to Shiloh Springs. Why couldn't he get it: she wasn't coming back. All those bridges were burned, not even a splinter left behind.

Setting the bottle of water beside her thigh, she twisted her hands until the rusty nail was between her thumb and her forefinger. She'd watched a video once that showed how to get out of zip ties, and one of the ways was to use something small and metal to force the clasp part loose enough to slide it up, and she'd be able to get her wrists free. She could do the same with the one on her ankles.

The biggest problem? How to do it without Mr. Bad Dude seeing her. With the blindfold on, she'd basically be working at a disadvantage, because she couldn't see. She'd managed to move it up a little, so she could see a bit underneath it, like the dirty floor beneath her, but she had no idea where her kidnapper was in the space, or even where she was. Or if there was anybody else around, like a second bad guy.

Going by feel alone, she maneuvered the tip of the nail into the slide mechanism of the zip tie around her wrist. It had already taken several precious minutes of maneuvering the slide end around her wrists to get it into a position where she could reach the clasp.

Wiggling the nail back and forth, she thought she felt it loosen the smallest amount. She tugged more and realized she could slide a thumb free. Not enough to get them off easily, but it was a start. Of course, it'd be a whole lot easier if she could slide the blindfold up and see what she was doing, but beggars can't be choosers.

Pulling her legs up, she placed her hands against her bent knees, hoping her bent legs would obscure her movements. She knew she'd only have one shot at getting away, and she needed to be ready.

She froze when she heard Mr. Bad Dude's cell phone peel. He answered on the first ring, and she listened intently, knowing whoever was on the other end was the one responsible for her being in this lousy situation. Hands shaking so hard she almost dropped the nail, she clenched it tighter, listening closely.

"I thought you were on your way. How long is this going

to take? I didn't sign on to be a babysitter. This was supposed to be a simple snatch and grab, then turn her over to you."

*Huh, guess things aren't going quite to plan. Is that a good thing or a bad thing?*

Whoever was on the phone must have talked for a while because Mr. Bad Dude hadn't said another word. The silence was killing her. It took everything she had to not try and make a break for it. He might be distracted enough by the call for her to get a head start. But she had to play things smart. She might only get the one chance, and she couldn't afford to blow it.

"I don't like this. The price for the job just doubled."

Heartbeat racing, adrenaline coursed through her veins as she realized something just happened to send this situation spiraling out of control. She felt like a pawn in a chess game, with no way to determine who was the grand master of this private tournament. All she knew was if things went south, she was the disposable piece in this scenario.

"That's not what I agreed to when you contracted my services. I have performed the services required, and now you want to change the terms. Therefore, the financial terms need to be renegotiated. The price is now double."

The silence stretched out, and with it the blood pounded in her brain like a metronome, each beat deep and ominous. What the heck was happening? She wouldn't put it past Jared to hire somebody to grab her and then not want to pay when the bill came due. Trust him to leave her in the hands of a hired killer and try to nickel and dime him to death.

"I'm glad you understand the situation. When will you be arriving to take delivery of the package?"

Mr. Bad Dude's voice never rose in volume, but Tina had goosebumps along her skin from the total lack of emotion he displayed. This whole situation was nothing more than a contracted job for him, a quid pro quo, a service for compensation. Too bad she was caught in the middle of negotiations, when her very life lay on the line.

"You've got twelve hours. That's more than enough time for you to get here and take possession of the package."

*Package? Is that all I am, a commodity, a package for delivery?*

"I'll text directions as soon as you arrive in the state."

Tina heard footsteps drawing closer, and she slid the nail into her palm, fisting her hand around it. She pulled her wrists slightly apart and turned them until the zip tie bit into her skin, making them appear taut. Mr. Bad Dude stopped directly in front of her, and she held her breath, wondering what he'd do.

"You hungry?"

The question surprised her because it was the last thing she'd expected.

"Not really."

"Alright. If you change your mind, let me know. I don't have much, but I've got the basics, like peanut butter and jelly and chips."

"Comfort foods, gotta love it."

He chuckled. "I know, I eat like a kindergartener. We've got a bit of a wait; you might as well try and get comfortable."

When he walked away, Tina blew out a soft breath and went back to work on the zip tie. She needed to be ready, because when the moment presented itself, she was out of here.

It probably took less than two minutes to run from Rafe's office to Daisy's place, but it felt like his feet were dragging through wet cement. Every step felt weighted, keeping him from finding Tina. Rafe rushed through Daisy's front door first, Chance on his heels. Dusty stood off to the far right, in front of the hallway that led to the restrooms and also the door leading to the back alley. A dark-haired woman stood with him, speaking softly. Wringing her hands, she kept making the nervous gesture over and over, and Chance finally recognized her as the new waitress Daisy hired a couple of weeks earlier.

Dusty spotted them and motioned for them the minute they got through the door. Chance's stomach knotted, and he fought the anxiety attempting to morph into a giant monster, ready to consume him whole. He couldn't give in to emotion, not now. Once Tina was home safe and sound, then he could fall apart. Until then, he needed to be a rock.

"Boss, this is Jackie Gilbert. Jackie is the new waitress here. She was here when Tina disappeared. Jackie, why don't you tell Sheriff Boudreau what you saw?"

Jackie took a deep breath, and Chance again noticed her shaking hands. The paleness of her face was another dead giveaway she was scared.

"I'm not sure what I saw. I had been on shift for almost four hours, and since the rush had petered out, Daisy told me I could take my break. I figured I'd go out back for a quick smoke break." Reaching into a pocket, she pulled out a pack of cigarettes and a disposable lighter. "I've been trying to quit, but every once in a while, I get a craving, and this morning I gave in. I do remember when I went to go outside, the door to the alley was unlocked. I told myself to remember to mention it to Daisy, because with it unlocked, anybody could slip out without paying their tab." She gestured toward the back door. "I noticed right away, because you have to manually unlock it for it to stay unlocked. It's a little tricky."

Chance fisted his hands to keep from grabbing Jackie by the shoulders and shaking her, wanting to yell for her to get to the point. But this was his brother's gig, and he'd let him do his job. If he didn't get all the answers, Chance had no problem jumping in and asking questions himself.

"That's a good observation, Jackie." Rafe gave her an

encouraging smile. "Was there anybody in the hall, or going in or out of the restrooms? Somebody stand out, a stranger maybe?"

She shook her head. "Sorry, nothing like that. I slipped out through the door and lit up. That's when I saw a car parked in the alley. It wasn't directly outside the door, actually down several feet. I figured it was somebody making a delivery for one of the shops, dropping it off at their back door. I saw a tall man closing the front passenger door, then walk around and get into the driver's side. Honestly, I wasn't paying a lot of attention. I did notice the passenger side occupant was a lot smaller. I guess what caught my attention was the driver reached across and did up the seatbelt for the passenger, which seemed odd. I mean, whenever I ride with somebody, I put on my own seatbelt, right?"

"Another good catch, Jackie. You're really helping us. Think carefully about the man. Can you remember anything about him? Was he tall? Short? Young? Anything you can tell us will help."

"Honestly, Sheriff, I wished I'd paid more attention." She screwed her eyes closed, rubbing at her temples, and Chance worried she wouldn't be of any more help. With his legal training, he knew how important it was to treat witnesses with kid gloves, and Rafe's technique was flawless. But it felt like a waste of time, because she hadn't been able to tell them much they didn't know already.

"I can't tell you much about the guy, but I can tell you

about his car."

Chance drew himself upright at Jackie's declaration. "What about his car?"

Rafe shot him a glare, as if to say *let me handle my own investigation, thank you very much*. Chance returned his glare with his own *you're taking too long, get to the point* stare.

"A 2017 Toyota Avalon. White. Dark interior. Rental sticker in the right rear window." At the men's surprised looks, she replied, "I was kind of a grease monkey growing up, hung around with the car guys. I know cars."

"Did you recognize the rental sticker, what company?"

"Sure did," she answered, and spouted off the name of a national rental company. Might or might not help, because it could have been rented anywhere, but it was more than they'd had an hour ago. Chance's hand started to reach for his phone, intent on getting Ridge and Destiny working on the tip, but Rafe stayed his hand.

"Anything else you think might help, Jackie? Anything at all?"

"I can't be positive, because like I said, I thought it was just somebody making a delivery, but I think the person in the passenger seat was a brunette. Does that help?"

"Yes, thank you, Jackie. I'm going to let Deputy Sinclair get the rest of your statement." Rafe pulled a business card out of his shirt pocket and handed it to Jackie. "If you think of anything else, don't hesitate to call me. No matter what time, day or night, call. I appreciate your help."

"I wish I could have told you more."

Chance reached forward and laid his hand lightly on her shoulder. "You've helped a lot. Thank you, Jackie."

Spinning on his heel, Chance headed toward the door, Rafe hard on his heels. He'd barely made it through the door before his brother grabbed his arm, spinning him around.

"Don't go off halfcocked, bro. You've got to get a handle on this right now, or I'm gonna have to—"

"Have to what? How would you react if it was Tessa who was missing? I remember how you reacted when she was held hostage by two men with guns. Seems to me you were right in the thick of things. I can't—I can't stand by and do nothing."

"I know. But I can see the gleam in your eye, and you're getting ready to do something stupid. Let's take two minutes to make a couple of calls, starting with the car rental place. Maybe we'll catch a break."

"I keep thinking of her in the hands of some low life thug that Webster hired to grab her."

"You can't think like that; all it will do is keep you from making the right choices. Tina's strong and she's smart. She had to be to stay one step ahead of her ex all this time. She's not going to suddenly sit back and play the damsel in distress, waiting for somebody to ride to her rescue. Think about who we're talking about. You told me the first time you met, she brained you with an ice bucket. Do you think she's going to do less to somebody who snatched her away from her family and friends—from you?"

Chance drew in a long, shuddering breath. "Yeah, you're right. I just feel helpless. Tina's somewhere in the hands of somebody willing to kidnap her in broad daylight, with a diner full of people. He's either a professional or stupid. Either way, that puts her in a heap of trouble, and I'm sitting here twisting in the wind."

"Again, I doubt Tina is meekly sitting around, allowing any man to tell her what to do. I bet she's plotting and scheming a way to get free, and I'd bet my next year's salary the first place she'll head is straight to you."

Chance started walking as he digested Rafe's words. "You think so?"

"I swear. Now come on, let's go make a few calls and find your gal."

# CHAPTER SEVENTEEN

C hance and Rafe set up the conference room at the sheriff's station, listing a timeline on the white board. Dusty had returned with the witness statements, but nothing Chance heard gave them any information he didn't already know. Only the one from Jackie gave him a glimmer of hope, because sometimes rental cars were equipped with GPS tracking or LoJack capabilities.

Rafe stood at the front of the table, cell phone to his ear. He'd called the car rental company's corporate office and was explaining the kidnapping situation, and the urgency of trying to find out who'd rented the car, or any information they could use to track it, but from the look on his face, things didn't look promising. He was pretty sure even if they were able to identify the rental, the company wouldn't provide any information or track it without a warrant. That's where he came in, because he'd have that sucker signed the minute they needed it, even if he had to put the pen in Judge Willis' hand and guide it personally.

Sally Anne stuck her head in the doorway and waved at Rafe. Without missing a beat, Rafe pointed to Chance and

Dusty, keeping the phone to his ear. Chance followed Dusty into the hallway.

"I'm not sure if this is important or not, but Joel McAllister is here. He wants to talk to Rafe."

"Did you tell him Rafe's in the middle of a kidnapping and he can't talk to him now? Take a message, let him know it'll have to wait."

"No."

Chance stared at Sally Anne, shocked at her one-word refusal. It definitely wasn't like her to disagree, much less refuse to do what was asked. He noted the beads of sweat along her forehead and the mulish set of her jaw, and decided to play along.

"What's Joel need, Sally Anne? Is somebody hurt or in trouble?"

"Talk to him, Chance. He said he heard about Tina going missing, and—"

"Where is he?"

"Sitting at my desk." Sally Anne pointed toward the front, and Chance strode toward McAllister. He knew Joel. He was a good kid, and Rafe suspected once he graduated high school, got his head screwed on straight and thought about anything other than his girlfriend, he'd grow into a fine man. Joel had played a big part in helping with the hostage situation at the high school, alerting Rafe and the sheriff's office about the gunmen holding a classroom full of kids as collateral to get their guns and drugs.

"Joel, Rafe's dealing with a crisis right now. Can I help you with whatever you need?"

"Hey, Chance. Rachel called and told me about what's going on. She was at Daisy's when all the commotion broke out. Don't get mad, but she eavesdropped on y'all talking to Jackie about that lady going missing. She said something about a 2017 Toyota with a rental sticker in the back window. Was it an Avalon?"

"Yes." Chance's pulse sped up, a thrill of excitement racing through him. This was something; he felt it in his bones. Were they finally going to get a break?

"Tell me it was white." Joel's lips curled up in the beginnings of a grin.

"Oh, yeah, it's white."

"I'd been out at old man Grady's place this morning." A flush spread across his cheeks. "I kind of go out there once a week or so, just to keep the old dude company. Help a little around his place, because he's having a little trouble getting all the chores done."

"That's because you're a good kid, Joel." Dusty's deep voice sounded from beside Chance, startling him. He'd all but forgotten Dusty was there, so intent was he on hearing Joel's news. "Rafe mentioned Tessa noted Grady seemed to be lonely, because he kept getting calls to go out to his place for 'stuff.'"

"Joel, get back to your story." Chance wanted to shake the teen, get the words to spill from him, because his gut told him what Joel had to say was important in finding Tina.

"Right. Anyway, I'm heading back toward town and this white Avalon blew through a stop sign like the tires were on fire. I got pissed, so I turned around and followed it. Figured the jerk was gonna cause an accident. I trailed him for a bit, but I was low on gas, so I had to let him go. But I did get his plate number."

"Yes!"

Joel continued, "I didn't have anything to write with, so I took a picture of it. It's not the best quality, but it's definitely legible. Here." He shoved his phone at Chance.

There it was in living color. All the digits they needed to give to the rental company. He took off at a sprint down the hall, bursting through the conference room doorway. Rafe looked up at his sudden arrival, and Chance shoved the phone into his hand.

"That's the plate number for the Toyota Avalon."

Rafe's brow rose, but he didn't miss a beat, informing the rental company, who was still on the phone, about this latest information. Maybe they'd have a chance, if they could get them to stop dragging their feet and find the stinking car.

*Hold on, Tina, I'm coming.*

"I don't care about your policies and procedures, ma'am. I care about the fact that there's a kidnapped woman being driven away in your company's vehicle. You can either get on the ball and get me the GPS information, or I assure your company, and you personally, will be named in the prosecution of this case. Yes, I will get you a bloody warrant. Here's the license plate number for your 2017 Toyota Avalon. Get me that information."

"I'm on it," Chance pulled out his phone and hit the speed dial for Judge Willis. The old goat's number was in his phone from all the cases they'd worked together. After explaining the urgency of the situation, he got his warrant. It needed to be filed with the courthouse, but they'd get it to him ASAP.

This was the part of the job he hated. All the paperwork, the loopholes that allowed bad guys to slither through the cracks, all because a piece of paper didn't get signed, or didn't have a date that allowed criminals free reign.

"Judge Willis is getting the warrant as we speak," he told Rafe, who relayed the information to the rental company. He listened for a couple seconds more and then disconnected.

Rafe closed his eyes and pinched the bridge of his nose between his finger and thumb. "How'd you get the plate?"

"Believe it or not, Joel McAllister." Chance watched Rafe's eyes go round with shock. "It's a long story, and I'll tell you later.

"Fine. The rental company is trying to get the information, but they're telling me it can take up to seventy-two hours."

"What! Tina can't stay in the hands of a monster for seventy-two hours. We both know Webster's behind this. He might have his butt sitting in California, but he did this."

"Chance, calm down. I agree Jared Webster has the most motive, but first things first. We find Tina and bring her home. Then, you and I will take a little trip to San Francisco and have a chat with her ex. Make him see the error of his ways."

"I don't want to wait; I want to go after him right now. I know, I know," he added when Rafe started to interrupt. "Every minute she's gone, it's eating me alive. What if he's—"

"Don't go there, bro. You cannot think about anything but getting her back in your arms. You haven't said it, but I know you love her. No matter what's happened, it won't change the way you feel. Hang onto the fact we're going to get her back, beat the ever-loving crap out of her ex, and make sure he never even breathes her name again, and you will get your chance to tell her how you feel."

"I do love her. It kind of snuck up on me, you know? I wasn't looking for anybody when I met her. I was simply doing Shiloh and Lucas a favor, and meeting her turned my world upside down. She's funny and outgoing, and I can't imagine life without her."

"You won't have to. Stay focused on the fact she'll be coming home." Rafe pulled him in for a hug, and Chance held on tight, allowing the comfort and camaraderie to flow into him. He loved his family, loved the closeness they shared, and wanted to make Tina a part of that. Though she'd had her aunt and uncle to lean on, he had the feeling she had never been part of a family like the Boudreaus.

He turned when he felt a small hand on the center of his back, and found his mother standing there. Without stopping to think, he stepped into her embrace, feeling the warmth of her love flowing into him. Standing in her arms, he felt like a prepubescent kid again, looking to his momma to fix things, make everything okay with a sweep of her hand.

"It's okay, honey, everything's gonna be alright." Though her words were whispered, they were like a panacea to his soul. His mother never lied to him, not once in his entire life, and she wasn't about to start now.

Glancing over his shoulder, she asked Rafe, "Has there been any news?"

Chanced stepped back, already missing the feel of his momma's arms around him. He answered before Rafe could. "We've got the plate from the car we think drove off with Tina inside."

His mother's eyes rounded in surprise. "That's fortuitous. How'd you find it?"

"Believe it or not, Joel McAllister spotted it. He followed and snapped a picture of the license plate."

"That was quick thinking on his part."

Chance glanced over at his brother. "You might want to go out front and talk to him. Maybe give him back his phone."

Rafe clapped him on the back and walked from the conference room. Chance pulled out a chair for his mother, sinking onto one beside her.

"Tina's a strong woman. She'll keep her head. I expect she'll be home before you know it. Boudreaus are nothing if not resilient."

The corner of Chance's mouth kicked up. "Tina's not a Boudreau."

His momma patted his hand. "She will be."

Yeah, she was right, because once he got her back in his arms, he was never letting her go.

# CHAPTER EIGHTEEN

Tina managed to doze, leaning back against the wall. She'd considered lying on the floor, but after seeing the conditions in the bathroom, put the kibosh on that idea. Glimmers of light peeked through the edge of the blindfold, telling her it was still daylight, though she had no idea how much time had passed.

Stretching as much as she could with both her hands and feet wrapped with zip ties, she felt the nail still clutched in her fist. Thank goodness she hadn't dropped it, because she'd never have been able to find it with her line of sight restricted.

A lowered voice penetrated her half-awake state, though she couldn't make out the conversation. She figured it had to be Mr. Bad Dude, because he was the only person she'd heard a peep from since she'd been commandeered at the diner. Somehow, she got the impression he wasn't talking to his boss, because there was a sense of intimacy about the call. A softness in his deep voice, as though he cared about the person on the other end of the phone.

When the talking stopped, she leaned her head back

against the wall, and tested the give at her wrists. There was enough give she could slide them free, which meant she had to figure out a way to get her ankles loose.

Light footfalls sounded from across the room, followed by the closing of the door. Was Mr. Bad Dude in the bathroom? If he was, this was her best shot at getting away. If not and he caught her messing with her ties, she was royally screwed.

*It's now or never, girl. Go for it!*

Reaching up, she ripped the blindfold down around her chin and blinked, her eyes adjusting from the darkness and pulled her hands free from the zip ties. Using the nail, she wiggled into the clasp around her ankles, working it like she'd done for her wrist, and within seconds, she'd moved the slide enough to get one ankle free, and then the other.

Jumping to her feet, she sprinted toward the only door she saw that didn't belong to the bathroom. That one had a glow of light shining from beneath the bottom, so she discounted it immediately. Her hand slipped on the doorknob, and she wrestled with it to get it open, and flew through it the second it opened.

Daylight shone outside, and she took off running, knowing she only had seconds to put distance between her and her captor. Glancing over her shoulder as she ran, she noted the small cabin she'd been held in didn't look like a den of evil. It resembled one of those line shacks she'd seen in movies, where the cowpoke ended up when he'd been working the range far into the night, and couldn't make it back to the bunkhouse or got caught in a downpour. There weren't any evil vibes or sense of menace. Honestly, it reminded her of a weather-beaten tiny house. Wooden slats, with small windows on either side of the front door.

She stumbled over something in her path and almost faceplanted into the dirt, but managed to right herself and keep running. Fear gripped her, knowing any second Mr. Bad Dude would notice she was missing and start hunting her. Right now, she was in the middle of an open patch of flat land. In the distance were trees, reaching toward the heavens, a place where she'd have a fighting chance at eluding capture, but only if she made it that far.

Putting on a burst of speed, she raced toward the tree line, praying with every step. A painful stitch in her side made her wince, but she refused to give in, placing one foot in front of the other. A shout from behind her had a rush of adrenaline pouring into her blood stream, and she refused to look behind her. If she saw Mr. Bad Dude closing the distance, she'd probably pee her pants.

"Come back here!"

Ignoring his shout, she kept putting one foot in front of the other, breath heaving in and out of her lungs. Her heart felt like it was going to burst in her chest, but she couldn't give up. This was her only chance. When the sunlight dimmed, she glanced upward, noticing several big dark clouds had moved closer, making the air feel heavier, humid.

The pounding footsteps behind her sounded closer, and she wanted to scream because there was no way she'd make it to the tree line and be able to hide in the dense forested growth. A sob caught in her throat, though she refused to give in to the despair, because she couldn't. She couldn't quit, not until her last breath.

A string of curses sounded behind her, and she glanced over her shoulder, noting Mr. Bad Dude on the ground, hands wrapped around his ankle. His gaze caught hers, something unreadable in his stare.

Swinging her head around, she continued running toward the trees, hoping the fall would slow him down enough to give her a good head start. While she knew he'd probably catch up to her eventually, any chance at freedom was better than giving in and giving up.

A droplet of water landed on her forehead and she glanced toward the sky. The clouds were thicker and darker, the sun obscured behind their roiling beauty. As far as she was concerned, a downpour at this point might give her a ghost of a chance, because the rain and thunder could cover the sounds of her feet stepping on the fallen, dead leaves.

"Tina, be reasonable. You know I'm going to catch you, so what's the sense in running? Use your head. Storms in Texas are dangerous. You're going to get hurt."

*Does he really think I'm going to answer him? Does he think I have stupid tattooed across my forehead?*

Weaving between two tree trunks, she paused long

enough to see Mr. Bad Dude closing the distance between them, though he was favoring his left leg as he did a kind of hobble-run. His long-legged gait still ate the distance between him and the stand of trees, and she couldn't afford to rest, even for a second.

Recognizing the trees as live oaks, because Chance had pointed some out to her around the Big House, she knew they'd provide some protection from the rain, but it would only be a stopgap measure. She still had no idea how far away from Shiloh Springs she was. Maybe she'd find a house somewhere close by, though judging from the fact the line shack didn't look like it had been occupied in a while, she wasn't holding out hope.

The stitch in her side got worse, and she knew she'd have to take a breather sooner or later, because it was slowing her down with every step. Her feet were dragging through the brush scattered across the forest floor while rain pelted her, drenching her within minutes. Though the temperature had been moderate for the past couple of days, being soaked to the skin sent a chill racing through her.

"Tina! There's nobody around to help you but me. I picked this place because it's so far off the beaten track, hardly anybody even knows it's here. I promise I'm not angry. There'll be no repercussions."

"Yeah, right," she muttered under her breath. "Thanks, but no thanks, I'll take my chances out here."

The ground beneath her feet made running harder and

harder, her shoes sinking into the newly developed mud. The torrent continued and a loud rumble of thunder reverberated, making the ground tremble. Whipping her head around, she looked for the clearest path, and headed in the opposite direction. No way was she making it easy for her captor. Maybe if she was lucky, the hard rain would wash away her footprints, and he couldn't track her easily.

Pushing her hair off her forehead, she jogged forward, each footstep taking her farther from the line shack. Farther from Mr. Bad Dude. Farther away from Jared getting his hands on her. The thought of being at the mercy of her ex-husband made her skin crawl, giving her a new burst of energy. The thought was abhorrent, filling her with dismay.

When long arms wrapped around her, lifting her from the ground, she screamed, struggling and fighting against Mr. Bad Dude's hold. How had he caught up so fast?

"Stop fighting or I'm going to have to knock you out." He muttered a curse when she reared back, trying to headbutt him. "Do that again, and you'll regret it."

Figuring it best to stop struggling, at least for the moment, Tina stilled in his arms. Felt him take a deep breath and loosen his hold.

"Tina, I don't want to fight you. I like you; you seem like a decent human being, and they are few and far between. Let's not make things difficult. I give you my word, I'm not going to hurt you, and I won't let anybody else hurt you, okay?"

"Don't lie. I'm nothing but a paycheck for you, and as soon as you get your money, you're gone and I'm back in the middle of a living nightmare."

He pulled in a deep breath and gave her an inscrutable look. "Things aren't always what they seem. And for the record, I don't lie. Ever."

When he wrapped his big hand around her wrist, she didn't fight, knowing it was useless. She'd taken her shot at freedom and fallen short. Didn't mean she was giving up, simply retreating and determined to come up with a new plan.

Once they arrived back at the line shack, he scrounged around, finally locating a ratty-looking blanket, which he handed to her. She wrapped it around her shoulders, pulling it close. Now that she wasn't moving around, the wet clothes stuck to her like a second skin, and she was freezing.

"If you give me your word, I won't restrain you again."

Tina's head jerked up at his words. He looked serious and gave her a brief nod.

"I promise."

"We'll only be here for a few more hours anyway."

The rain pounded on the corrugated metal roof, the sound deafeningly loud in the confined space. Though its interior was darkened because of the storm raging outside, she had sufficient light to study his face. Not because she wanted to be able to pick him out of a lineup later, though that did play a part, but because she found herself wondering about him. Tall, probably just over six feet, he was built like a football player, obviously fit and in good shape, because he'd chased her down pretty darned quick. Dark hair was plastered against his head, and surprisingly blue eyes held a word of weariness. An old soul in a young body. If she'd met him under different circumstances, and before she'd met Chance, she'd have probably gone out with him. Go figure.

"Where are we?"

The corner of his lip quirked up. "Where do you think we are?"

"Somewhere in Texas. I wasn't out long enough for us to get out of the state, at least I don't think so. Plus, those were live oaks out there, and I know they grow all over Texas."

"Pretty observant. Yes, we're still in Texas. I'm not going to tell you where."

"Didn't think you would," she added with a smile. "I hope you can live with your conscious. You know what you're doing is wrong."

"I don't have a conscious. It was killed a long time ago." He pulled out his cell and glanced at the screen, frowning at whatever he read.

"Something wrong?"

"Isn't there always?" He hit a key and put the phone to his ear. "What kind of game are you playing?"

She watched his face, his jaw tightening with every word said on the other end of the phone, the blue in his eyes growing colder by the second. Looked like somebody pulled the tiger's tail, and was about to get a mouth full of teeth in their backside.

"No, I'm not changing the terms *again*. No, I am not driving to Dallas with Ms. Nelson. You will meet me, as we agreed, or the deal is off. Which means, I give all the information regarding your name, the amount of money you agreed to spend for her apprehension, and another few details you might not know I'm aware of."

As he listened to the other person, he suddenly chuckled, the sound filled with humor. "You'd be surprised what I know. Unlike you, I do my homework, and I know exactly what you've done. Fulfill your end of our contract, and the information stays silent. Cross me at your cost."

Without another word, he disconnected, and stuck the phone back in his pocket.

"Problems?"

"Nothing I can't handle. I get annoyed when people try to change things mid-job. You make an agreement, you make your payment, you get your goods. It's simple business."

She shook her head, tugging the blanket closer. The clothing had started to dry, but still felt clammy against her skin. It sounded like the rain was easing a bit, but the lightning continued illuminating the shack, the flashes brilliant, though sporadic. Booms of thunder shook the walls, and she wondered how long before it rolled past. Chance had mentioned weather in Texas tended to be schizophrenic, changing several times a day.

"Gee, sorry I'm causing so much trouble. Easiest way out would be to let me go. Let me pay your fee, and you can walk away. I won't identify you or press charges. You'll have time to get out of the country. That's what you said you were going to do anyway."

"No can do, Tina. I have to see this through to the end."

Raising her hand, she brushed the damp hair off her forehead. Though she'd given her word not to escape, any promise made under duress didn't count as far as she was concerned. Her stomach rumbled and she blushed, knowing he could hear it all the way across the room, because he chuckled. Standing, he walked over to a cooler she hadn't noticed before, pulled out two sandwiches, and handed one to her.

"Thanks."

"Wish it was something a little fancier, but it won't be long. A few more hours."

"And I've lost my appetite."

"Eat it anyway, you need to keep up your strength. You expended a lot of energy with that mad dash earlier. And your body needs the fuel to keep you warm."

Unwrapping the sandwich, she bit into it, chewed and swallowed, though it tasted like sawdust. She knew he was right; she'd need all her strength to deal with Jared.

She leaned back against the wall and started making plans. Because she had no intention of staying within Jared's clutches. No matter what it took, she'd find a way to leave him again. She didn't belong with him. She really never had, her infatuation with him nothing more than a girlish crush, though she'd thought it was true love.

Now she knew better, because she knew what true love felt like. She'd found it with Chance, and it didn't matter what it took, or how long, she'd find her way back to the man who'd made her realize that love was something she'd been missing her whole life, and she didn't want to waste another minute without him.

People said home was where the heart is, and she'd found her heart in Chance, and she wasn't letting go. She was coming home.

# CHAPTER NINETEEN

"Hello?"

"Chance, it's Destiny. Something weird popped up in my searches, and I'm not sure what to make of it. Well, a couple of somethings actually, and I feel bad I didn't tell you sooner."

"Does it have to do with Tina?" Something in Destiny's voice had him sitting up straighter, and he leaned an elbow on the conference table, and glanced at Rafe.

"In a roundabout way, yeah."

"I'm going to put you on speaker. Rafe's here with me, and he probably needs to hear this, too."

"Alrighty. First, let me say this may not be connected at all with Tina's disappearance. But I told her about it, and now she's gone. I was going to tell you, but then I talked to her and we decided not to say anything. It's only a guess anyway, but my gut's telling me it's related, and—"

"Destiny, we don't have time for a long explanation. What did you tell Tina?"

He heard her deep sigh through the phone, knew she was getting her thoughts together because he'd interrupted her spiel.

"You know I went to see Tina. I talked to her about the stuff I found when I did the deeper dive into her background."

"I forgot about that with everything that's been going on. You never gave me the report." Chance glanced at Rafe, who shrugged.

"Look, I know you're paying me, but when I dug deeper, I realized Tina wasn't some bad guy who was trying to take advantage of you or your family. What I found was a woman who'd been taken in by somebody who's a user and an abuser."

Destiny's words stabbed at him like a knife. Though he'd suspected, Tina hadn't given him any details about her life at Jared's hands. Had he laid his hands on Tina in anger? Raised his hands in violence to the woman he loved?

"Abuser? Are you telling me Jared Webster hit Tina?" Chance was surprised he spoke so calmly, since inside he was a seething volcano ready to explode.

Destiny's voice was filled with anger when she said, "I shouldn't say this with the sheriff listening, but if I ever meet this jackass face-to-face, you'd better pray I don't have a gun, because I'd blow his bloody head clear off his shoulders."

"Hold it together, bro. We need to find out what Destiny knows before you blow your stack." Rafe's voice held a soothing tone, and he allowed it to seep into his consciousness. He knew Rafe was right. He could hunt Webster down later. Right now, every ounce of his focus needed to be on finding Tina.

"Tell me."

"Chance, this guy zeroed in on Tina like a heat-seeking missile. I talked to a couple of his former classmates. They said he was a petty little dilettante who was on the verge of flunking out, because his grades sucked. Along comes Tina, who's flying through her classes, getting the best grades, and he hires her to help tutor him. Things quickly progressed along to seduction, and he swept her off her feet. She helped him ace every class, while her own grades suffered."

"I really hate this guy," Rafe interrupted. "Bet he's a lousy doctor."

"Actually, from what I've gleaned, he's an amazing surgeon. It was his test taking abilities that sucked. Anyway, he swept Tina off her feet and they married. After that, things started happening. Little things at first, like missing classes, you know what I'm talking about. ER visits for clumsy accidents. But the kicker, the one that brought everything to a head, was when he slammed her hand in the car door. Deliberately."

Chance sprang from his chair and paced a couple of feet, turned and slammed his fist into the drywall. Dust floated from the hole he'd punched in the wall.

"What was that?"

"Nothing important," Rafe answered. "Just a problem with the wall."

Destiny chuckled. "Gotcha."

"How do you know it was deliberate?" Chance's voice came out in a deep growl. "Was there proof?"

"If you consider an eyewitness proof. The cops were called, and Tina was rushed to the hospital. She had surgery on the hand. Honestly, she's lucky she still has use of her hand. At least that's what I gathered from looking at her chart. Oh, who wants to guess what Tina wanted to do when she graduated?"

Chance stared down at his bloody knuckles. "She wanted to be a surgeon."

"Bingo."

"I'm going to kill him."

"Destiny, you didn't hear that. Bro, do not make threats of murder in front of the sheriff in his own office. Off the record, I'll help you dispose of the body."

"I think that was the last straw for Tina. She'd already dropped out of medical school, but planned to go back after Webster's career was established. She even worked in the psycho's office, helping him build up his patient list. With one deliberate act, Webster took away her dream. Guess he couldn't stand the competition."

"You showed the file to Tina? How'd she react?" Chance leaned back against the wall he'd just pummeled, wishing Tina were here. He ached to hold her in his arms, show her she was loved, adored, and she'd never be hurt again. He refused to believe she'd never be in his life again.

"At first, shocked I'd found out everything. But she didn't care if I gave the file to Chance, left the choice up to me. I decided she'd been through enough, and didn't need or deserve to have her whole life boiled down to a few pages of information you didn't really need. You know she's not a danger to your family. She's not going to hurt anybody, and I made the call not give you the information. That's on me."

"I get it, Destiny. You said there were two things. What's the other?"

She was silent for several beats, until Chance was ready to crawl out of his skin, when she finally came back on the phone. "This one is pure supposition on my part. When I found out what her lousy ex pulled on her, I assumed the apple didn't fall from the tree, so I did a little unethical digging into Jared Webster's parents."

"And?" Rafe leaned forward in his chair, his gaze meeting Chance's. "Were you right?"

"Randolph Webster comes from old money, but he didn't let that stop him from being a workaholic. His employees liked and respected him. Now, if we're talking about his wife, that's a whole different scenario."

"A real piece of work, huh?" Chance kept his mouth shut, letting Rafe lead Destiny where he wanted her to go, though he wished she'd get to the point, because he needed to stop sitting on his backside and get out there and find Tina.

"Let's just say Mommy dearest makes Ms. Patti a candidate for sainthood. She thinks she deserves everything, and she's not above doing some pretty shady things to make sure she's never denied. Jared is a chip off Mommy's block."

"What does this have to do with Tina?" Chance couldn't hold back any longer. "She hasn't had contact with the Websters for years."

"True. But I discovered something while I was digging, and I don't know, it set off my radar. I sometimes get hunches when I'm doing a dark web search or digging for info, and most of the time I'm right. In this case, I don't want to be right, but—"

"What'd you find?"

"That's just it. I didn't *find* anything. Randolph hasn't been to the office for weeks. Liliana Webster, who's known as a social butterfly and never out of the limelight, is into anything and everything to keep her name front and center, hasn't been to any event in the same amount of time. Randolph was in the middle of some big-time negotiations, and he *supposedly* went out of the country. But if he's out of the country, why isn't he using his credit cards? The only activity on the personal or business cards has all been done by Liliana Webster. Now, the dude could be sick, and the family is covering. Maybe he's run off with a mistress, though there hasn't been a whisper of him being unfaithful. Could be he cracked, had a manic event and they put him in an institution. But…"

"You think he's dead."

"Yeah, I think he's dead and the family's covering it up." Chance was starting to see a pattern and didn't like where his thoughts led. Because if he was right—and he really hoped he wasn't—Tina was in a lot more trouble than he'd first thought.

"I'm kind of following this, but I don't get the connection between Randolph being missing and Tina. She wouldn't know anything about her former father-in-law being incommunicado. Why would the family not notify the authorities if Randolph was dead? Unless—"

"Unless they were responsible for his death? That's my guess too, Sheriff." Destiny's answer was met with stony silence. Every implication sped through Chance's mind, and he didn't like the way things were adding up. He also hated the fact that Tina had known this information and hadn't told him.

"We're jumping the gun here," Rafe's voice broke into Chance's thoughts. "We don't know anything's happened to Webster the elder."

"I know, but I've got a bad feeling. Can you have the authorities in San Francisco do a welfare check on Randolph Webster?"

"I can contact the San Francisco Police Department, do an unofficial inquiry. I'll be right back." Rafe stood and walked out of the conference room.

"I wish I'd said something sooner. Is there something else I can do? I want to help. I really like Tina, and it's pissing me off that somebody thinks they can get away with grabbing her practically off the streets."

"I know, Destiny. Keep checking into the Websters. I know they're involved in this. I find it suspicious that Tina went for months without Jared getting close and suddenly ramped up his efforts to find her. Why?"

"Good question. Hang on a second." Chance heard rapid-fire keystrokes, and knew Destiny was working her personal magic on the keyboard. He got that unique feeling he always got when a case came together, when all the pieces fell into place and he knew he'd get a conviction. The instinct that came with finding the missing puzzle pieces to make the picture as a whole come into focus. There was one key thing missing, and if they could find it, they'd figure out where Tina was, and find her.

"Your instincts are spot on, big guy. I'm checking Jared Webster's bank accounts, and it looks like for the past year he's had a private investigator on a monthly retainer. Then a month ago he took out two cash withdrawals, one for twenty thousand and one for fifteen thousand. Since it's cash I can't track it, but that's about the same time Tina started having issues, right? Man, I wish I could get my hands on his laptop. I already looked at his office computer, but there's nothing on it."

"I still trying to figure out where the connection is between Tina and Randolph Webster, other than his being her ex-father-in-law. As far as I know, she didn't keep in touch with him after the divorce."

Rafe walked back in and sat in the chair he'd vacated earlier. "The SFPD is going to do a welfare check, and they'll get back to me. The inspector I spoke with did remark they'd done a welfare check on Randolph two weeks ago. His wife said he was out of the country on business. Since they've been having some problems in the city and are stretched thin, he never followed up."

"There's something about this whole situation that stinks. People acting out of character. Webster's apparent added push to find Tina." Destiny paused for a beat and added, "Oh, did you know Webster showed up in Portland?"

"Wait—what? When was that?" Chance shot a glance at Rafe, who shrugged. Guess he hadn't known about that little tidbit, either.

"The morning I met with Tina. He flew into Portland that morning and we all know why he was here. He's still looking for her."

"Thanks for all you've done, Destiny. I appreciate you going above and beyond what I asked for. Let Rafe or I know if you find anything else."

"Will do. Call me when you find her."

Chance disconnected the call and leaned his head back, staring at the ceiling. All the pieces were falling into place, and if he had enough time, he knew he'd figure it out. He was good at puzzles, and that's what they were dealing with. Only they didn't have time to deal with the intricacies of manipulating the pieces to fit them together. His gut told him Tina was running out of time, and if they didn't find her soon, all would be lost.

"What are we missing, bro? I know it's staring us in the face, but I can't see it."

"So, let's figure it out while we wait for the call from the SFPD."

Rafe stood and walked to the white board, picked up a marker, and drew a big broad line down the side not containing the timeline they'd written up when Tina went missing. He began writing down the facts they'd gathered from Destiny's phone call.

It all lead back to Webster, somehow, some way, and if he could connect the dots, he'd find Tina.

He had to, before it was too late.

# CHAPTER TWENTY

The rain quit as quickly as it had moved in, and now the sun shone brightly, though Tina knew it wouldn't for much longer. Pretty soon, the shack would be plunged into darkness, and she hadn't spotted any handheld lanterns or even a flashlight. She dreaded being stuck out in the middle of nowhere after dark, because nature was out there. All kinds of creepy crawlies were out there. She was a city girl through and through, and the thought of bugs—or worse—getting in through the holes in the walls gave her the heebie-jeebies.

Mr. Bad Dude had gotten another call, about half an hour ago, and when he'd hung up his eyes lit with a gleam that scared her. If she had to wager a guess, his money had come through. Which meant her luck had just about run out.

"Shouldn't be long now, Tina. Everything's gonna work out exactly the way it should."

"Easy for you to say," she groused. "You're not being held against your will because somebody else can't take no for an answer. I swear I have the worst luck. Or maybe it's just that all men stink, present company included."

His deep chuckle rumbled through the small confines. Glad he was having a good time, because the reality of her situation rode heavy on her shoulders. After all her moving around, hiding to avoid him, she was ending up back with Jared—right where she'd started. It didn't seem fair.

"I need to make a call." He stared at her until she felt a chill race down her spine. "Don't make a sound, understand? I want you to shut your mouth and listen. Not a peep."

She nodded, swallowing down the sudden fear assaulting her. Mr. Bad Dude had been nice enough that she'd let her guard down, but that single stare reinforced he wasn't the good guy in this situation. He'd cornered her in Daisy's place, strongarmed her into his car after drugging her, and chased her down when she'd tried to escape. Just because he hadn't beaten her did mean he was a good guy. Seemed like his sole focus was keeping her until he got his money and turning her over to Jared.

He slid his fingertip across the screen, and she realized she could hear the phone ringing. Wait a second—he wanted her to hear whoever he was talking to? What was going on?

"Hello?"

"You want to find Tina Nelson?"

"Who is this?"

*Hold on—wait—was that Rafe's voice? Why would Mr. Bad Dude call Rafe? Did he want to get caught?*

"Tina Nelson is at the line shack on the northwest border of the Boudreau property. I assume you know where it is."

"Of course I know where it is. Why should I believe this isn't a crackpot sending me on a wild goose chase?"

Mr. Bad Dude walked over to stand beside where Tina was sitting. He turned the phone toward her, the speaker still on. "Tell Rafe you're here and you're safe."

"Rafe, I'm okay."

"Tina!"

"Chance!"

"Baby, hold on. I'm going to find you, I swear. I love you."

"I love you, too."

"Aw, you're so sweet you're giving me diabetes. You've got an hour to get here. Any longer, and everything will be shot to pieces. I'm already regretting calling you. One hour."

With a quick slide of his finger, he disconnected the call.

"Why?"

"Because I'm an idiot. A sentimental fool who's letting his heart rule his head, something I never do. I can't believe I just did that. This whole job has been screwed up from day one, and I just put the final nail in my coffin."

Tina shook her head, not understanding him, or why he'd called Rafe. How did he even know Rafe? The bigger question, was she really on the ranch? Was the Big House nearby? None of what had happened in the last few minutes made any sense. Was Mr. Bad Dude summoning Rafe and

Chance into a trap?

"I don't get it? Why tell them where we are?"

He barked out a rough laugh. "Because I'm a fool. I can't believe I found myself pulled into the Boudreaus' world again."

*Again?*

Before she could ask, he held up a hand, and seemed to be listening for something. A scowl crossed his face, and he reached behind him and pulled out a 9mm from his waistband. Her eyes widened, because he hadn't pulled a gun the entire time they'd been at the shack, not even when she'd escaped. The presence of a gun seemed to ratchet the tension in the space, the element of danger invading her very soul.

"They're early. I figured the weather and the secluded location would slow them down. You'd better pray Rafe and Chance are on their way, or we're screwed."

The slamming of a car door had Tina scrambling to her feet and moving to stand behind Mr. Bad Dude. The door swung open, and a figure stepped into the room, silhouetted by the twilight sky behind them. Tina blinked once, and then again, not sure if she was seeing things.

Because the figure standing before her wasn't Jared, her ex. It might have been easier if it were. No, it was worse.

It was her monster-in-law, Liliana Webster.

"Are you sure you didn't recognize the voice?"

"Chance, you've asked me that a half dozen times now. The only voice I recognized was Tina's. I'm still trying to figure out why he called. There hasn't been a demand for ransom. And you heard Tina. She sounded fine. Dude, she told you she loves you. I don't think her kidnapper forced her to say those words."

"Can't you drive faster?"

Chance glanced at the speedometer, the needle inching closer to one hundred miles per hour. They were running with lights and sirens, people getting out of the way as they approached, though there weren't many folks on the roads. He was surprised Rafe was keeping up the speed, considering the road conditions, but he didn't care. All he could hear was Tina's voice, repeating over and over in his head, saying she loved him.

"I called Dane. We're lucky; he just got back to the Big House. He's taking the ATV to the line shack and will keep watch until we get there." Rafe drew a deep breath when he skidded on a slick section of roadway before he straightened. "As soon as he gets there, he'll scout things out and call. I told him to call you, since I'm kind of busy here."

It helped knowing his brother would get to Tina fast. Dane knew the ranch better than anybody, had explored every nook and cranny, each hill and wild pastureland, because he loved the place. There wasn't anywhere on the ranch anybody could go where Dane couldn't follow. One thing bothered Chance, though. After the whole incident with Jamie's kidnapping, they'd beefed up the security on the ranch, including additional cameras and motion detectors. How'd anybody gotten on the property without an alarm going off?

"I have no idea, but you can bet I'm going to find out," Raf answered, and Chance realized he'd asked the question aloud.

When Chance's phone rang seconds later, he answered before the ring ended, immediately putting it on speaker.

"Dane? What do you see?"

"There's definitely people in the line shack. Can't say how many. There's a white sedan parked around in the back. Toyota Avalon, which is the rental you're probably looking for. A black Mercury pulled up a minute ago, a driver and one passenger. I couldn't see much because it's getting dark, and I can't get closer without being seen."

"So, we've got at least four people in the line shack. The two who came in the Mercury, Tina, and the man who snatched her."

"Actually, only three inside. The driver of the Mercury helped the passenger to the door and then got back in the car. The passenger was a woman." Dane's voice lowered to a whisper. "I'm going to try and circle around through the trees, see if I can come up on the back of the line shack, and look in one of the windows."

"Only if you think it's safe. Otherwise, you keep your

distance, you hear me?" Rafe's voice brooked no argument.

"I'll be careful. Don't want to spook anybody in case there are weapons involved."

Chance swallowed at his brother's words. "Are you armed?"

"What do you think?"

"Be careful. We're about fifteen minutes away."

"Gotcha. See you soon." With that, Dane disconnected, and Chance swallowed, feeling helpless.

"A woman? I would've bet it was Jared Webster who'd had Tina taken. Course, he may still be orchestrating things from a distance. Wouldn't surprise me. It seems to be his M.O."

"I bet it's Liliana Webster."

Rafe's head swung toward Chance for a few seconds before he looked back at the road. "The mother-in-law? You think she's doing Jared's dirty work?"

"No. I think she's the one who's been pulling the strings the whole time. Tina called her monster-in-law, and Tina gets along with everybody. Which means Liliana is really bad news. If Jared is under Mommy's thumb…"

"She might not want Tina back in the picture. Nope, still not seeing it. There's got to be something more."

"Maybe there is." An awful fine piece to the puzzle clicked into place in Chance's brain, and he felt an overwhelming sense of dread, because if he was right, Tina was in a whole heap of trouble.

"Don't leave me hanging."

"I'm trying to add up all the pieces. Jared stepped up his search for Tina the last few weeks. Liliana Webster dropped out of public view around the same time. Randolph Webster hasn't been seen by his home staff or office personnel, either. Are you seeing the pattern?"

"Chance, spell it out. I'm concentrating on not killing us before we get to the ranch. I don't have time to analyze the way your brain thinks."

"It all ties back to the Websters. What is the most important thing to the Websters? Wealth and privilege, which equals power. Jared only got as far as he did in medical school because he came from a powerful family, at least until he latched onto Tina, right? Without her, he's lost a lot of what made him successful. Liliana Webster loves the spotlight, doing her charity work, being a leader of fashion and the country club set. Again, wealth and privilege, all brought about by marrying into the Webster family fortune. Wonder if she had any before latching onto old Randolph? Being with him brings that prestigious lifestyle. Then we have Randolph Webster. He inherited family money, yet he worked. From what Destiny said, he's a workaholic, spending more time on the job than at home with the missus."

"I'm following you so far. Keep going."

"Randolph's different from Jared and Liliana in the fact that people actually like him. Tina mentioned he was the only good thing about marrying into that family. She cared for him. Said he was the only thing about her marriage she missed."

Chance fell silent, weighing his next words carefully. Because the direction of his thoughts seemed so outrageous, so outlandish as to be improbable. But it was the only thing that made sense, given what he knew.

"You can't stop there. Yeah, they're all a bunch of rich jerks. Most rich jerks don't resort to kidnapping their ex-wives."

"They do if there is money involved. I'm going out on a limb here, because everything I'm going to say is a wild guess, but it makes sense. We know Randolph liked Tina, right? They got along well. What if Randolph didn't go out of town? What if he really is dead, like Destiny proposed? Maybe there was an accident. Shoot, maybe he had a heart attack or a stroke."

"I'm following you, but I still don't see what Tina has to do with any of this." Rafe sped past the driveway turnoff to the Big House, heading further down the asphalt toward the northern border of the property. It was getting darker outside, and he flipped the headlights on, casting light in front of them that glistened on the wet roadway.

"I'm getting there. What if Liliana or Jared, maybe both, found out Randolph wrote Tina into his will? That would make them angry, right? Tina was an ugly blip on their otherwise perfect lives. Only good old Randolph didn't feel the same; he truly cared about Tina. Let's play out one scenario. Liliana finds out her husband included Tina in the will, maybe leaving her a large chunk of the family fortune. It would infuriate the woman, who considered herself Randolph's sole heir. Jared's got his medical practice, the hospital, and probably a trust fund, but without her husband's money, Liliana's lifestyle goes bye-bye."

"Son of a—that actually makes a twisted kind of sense. Mommy dearest wouldn't want her son's ex to have any of their money. She'd probably think Tina didn't deserve a penny because she dared leave her precious baby boy." Rafe slammed a hand onto the steering wheel.

"What if—and here's where I'm guessing—they've been able to keep Randolph's death under wraps? If his death hasn't been reported, then the will hasn't been read. If Liliana can get Tina out of the picture before the will goes into probate, Tina gets nothing. Liliana gets everything, and her lifestyle remains exactly the way she wants."

Rafe's foot smashed against the accelerator at Chance's final statement. Chance grabbed onto the armrest with one hand and slammed the other against the dashboard at the sudden leap forward.

"I'm never going to understand rich people and their love of money. Life shouldn't revolve around things. People worshipping the almighty dollar above everything else. I bet Tina hasn't got a clue what's going on."

"If we're right, she's in more danger than we imagined."

"We're almost there, bro. Hang on."

Chance closed his eyes and did the only thing he could. He prayed.

# CHAPTER TWENTY-ONE

"Liliana? I don't understand. Where's Jared?"

Liliana flipped her blonde hair over one shoulder and stepped inside the line shack, looking down her nose at what Tina was sure were accommodations below her standards. Nary a muscle moved on her ex-mother-in-law's face, and she guessed Liliana must've had work done recently. While she'd been married to Jared, one of her secret hobbies was guessing what Liliana's next plastic surgical procedure would be.

"Jared's at home, exactly where he should be. The hospital depends on him, you know. He can't just traipse all of the country, trying to find you." She looked down her nose at Tina, before brushing a nonexistent piece of lint from her jacket. The dark navy suit probably wasn't the best choice for Texas in a thunderstorm, but Liliana never had cared about what was practical; she was all about what worked to enhance her status.

"I never asked him to follow me. As a matter of fact, I made it perfectly clear I wanted him to leave me alone. He never seemed to get the message."

"It's my son's one fault. Once he met you, he became obsessed." She gave Tina a measured glance from head to toe, and from her moue of distaste, found her wanting. Not that she hadn't seen the same expression on Liliana's face almost every day from the time Jared proposed. Too bad she'd been so infatuated with him that she'd ignored all the warning signs that his mother was crazy as a one-legged man in a butt-kicking contest.

"Ladies, as much as I'm enjoying your family reunion, I think we need to conclude our business and be on our way."

"I agree. Tina, I've made arrangements for us to fly back to San Francisco immediately. I have my private plane at an airport outside Dallas, ready to leave as soon as we arrive. Please don't cause any trouble, or I'll have you knocked out."

"I'm sick and tired of people pumping me full of drugs. Well, I've got news for you, lady, I'm not gonna stand by and let you drug me."

Liliana's cold smile sent chills down Tina's spine. "Who said anything about drugs?"

The implication was crystal clear.

"My job is done." Mr. Bad Dude crossed his arms over his chest, though Tina' noted the slight tic in his jaw. His posture might be causal and relaxed, but standing this close, she couldn't help noticing the muscles bunched beneath his shirt sleeves.

"I'm afraid we aren't quite finished, Mr. Jones."

*Jones? Why don't I believe that's his real name?*

"I'm afraid it is, Mrs. Webster." Liliana's eyes widened at the use of her name.

"How'd you know my name?"

His smile was even colder than Liliana's had been moments earlier. "I never take a contract without knowing everything about the parties involved." The slight hesitation after his words had the tiny hairs on the back of Tina's neck standing at attention, before he added, "And I mean *everything.*"

Every ounce of color drained from Liliana's face, though she rallied quickly, and she put on what Tina always called her public persona. The sweet butter wouldn't melt in her mouth smile that never reached her eyes, and her backbone of solid steel. When she got like this, Tina tended to steer clear of her, because she scared her. Like a swaying cobra hypnotizing its prey, Liliana lured people into believing she was meek and defenseless. Tina knew better.

"Please do not think you are in a position of power, Mr. Jones. Since you know who I am, you are aware of the power I have available to me at the snap of my fingers. You will do what I say. I'll make sure you are compensated appropriately."

The look of hatred Liliana shot Tina wasn't anything new, but there was an almost gleeful satisfaction in her eyes. She'd never understood why Liliana hated her so, had from the day she'd met her.

"Ah, you're wanting to negotiate an addendum to our

contract, Mrs. Webster. That could be arranged if the price is right."

Tina took a step back, a small gasp escaping her lips. As stupid as it seemed, she'd started to like Mr. Bad Dude, or Mr. Jones, or whatever he called himself. Had actually felt like there was a chance he'd help her. How stupid was that?

"I need Ms. Nelson," Liliana's lips curled up at the use of Tina's new name, "to have an accident."

Tina's breath caught in her throat at her words. "What?"

"Shut up. I am sick of you. Everything I've had to do is because of you. I curse the day my son brought you into my life. Into my home. You and your siren ways, seducing him into believing you were good enough for him. You are nothing but trailer trash, and I'm going to make sure that you end up back in the gutter where you belong. Or at least your body will."

"I'm not an assassin, Mrs. Webster. I'm a businessman. I'm not going to kill anyone, certainly not Ms. Nelson."

She whirled toward him and flung a hand in his direction. "You're willing to kidnap her, hold her hostage, but you draw the line at ending her? What are you, a coward?"

"Believe what you will. Murder is a line I have never crossed."

"Not even for half a million dollars?"

Tina felt the tension in the room ratchet higher, as Mr. Bad Dude straightened to his full height.

"Please…" Tina's voice caught in her throat when he

held up his hand, never glancing her way.

"You're willing to pay half a million dollars to have your daughter-in-law murdered?"

Liliana simply quirked her brown, a reptilian smirk on her lips. "Murder is such an ugly word."

"Accurate word, though."

"Why, Liliana? I haven't been a part of your life, of your family, for years. Why are you doing this now?"

Completely ignoring Tina, she squared off with Mr. Bad Dude. "Do we have a deal?"

"How do you want it done? Double tap to the head? Or do you want it to look like an accident?" He folded his arms over his chest, and that's when Tina noticed he'd slid the gun back into his waistband. Turning his head toward her, he gave her a slow wink.

"I don't care, as long as her body is found after the fact. There needs to be proof that she's dead."

"Your money, your job. Do you want to watch?"

Liliana recoiled, as if he'd struck her. "Heavens, no. I'm not a ghoul. I simply need her out of the picture."

"You must really hate her."

"You have no idea. She broke my son's heart. Jared adores the ground she walks on, thinks she some fairytale princess. He treated her with kid gloves, and she walked away without a backward glance."

"Are you insane?" Tina exploded around from behind Mr. Bad Dude, ready to scratch Liliana's eyes out. "You think Jared treated me like a princess? I don't think princesses get slapped in the face. I haven't heard of any princesses who've had the bones in their arm cracked by having it slammed against the wall. I don't know a single princess who had all their dreams of being a surgeon cut short because their husband deliberately slammed their hand in a car door. I will never have the full use of my hand again, never be able to do the intricate work of operating on anybody ever again. That's not the acts of a saintly prince. Jared was an abuser, and I saved my life by leaving him."

"Liar!" Liliana took a menacing step toward her, but Tina stood her ground. She'd never back down from her, never again allow her former mother-in-law to walk all over her like a doormat.

"Ladies, ladies. Calm down."

Mr. Bad Dude turned and put his hands on her shoulders and guided her back a couple of steps. Leaning in close, he whispered, "Trust me."

Tina pulled in a shuddering breath, her whole body shaking with anger. How dare Liliana act like *she'd* done something wrong? Did she honestly believe Jared had been the wronged party?

She gave him an imperceptible nod and took one final step back. For now, she'd follow his lead, but she wasn't about to let Liliana kill her. She'd fight until her final breath, because she wasn't going to give up, not now that she had something to live for.

# CHAPTER TWENTY-TWO

Rafe cut the headlights and pulled over behind a stand of trees not far from the line shack. They'd need to go the rest of the way on foot because they didn't dare pull closer. The sound of the engine might clue the kidnapper to their arrival. Even though they'd gotten the call on where to find Tina, Dane's account of another car showing up complicated things.

"We walk from here."

"I'm going to text Dane, find out what's happening." Chance whipped out his phone, pressing the keypad while he spoke. His heart was in his throat, fearful Tina might be hurt. He didn't dare contemplate any option other than she was still alive.

Dane answered almost immediately.

"Bro, Dane said he caught a couple of guys sneaking up on the shack. One of them had already taken out the driver, left him tied up in the back seat of the town car."

When his text alert sounded, Chance looked down and read the message out loud.

*"Took out the two guys. Tied up in trees behind shack. I'll*

*cover the back. Be careful."*

Walking around to the back of the car, Rafe opened the trunk and pulled out a Kevlar vest and handed it to Chance, who shrugged it on. Pulling on his own, Rafe then pulled two shotguns out, handing one to Chance before closing the trunk with a quiet click.

"I'm having serious doubts of letting you come with me. You need to keep your head, no matter what's going on inside."

"Stop wasting time. I'm not going to rush in, guns blazing. Have you ever known me to lose my cool?"

Rafe's shoulders shook with silent laughter, and Chance realized he'd left himself wide open with that crack.

"Sorry, bro. I'd answer your question, but we don't have enough time."

"Jerk." Chance turned his back and started walking, doing his best to avoid the mud puddles, not needing to lose time digging out a stuck shoe. The earlier downpour had tapered off to a soft drizzle, the sky still dark with heavy clouds. Thunder rumbled in the distance, giving the woods an ominous feeling.

Rafe shouldered past him, putting a finger to his lips in a shushing motion. What did his idiot brother think he was going to do, race through the trees like a moose in heat? He'd never do anything to put Tina's life in danger.

Within minutes, he was soaked to the skin, but within eyesight of the line shack. One thing had been bothering him, ever since they'd gotten the phone call. Why would the kidnapper bring Tina back onto Boudreau land? It didn't make sense. But then, nothing had made sense about this whole mess from the beginning.

"Bro, when's the last time you came out this way? I haven't visited this line shack in years."

"Me, either," Rafe answered. Some of the hands might have been out this way, but unless Dane's been here, it probably sits abandoned."

"But with a chance somebody might drop by, why do you think the kidnapper brought Tina back here? Practically right under our noses. Is he taunting us, trying to rub it in our faces that he snatched her right in the middle of town?"

"Doesn't matter, we'll get the answer to that when we arrest him. Now, quiet."

Chance rolled his eyes, then followed his brother, moving closer to the line shack. Knowing Dane had their six, covering the back of the line shack made it easier, because nobody could sneak up on them from that direction.

As soon as they approached the edge of the tree line, the black town car stood out in front of the shack. It meant that the driver was still incapacitated in the back, and nobody had attempted to leave before they'd arrived.

"How do you want to do this?"

"I'm going to try and get across the open space, and get close to the window, see if I can get a glimpse inside. You stay here."

"Seriously?" Chance shot his brother a death stare. "I'm not sitting on the sidelines while Tina's in that cabin in danger. You don't like it, you can stay here."

Without another word, Chance took off at a low sprint, staying low, and running straight for the line shack. He could hear Rafe running behind him, his footsteps slapping against the wet dirt and grass and leaves. The rain fell heavier, not the deluge from earlier, but enough to chill his skin.

When he reached the shack, he placed his back against the wooden slats, looking around. Dane said he took care of two guys, but were there more hidden? He scanned every inch he could see, but there was no movement, no hint anybody other than he and Rafe were outside.

Rafe's back landed against the wood by Chance's side, and he jerked his head toward the right.

"Stay here, see if you can hear anything. I'm going to sneak around the back, come up on the other side. Do not, under any circumstances, go inside. Hear me? I'm not kidding. No matter what you hear or see, stay put. Don't make me arrest you when this is all over."

"Go."

Rafe gave him another glare and slipped around the side. After what seemed like an eternity, his brother eased around the corner, his back against the wall on the other side, like a bookend to his own position.

"Anything?" Rafe mouthed the word.

Chance shook his head. Rafe eased closer to the window beside the door. The line shack wasn't new and definitely wasn't in the greatest shape, the boards weathered and gray, the caulking around the windows cracked and falling out in chunks.

Chance could hear voices inside. Sounded like two females and one male, but he couldn't make out what they said. He watched Rafe begin picking at the caulking around the window closest to him, and immediately started on the one closest to him. If they could hear what was going on, it might give them a fighting chance to shut things down without any bloodshed.

"You must really hate her." Definitely a male voice, but who was he talking to?

"You have no idea. She broke my son's heart. Jared adores the ground she walks on, thinks she some fairytale princess. He treated her with kid gloves, and she walked away without a backward glance."

Chance looked at Rafe, who raised his brows. Was that Liliana Webster? It had to be since she was talking about her son, Jared.

"Are you insane?" Chance gave a shuddering breath when he heard Tina's voice. Though he couldn't see her, she sounded okay. Angry but okay.

"You think Jared treated me like a princess? I don't think princesses get slapped in the face. I haven't heard of any princesses who've had the bones in their arm cracked by having it slammed against the wall. I don't know a single princess who had all their dreams of being a surgeon cut short because their husband deliberately slammed their hand in a car door. I will never have the full use of my hand again, never be able to do the intricate work of operating on anybody ever again. That's not the acts of a saintly prince. Jared was an abuser, and I saved my life by leaving him."

Chance's head fell toward his chest, realizing the pain and the heartbreak Tina had endured during her marriage to Jared Webster. How strong she must've been to not only make it through, but to survive and thrive. She was amazing.

"Liar!" Liliana's screech would've been heard, even without the missing chinks in the caulk. Guess Tina must've hit a nerve.

"Ladies, ladies. Calm down."

He hated they were working blind, without a clear line of sight into the shack. The windows were single-paned, older than dirt, and were covered with what was probably years of grease and grime. Visibility was obstructed, and they still wouldn't have been able to see much, because of the oilcloth covering most of the panes.

"What do you want to do?"

"We wait."

Chance didn't like Rafe's answer.

"Mrs. Webster, I'm afraid I'm going to have to decline your proposal. While I fulfilled our previous contract, I find the terms of your new job unacceptable." The male voice sounded calm, businesslike, and eerily familiar. Chance had heard that formalized style of speech before, but where? When?

"Do you want more money, is that it? Fine, one million dollars."

"One million? Liliana, why is it so important for me to die? I haven't done anything to you or Jared. I moved away and stayed away. I can't help that Jared won't accept our divorce."

"You stupid cow," Liliana's voice sneered. Chance wanted to storm the door just for the insult alone, his insides icy with fear at Tina's statement. Liliana wanted her dead. Not simply kidnapped and out of the way. She wanted Tina's life over. He'd show the murderous old crow.

Rafe slammed a hand against his chest, blocking the door. Chance hadn't even realized he'd moved, his hand inches from the doorknob.

"Wait!" Though he didn't say the word aloud, Rafe's message came through loud and clear. It took every ounce of Chance's willpower to keep from kicking the door open and slamming inside, taking out the miserable, worthless woman who dared threaten Tina.

"I told my son he was making a mistake marrying you. He could have married anyone, and he chose a useless piece of trailer trash who couldn't even finish school."

Tina's laugh was sarcastic and bitter. "You're right, I didn't finish. I never got my degree because your son wanted me to help him. He was on the brink of flunking out of med school. I helped him pass his tests. I helped him build his practice. I might not have your money and cachet, but I was loyal to Jared. Right up to the point where he decided I made a good punching bag."

"If my son ever touched you, I'm sure you deserved it." Liliana's voice rose with every word. "Mr. Jones, is your refusal your final decision? Because I have someone waiting outside who will be more than happy to do the job."

"Mrs. Webster," the calm male voice spoke, his suddenly icy tone sending a chill down Chance's spine, "you don't have enough money for me to kill Ms. Nelson. And I think you'll find your *driver* is otherwise occupied at the moment."

"What? That's impossible."

"Woman, you've overestimated your power. I think you'll find your bank accounts inaccessible. Not only do you not have the million dollars to pay me, but you also haven't got a single dime to your name. All your accounts have been frozen, along with your husband's business accounts, as well as your son's."

Chance looked at Rafe, who stared back. What in the world was the guy talking about? Who was he? Was he bluffing, trying to throw Liliana Webster off her game?

"Rafe, you out there?" Mr. Jones' voice sounded loud and clear.

"I'm here."

"You hear everything?"

"We heard enough. I'm coming in."

Rafe flung the shack's door open, and it banged against the wall. Chance stood behind him, his gaze going straight to Tina. She stood behind and to the left of a tall, dark-haired stranger, his stance protective. None of this mess made any sense.

Behind Tina, he spotted Dane standing outside the window, which was cracked open just enough for the barrel of a shotgun to peek beneath. Trust his brother to have his own handle on the situation. Liliana Webster wouldn't have made it anywhere near Tina.

"Rafe, you need to place Liliana Webster under arrest for solicitation to commit murder for hire. Her driver, too."

"Under whose authority?" Rafe shot back.

Mr. Jones slowly reached into the rear pocket of his jeans and pulled out a folded leather case and showed it to Rafe. One look at the ID and Rafe started chuckling. Taking it in one hand, he passed it to Chance.

Chance looked at the ID, then at the man it belonged to. He knew his mouth hung open, but he couldn't have been more surprised if a sinkhole opened beneath his feet and sucked him under.

"Are you joking?"

"Afternoon, Chance. Good to see you, too." Mr. Jones took his ID back and slid it into his pocket. "Who'd you have covering the back?"

"Dane."

"Ah, good choice. Rafe, we should head to the sheriff's office and get all the official paperwork handled." Mr. Jones reached into a backpack on the floor and pulled out a set of zip ties. Tina snickered when he handed them to Rafe.

Without a word, Rafe slipped the zip ties on Liliana Webster's wrists while she struggled to break free. Chance knew there wasn't a chance Rafe would let her get away. Not after he'd heard the same thing Chance had, her offering a million dollars for Tina's death.

"Let's go, Mrs. Webster." As Rafe began marching Liliana outside, Chance heard him begin reading her the Miranda rights. He'd make sure she got them repeated when they got to the station, because he absolutely would not let her skate on a technicality.

Leaning his gun against the wall, he opened his arms and Tina rushed forward, wrapping her arms around his neck and her legs around his waist. He squeezed her tight, adrenaline soaring through him now that the danger was over. Tina's body trembled, and he needed to get her home.

Where she'd never be in danger again.

# CHAPTER TWENTY-THREE

"I can't believe your former mother-in-law tried to get you killed." Beth leaned her shoulder against Brody's, smiling softly at Tina. "My previous in-laws aren't exactly role models for congeniality, but they never put a hit on me."

Tina slid her hand into Chance's, threading her fingers with his. It was hard to comprehend everything was over. Well, except for sweeping up all the pieces scattered across several states. The San Francisco police had picked up Jared, and he was swearing up and down he didn't have an idea what his mother attempted. He also denied having anything to do with the threatening message left on Tina's apartment wall.

Several hours had passed since her rescue. Rafe and Antonio were at the sheriff's office, trying to make sense of everything and dealing with the fallout. Liliana had been arrested, and Antonio had contacted Derrick Williamson, his boss at the FBI office in Austin, because this case was going to be big news. The shock waves were expected to make national and possibly international news, because of the notoriety of the parties involved.

Chance hadn't left her side for a second. They still need-ed to make statements, but Rafe agreed it could wait until he'd processed Liliana, Mr. Bad Dude AKA Mr. Jones, and Liliana's driver. Wrapping her head around Liliana wanting her dead still hadn't sunk in. Chance had explained his theory about Randolph being missing, probably dead, and his crazy supposition that Randolph had left her everything in his will.

Now, several hours later, pretty much everybody gath-ered at the Big House or were on their way. The love and support these people shared might be overwhelming at times, but it was the truest form of love she'd ever felt. Nobody cared they didn't share a direct blood link; they had something better. Something stronger.

"Auntie Tina, can I get you some cookies? Me and Mommy made them and they're really good."

"Thank you, sweetie. I'd love a cookie." Tina knew Ja-mie didn't understand all the underlying tension filling the room, but she knew Tina seemed to be at the center, and in her own childlike way she wanted to make Tina feel better. She was such as sweet little girl, and she adored her.

When she came running back into the room, she clasped a cookie in each hand, handed one to Tina, and held the other one out to Chance. She nibbled her bottom lip between her teeth, concentrating hard on making sure she didn't drop it.

"How about you eat that one, Jamie? I'll share this one with Auntie Tina." Chance winked at Tina, emphasizing the auntie thing, and she felt a little fizzle of awareness in the pit of her stomach. One of those *if only* moments.

"Okay." She skipped away, after taking a huge bite out of the oatmeal raisin cookie.

"Here," Tina passed the cookie to Chance. "I didn't really want a cookie, but…"

"Eat it anyway, sweetheart. You haven't had anything since this morning."

She took a small bite of the cookie before asking, "What do you think's going to happen now?"

"I suspect the FBI and the San Francisco police are going to try and locate Randolph. I hate to admit it, but I think he's dead and has been for a while." Chance's voice was somber, and she nodded.

"I think you're right. Randolph would never leave without letting his office know where he was headed, and make sure they could contact him. He was a very conscientious and diligent boss. Do you think Liliana had him killed?"

Another shiver ran down her spine because the whole ordeal was finally sinking in, the reality of how close she'd come to losing her life. Liliana had tried to order a hit on her. She'd wanted her dead. Even though they'd never gotten along from day one, she'd never imagined the depth of the other woman's hatred. It defied explanation.

"I have no idea. Hopefully, Rafe and Antonio will have

answers for us once they finish questioning her. I hope the feds plan on throwing the book at her."

Tina made a scoffing sound. "She'll lawyer up so fast, you'll never get a straight answer out of her. Liliana will always think about herself first. Self-preservation will kick in. She'll try and make a deal. And she's got some powerful friends."

"Who will probably scatter like rats abandoning a sinking ship the minute they catch a whiff of the scandal attached to Liliana now. I've seen it happen over and over. When you're questioned by law enforcement, especially the feds, it doesn't matter who you are or how much money you've got, people will turn their backs on you. It's human nature."

She leaned her head on his shoulder, and watched the others gathered at the Big House. Tessa had shown up around the same time as Brody and Beth. Even with all the drama, Beth seemed to glow. Was it only earlier today she'd heard the exciting news about the baby?

"Did Rafe say anything about Mr. Jones?"

"You mean the guy who kidnapped you?" At her nod, Chance scowled. "I haven't heard anything. Chances are good the feds will take over. That's gonna happen anyway, because of the family connection at the sheriff's department, which is why Williamson is on his way."

"I know it's weird for me to say this, but he was actually nice to me. Even when I escaped, he didn't—"

"Escaped?"

She ducked her head, hiding her eyes. Had she forgotten to tell them about that little detail? Oops.

"I'd been tied with zip ties. When he let me use the bathroom, I found a loose nail, and when Mr. Bad Dude, I mean Mr. Jones, was distracted, I used it to get out of the zip ties and ran. Made it all the way to the trees, but he caught me."

"Tina, he could have hurt you."

"But he didn't. He fed me, gave me water, and he was actually nice. I think he was trying to make sure Liliana didn't hurt me, if that makes any sense."

Chance slid his arm around her shoulders, nodding when his father walked into the room, his momma coming in right behind him. She immediately crossed the living room, and sat down on the couch beside Tina, pulling her into her arms. Rocking softly back and forth, she didn't speak, simply offered her comfort, and Tina let out a deep sigh. For the first time, after the whole crazy ordeal, she felt like everything was really over.

She was safe.

She was home.

"I talked to Rafe a few minutes ago. He thinks he and Antonio are going to be in town for the rest of the night. Randolph Webster is dead. They found the body in a freezer in a storage unit rented by Liliana Webster. SFPD didn't see any obvious cause of death, but will have to wait for the autopsy."

"I'm sorry. Randolph always treated me well. He was a good man."

Tina looked around the living room of the Big House, at the faces of all the men and women—and even little Jamie— who'd become such an integral part of her life. So long ago, she'd felt alone, her only friends the people she worked with at the coffee shop, especially Renee. How her life had changed in a matter of weeks.

"What happens now?" Tessa asked the question, carrying in a tray overflowing with coffee cups and passing them around. "I realize there's going to be all sorts of jurisdictional stuff to be straightened out, but can we relax, knowing Tina's going to be safe?"

"I think so," Chance answered, accepting one of the coffee cups and handing it to Tina, then taking one for himself. "It'll probably take a long while, with a lot of legal wrangling, but she's going to be fine."

"Good. I want all my family safe." Ms. Patti patted Tina's back, and stood. "I'd like five minutes alone with Liliana Webster. I guarantee Tina wouldn't have anything to worry about after that."

Douglas chuckled. "Down, tiger."

"I'm just saying, nobody messes with one of mine. Especially somebody who raises a lousy son like she did."

The lighthearted banter continued for several minutes before Ms. Patti clapped her hands together and proclaimed. "Y'all settle in. I'm going to fix us something to eat."

"I'll help, Momma." "Me, too." "I could eat." The women followed Ms. Patti into the kitchen, leaving Tina and Chance on the couch. Douglas and Brody sat in the two armchairs, resembling two bookends, seated but still on guard duty. She doubted anybody would be dropping their guard anytime soon, and a tinge of guilt spread through her.

"Don't."

"Don't what?" She looked at Chance.

"You have nothing to feel guilty about. You didn't ask to have an abusive monster for a husband. You didn't ask for your former mother-in-law to turn out to be an even bigger monster than her son. Having a big heart and trusting soul doesn't make any of this your fault."

"He's right, Tina." Douglas' deep voice drew Tina's attention. Before he could say more, Shiloh and Renee walked through the front door. Tina sprang to her feet and ran across the living room, straight into her friend's arms. Renee's eyes were red-rimmed from crying.

"I'm so, so sorry. Are you okay?"

"I'm okay, I promise."

"I still reeling from everything. Can you believe how much has happened to us in the last few months?" Renee couldn't seem to stop hugging Tina. "How strange is it that both of us were running from our pasts, ended up working together, then wound up in Shiloh Springs?"

"Pretty big coincidence."

"I don't believe in coincidences." Ms. Patti walked back

in from the kitchen, wiping her hands on a tea towel. "You were meant to meet my sons. You were meant to be a part of this family. Now, anybody who wants to eat, food's ready. Get a move on before it's all gone."

"What'd you make, Momma?" Lucas gave an exaggerated sniff. "Is that lasagna?"

"Yes."

"Outta my way. I'm starving." With an arm around Renee's waist, he shot Tina a smile, and headed toward the kitchen.

Douglas moved to stand beside Tina. "You'll have to forgive my son. That one, he's always been ruled by his stomach."

"Dad," came Lucas' aggrieved response from the kitchen.

"You need to eat, Tina."

"I will, Ms. Patti. I'll be right there." Tina gave her a tentative smile, not having the heart to tell Ms. Patti she wasn't hungry. When Chance moved to stand behind her and slid his arms around her waist, she leaned back against him, simply allowing the feel of his embrace ground her.

A sharp rap sounded on the front door, and Chance stepped back to answer it. Tina gasped when she saw who stood on the other side.

*Mr. Bad Dude.*

Tina took a step forward, looking into his face. "What are you doing here? Why aren't you in jail?"

Chance drew back his arm, and his fist flew toward the

other man's face, and Tina bit back a scream. The punch never connected, as Mr. Bad Dude caught Chance's hand inches from his face.

"No free shots, Boudreau."

Chance glared at the other man, anger radiating from him. Tina had no clue what had set him off, but she'd find out later. Right now, she wanted to find out why Mr. Bad Dude had shown up on the Boudreaus' ranch.

"I'm here to explain what's going on, and my part in it, if you'll listen, Ms. Nelson."

*Answers? Somebody finally has some answers for what I'm dealing with? Heck, yeah, I want to hear this.*

"Both of you, no fighting. You really know what's going on?"

Mr. Bad Dude chuckled and released Chance's fist. "No fighting, but for the record, I didn't throw the first punch."

"This time," Chance muttered under his breath. He stepped back, putting his arm around Tina's shoulders, and motioned for the other man to enter.

"You'd better have a good explanation for snatching Tina from the diner. I don't care that we've got history, hurt her again and I will end you." Chance moved his hands to the top of her shoulders, his touch possessive and a clear indication to the other man to watch his step. Tina hid her smile at his macho display.

As Mr. Bad Dude stepped inside, he removed the buff-colored cowboy hat, and she caught sight of the beginning of a shiner around his left eye.

"What happened?" She pointed toward it.

"A misunderstanding. It's been cleared up."

Chance didn't comment, but she couldn't miss the smirk on his lips.

The sound of multiple voices, one talking over another, came from the kitchen and Tina caught the surreptitious glance the other man cast in that direction, an almost wistful expression on his face, before he quickly covered it and walked toward the living room.

He stopped in the center of the room and turned to face Tina. "My name is—"

"Brian?"

Ms. Patti stood in the opening of the living room, her hand in front of her mouth. Tina watched as tears filled her eyes as she struggled to keep them from falling.

"Hello, Ms. Patti."

Without another word, Ms. Patti raced across the living room and flung her arms around Brian, wrapping them around his back, her head resting on his chest. His arms pulled her close, and Tina watched him swallow several times, his eyes closed. She'd bet if they were open, they'd be overflowing with a myriad of emotions.

"I can't believe you're here." Ms. Patti pulled back and wiped at her tears. "I've always wondered—"

"It's a long story. Maybe—maybe we can talk about it sometime?"

"Anytime you want, Brian." Her hand crept up and cupped his cheek, the look of love on Ms. Patti's face making her glow like she'd been lit from within. Tina had no idea who Brian was, other than the man who'd held her hostage, but apparently Ms. Patti knew him and cared about him.

Tina glanced at Chance when he let out an expletive. "Why, Newkirk? What's going on? You haven't been around for over fifteen years, and now you're in the middle of this?"

"You know Brian?"

"Honestly, I didn't recognize him at first. Wasn't until I saw his name on his ID that all the pieces fell into place. Brian used to live here. We both came to the Big House about the same time. There were some problems, and he ended up not staying. Once he went back into the system, we never heard from him again."

Ms. Patti sniffled and again patted Brian's chest. "I never forgot you, not for one second."

"Neither did I." Douglas walked up behind Ms. Patti, placing his hands on her shoulders gently. "We've prayed for you every night."

"I'm really confused. Brian used to live here?" Tina kept looking from Chance to Brian to Ms. Patti and Douglas. Was he one of the lost ones she'd talked with Ms. Patti about? She knew the Boudreau matriarch was heartbroken about the boys who'd ended up not staying on the ranch, not becoming part of their family. There weren't many, but those few lost souls weighed heavily on her heart.

"I did." Brian answered. "It was a long time ago, but I never forgot the Boudreaus." He turned to Douglas. "I'm here to talk to Ms. Nelson, explain to her why I grabbed her out of Daisy's place."

"Yeah, I'd like to hear why you kidnapped her, drugged her, and scared her half to death. I doubt you've got a good enough explanation to keep me from prosecuting you. Oh, yeah, and ripping off your arm and beating you to death with it." Chance's aggrieved tone almost had Tina smiling, but she bit her cheek to keep from letting it show. He was cute when he got all defensive.

Brian reached into his jeans' pocket and pulled out a leather folder and flipped it open, displaying an FBI shield.

"You've got to be kidding me!" Lucas let out a loud chuckle. "You're a fed?"

Brian gave a sheepish grin. "Yeah."

"I've got a hard time believing it." Chance ran a hand through his hair. "When we were kids, I'd have pegged you as a candidate for Huntsville, not a job with the U.S. government."

"I finally got my head on straight. Can we talk about that later? I don't have a lot of time; I'm flying out in the morning."

By this time, Renee, Brody and Beth were all standing just outside the kitchen, their whispered voices like buzzing bees in the background. Tina figured they were as shocked at seeing Brian Newkirk as Douglas and Ms. Patti.

"Everybody sit." Douglas moved to an armchair and eased Ms. Patti onto it, and then sat on the ottoman positioned in front of it. The others poured into the room, filling up the rest of the chairs and the sofa.

"I hadn't planned on talking with anybody but Ms. Nelson and maybe Chance."

"You can talk in front of everyone. They've all supported me throughout this whole disaster, they might as well hear it firsthand."

The corner of Brian's lip kicked up. "I'm not surprised. Boudreaus are nothing if not loyal to a fault." The wistfulness in his voice was poignant, striking a chord in Tina's chest. Maybe he missed being a part of the Boudreau clan?

"I'm going to give you the Reader's Digest version, because a lot of the information is confidential, part of an ongoing investigation."

Chance rolled his eyes, squeezing Tina's hand. "Get on with it, man."

"The FBI has been looking at the Websters for several months now. Randolph Webster had some shady dealings with some overseas individuals, and a little matter of money laundering. During our investigation, it came to light that Jared Webster was obsessed with Ms. Nelson."

"You might as well call me Tina. You did at the line shack."

Brian gave a brief nod and continued. "We've kept a close eye on Dr. Webster, along with the less-than-ethical investigators he sicced on you. We're also aware of your fraudulent identification. You'll need to get that taken care of ASAP. Either change it back to your legal name, or have your name changed through the proper channels."

"I didn't have a choice," she protested. "Having a new identity was the only way to stay one step ahead of him."

"We're aware. We're also aware of Dr. Webster's abuse. If you'd have gone to the authorities, reported him, we'd have been able ensure he couldn't continue harassing you. Because there was no official record, our hands were tied."

"Get back to Randolph Webster." Lucas leaned forward on the sofa, his elbows resting on his knees. "International money laundering carries a pretty harsh penalty. How close were you to arresting him?"

"Close. Then he disappeared. Of course, we've had eyes on Liliana, too. What a narcissistic, sadistic female. Don't get me started on her." Brian gave an exaggerated shudder. "We intercepted a message that she wanted to find Tina. The amount of money she offered would have drawn out every low-life mercenary in the western hemisphere. Because we knew Tina had come to Shiloh Springs, I got shanghaied into coming up with a solution. They thought, and rightly so, because I was familiar with the terrain and many of the people, I'd be the best choice for keeping her safe."

"I don't understand. You kidnapped Tina right in the middle of town. How was that keeping her safe?"

"The FBI got wind of Liliana was getting desperate, and

she planned to offer a huge bounty on Tina's head, found dead or alive. I'd already taken the initial contract and kept feeding Mrs. Webster just enough bogus info to keep her on the hook. Something happened, because she became frantic, desperate in her efforts to find Tina. I'll be honest, I don't have any idea why she suddenly accelerated her timetable, but her recent messages were heartless and cold. There's no humanity in that woman."

Chance raised his hand. "We have an educated guess about why she needed Tina out of the picture. It's an educated guess, but we think Randolph wrote Tina into his will."

Brian's eyes widened, and then he nodded. "Makes sense. It also explains why she offered me half a million dollars to kill Tina."

A collect gasp swept through the room. "Is that why you called Rafe?" Chance asked.

"No, she didn't make the offer until after she arrived at the line shack. I called Rafe because I wanted him to know where everything was going down in case Mrs. Webster pulled a fast one and showed up with hired guns."

"Why didn't you have back up?"

"I didn't need any. I figured I had Boudreau brothers for back up. Why do you think I picked a building on your land to hold Tina?" Brian held up a big hand when Chance took a step forward. "Just kidding. There were agents in place. Surprised you didn't catch sight of them."

"I did." Dane walked from the kitchen into the living room. "Course, nobody bothered to tell me they were feds. "You might want to collect the two guys I left tied up about fifty yards behind the line shack."

Brian burst out laughing, his big shoulders shaking. "I knew I could count on y'all. I've kept tabs on everyone here, and I knew you'd circle the wagons to protect one of your own. Something your parents taught you well."

Dane sighed, and turned back toward the kitchen. "I'll go and turn 'em loose."

"I'll go with you, son." Douglas stood and pressed a kiss against Ms. Patti's forehead. "We'll be back soon."

She made a shooing motion.

"I need to go. Rafe's got my official statement, as well as my FBI affiliation and involvement in the case. If you've got questions, I've left contact information with him." Brian turned to face Ms. Patti. "It's so good to see you again. I've really missed you. If you need anything—*anything*—don't hesitate. I'll come running."

Ms. Patti stood and held out her hand. "The same goes for you. If you need me—need us—we're here for you."

Tina watched Brian swallow several times and sympathized. Being around the Boudreaus tended to be overwhelming, especially when they turned all their love and attention on you. If Brian's reaction was any indication, living with the Boudreaus when he was younger, even though he'd been one of the ones who "didn't stick", they'd made an indelible impression that remained long after he'd left. She had the feeling it would be the same with her. She knew she'd never forget them.

Tina and Chance walked Brian to the door, while everybody else headed back into the kitchen. She overhead Beth whisper to Brody she was going to check on Jamie, who'd fallen asleep earlier. Stepping out onto the front porch, Chance held his hand out to Brian.

"Thank you." He gave a half-hearted laugh. "Seems strange thanking you for abducting my girl, but you did keep her safe."

*His girl?*

"Things will probably be crazy for the next few weeks, while jurisdiction gets straightened out and the autopsy on Randolph comes back. If you're right about his will, who knows what kind of catastrophe that's going to cause, especially if he was doing money laundering. Forensic bookkeeping is out of my wheelhouse."

"I don't want his money. I never wanted any of their money."

"I understand, Tina. It'll all get worked out, but you may be tied up for months getting this whole mess straightened out. At least you've got this big lug to help you out. Have him put his big brain to use. Seriously, he's a good man to have your back."

"I know." Tina wrapped her arm around Chance's waist, snuggling against his side.

Brian turned to Chance. "Take good care of her. She's a keeper."

"I intend to."

Without a backward glance, Brian bounded from the front steps, climbed behind the wheel of the white Toyota Avalon, and drove off. She watched until he was out of sight, marveling at the turn of events the day had taken.

So why did she have the feeling the surprises weren't over yet?

# CHAPTER TWENTY-FOUR

"That was a surprise."

Chance stared down into Tina's upturned face, noting the seriousness of her expression. Today had been a rough one, more so on her than anybody. He wasn't surprised she'd handled things like a champ. If it had been him, he'd probably be curled up in the corner, rocking back and forth at this point.

"Hmm?"

"Finding out Mr. Bad Dude actually turning out to be a good guy. Add in he apparently knows your family well, it makes you stop and think. Can't be a coincidence."

"I haven't seen Brian in years. An FBI agent; I'd never have pegged him as being part of the establishment. I figured he'd end up on the other end of the spectrum, behind bars. Knowing that he kept tabs on us feels kind of weird."

"Sometimes we don't know what we've got until its gone. I think he feels that way about Douglas and Ms. Patti." Tina walked across the front porch and sat on the swing. She drew in a deep breath and stared out at the starlit sky. His breath caught at how beautiful she looked, silhouetted by the moonlight and the golden glow from the ambient light from the window.

"I get the feeling he's not going to stay a stranger, now that he's reconnected with them."

Sitting beside her, he started the swing gently rocking, setting up a gentle rhythm. He was still wound tight, the events of the day catching up to him, making him realize how close he'd come to losing Tina.

"I guess I'll be able to head back to Portland soon."

"Do you want to?"

She shrugged, her shoulder brushing lightly against his. "I don't know what I want. I have an apartment, a job. At least I think I still have a job. I haven't talked to Gertie yet."

"Have you considered other options?"

"Like what?"

"Staying here in Shiloh Springs. Now that you can settle in one place without worrying about your ex, you can live anywhere. Renee is here. You've gained a lot of friends here. My parents adore you."

"And I adore them."

They rocked quietly for a moment, the silence not uncomfortable, yet Chance felt a sense of anticipation. She hadn't directly said no to staying, but she hadn't said yes, either.

"I want you to stay, Tina."

"Why?"

*Why? What does she mean why?*

"Why do *you* want me to stay, Chance?" Tina turned to face him, and he read the indecision in her face. He knew his answer could be the deciding factor of whether she stayed or whether she left. The make or break it moment, and suddenly the words dried up. The man known for his oratory skills in the courtroom, who had an outstanding conviction rate because he could convince juries with his words, found himself unable to speak.

Because this one moment was more important than any legal case he'd ever prosecuted. If he didn't tell Tina what he felt, make her understand how important she was to him, he could and would lose her.

"I don't want to screw this up, Sunshine. I've had a pretty good life. I have a family who loves me, and I love them. I've got the job I've always dreamed of, and a community who respect me and trusts me. And I want to share it with you. I want to see your face every day. Watch you smile. Hear you laugh. I want to know that you're happy. And if that means you going back to Portland, then I'll go with you."

"What? Chance—"

He gently placed a finger against her lips, because he wasn't finished. The three words he needed to say, the three words he wanted her to hear; he hadn't said them yet.

"I love you. Everything else is fluid, movable, changeable. My love isn't. It's yours forever." He smiled and cupped her cheek, before rubbing his knuckle softly against her skin.

"If you'll have me, I want to spend every day with you for the rest of our lives. Whether it's in Shiloh Springs or Timbuktu, as long as you're there, we can make it work."

When her eyes welled with tears, he knew he'd screwed up. Assumed she'd feel the same way he did. What an idiot!

"Chance, you're not an idiot." Her sweet smile let him know he'd said that out loud. Yep, he really was an idiot. "I don't think I've heard anything so sweet in my entire life. I'm the idiot for thinking I could walk away and leave you behind. Somehow, you've managed to work your way into my life and into my heart. I can't imagine spending the rest of my life without you. Oh, Chance, I love you, too!"

Tina flung herself into his arms, wrapping hers around his neck, and pressing kisses all over his face. He knew he was smiling, probably grinning from ear to ear, but he didn't care. At this moment, he was the king of the world, because the woman he loved, the woman who was the center of his world, loved him, too.

Taking her face between his hands, he kissed her, pouring everything he felt into the press of his lips against hers. She responded, leaning into him and parting her lips, allowing him to deepen the kiss, a sweet tangle of teeth and tongues.

He finally eased back, catching the dazed expression on her beautiful face. If there'd been a mirror handy, he'd probably find a matching one on his face. And he didn't care a lick, because he'd won the lottery with the amazing woman in his arms.

Sliding off the porch swing, he knelt on one knee and took her hands between his. Her eyes rounded in surprise.

"I hadn't planned on doing this tonight, and I don't have a ring or anything to give you except all the love in my heart. Will you marry me?"

"I don't care about a ring. All I care about is that you love me. Yes! A thousand times, yes!"

Chance stood and swept Tina in his arms, spinning around, his heart overflowing with emotion. He couldn't contain them any longer.

"She said yes!"

The uproarious exclamations of joy coming from the Big House faded into the background as he kissed her, knowing that no matter what the future threw out them, they could handle it—together.

# CHAPTER TWENTY-FIVE
## EPILOGUE

Walking through the front door of the Big House, Derrick Williamson drew in a deep breath and smiled. It was evident from the scents filling the air, Ms. Patti had been busy in the kitchen. After the past few days, the whole craziness of Tina Nelson's kidnapping, the arrest of Lillian Webster, and the subsequent fallout from the discovery of Randolph Webster's body in her multimillion-dollar home in San Francisco, to say things had been a nuthouse would be an understatement.

Today the Boudreaus celebrated Tina's inclusion as part of their family with a barbecue, and he'd been invited, since he'd been part of making sure the Websters wouldn't be free to cause any more trouble for the lovely Ms. Nelson. He smiled, knowing that fact made one particular Boudreau happy.

"Where is everybody?"

Derrick's nine-year-old son Ian stood at his side, his ever-present video game in his hand. Seemed like no matter where they were lately, he always kept a tight grip on the device. He really couldn't blame Ian, that game had gotten him through some pretty ugly stuff in the past few months, including having his life upended. First Derrick's ex-wife decided she needed to go and *find herself*. Somehow finding her inner person didn't include having her son around. Then he'd moved in with Derrick, another upheaval of his life. It was a lot for a kid to handle. Though he was doing his best, Derrick knew Ian resented being treated like he was an unwanted toy, tossed aside when his parents got tired of playing with it.

"I think everybody's out behind the house. My e-mail said to come through the house and head out the kitchen door."

"Something smells good."

"So, let's go find everyone." Derrick gestured toward the kitchen door right as it opened, and Ms. Patti walked in.

"Derrick! Ian! Welcome to the Big House. Although today I think it should be called the Mad House." She smiled and made her way to the foyer and ushered them through into the kitchen. Opening the refrigerator, she reached inside and pulled out two big cellophane-covered bowls. One contained potato salad and the other cut fruit, the colors vivid and bright against the white container.

"If y'all would carry these out and put them on the table, I'll be right out. Most everybody's already here, so make yourselves at home."

"Thank you, Miss Patti."

Within minutes, they'd said their hellos and Jamie, Beth and Brody's daughter, had commandeered his son, insisting he needed to meet Otto, whoever that was. She grabbed his hand and practically dragged him away, Ian turning around once to meet his eyes, a slightly panicked expression crossing his face. Derrick figured it would do his son good to interact with the only other child there, even if she was a girl and a few years younger.

Across the large patio area, he spotted Chance seated beside Tina along with Brody and his wife, Beth. Standing beside the grill, Douglas was flipping burgers and hot dogs, along with steaks with an expertise which bespoke familiarity. A pretty blonde stood talking with Serena and Tessa. He'd been introduced to her once on a previous trip to Shiloh Springs, and remembered she was the only Boudreau daughter. Hard to imagine being the lone girl in a sea of testosterone-laden brothers.

"Glad you made it, Derrick."

He turned at Rafe's voice and couldn't help noting the dark circles under the man's eyes. They matched the one's on his own face. The last few days had been long, crazy hours filled with meetings and dealing with numerous government agencies besides his own. This whole fiasco with the Websters spanned multiple states, dealing with stalking, kidnapping, and attempted murder meant reams and reams of paperwork and red tape to wade through.

"Happy for the invitation. It gave me a chance to spend a

little time with my son. He's probably feeling neglected."

"Ian's here?"

Derrick pointed toward the corralled area beside the barn, where Ian stood beside Jamie, an old donkey chomping on the carrot she held. The only promising thing he noted was his son's video game was in his back pocket, and not in his hand. He couldn't remember the last time that had happened.

"Finally got word from the San Francisco police. Randolph Webster's official cause of death is being listed as a heart attack."

"You're kidding! I thought Liliana Webster killed him. Didn't she admit to poisoning him when she was questioned?"

Rafe nodded. "She did. Coroner said the poison never had a chance to work in his system, because he had a massive coronary. Granted, the poison would have killed him if the heart attack hadn't, so the charge of murder will probably be revised to attempted murder. Along with the other charges, including concealing the body, she's still going away for the rest of her life."

"What about the son? He made Tina's life a nightmare, stalking her across state lines."

Rafe made a scoffing sound, filled with disgust. "Idiot's still claiming he knew absolutely nothing about his father's death. That he didn't know his mother hid the body. Nobody believes him, but so far they haven't found any evidence to implicate him. As far as the stalking, there's an investigation ongoing, but for now he's still walking around free to go about his business. As far as we're concerned, he'd better keep himself far away from Texas if he knows what's good for him."

"Bet Chance feels the same."

"I do. I also have somebody keeping tabs on him. He so much as breathes across the state line, and I'll know about it." Chance moved to stand beside his brother, and Derrick couldn't help noticing how different they were. One blond haired, blue eyed and the other with dark hair and eyes. They couldn't be more different in looks, but one thing he'd come to know having worked alongside both with his dealings in Shiloh Springs for the FBI. Both were Boudreaus through-and-through. Not a bad thing, in his humble opinion.

"Momma told me you're looking for a place in Shiloh Springs. You thinking about moving to our town?"

"Not full time. We're looking at places for holidays and the weekends. I figured it would be good to have someplace to bring my son, where we can do things together outside Austin. The city can get a little much, cooped up in my condo. He already spends way too much time with a babysitter."

Understanding spread across Chance's face. "It'll probably do your son a world of good. And it'll mean you get to see Daisy a lot more often." His knowing smirk told Derrick he hadn't been quite as adept a hiding his interest in the pretty diner owner than he'd thought.

"You mean I'm not the only one who's noticed Derrick mooning over Daisy? I don't think he's eaten anywhere except the diner every time he's been in Shiloh Springs."

"Hey, I like the food," Derrick protested Chance's statement.

Chance slung his arm around Derrick's shoulder and leaned in close. "Daisy's been through a lot and she deserves somebody who'll treat her right. If you're not serious about her, best to not start something. We care about her, and don't want to see her get hurt."

Derrick stiffened and took a step back. "Message received."

"Don't take this wrong, Derrick, because we like you. Respect you. But Daisy's like family, almost a little sister."

*And with the Boudreaus, family is everything.*

Derrick could practically hear their unsaid creed. One thing about the Boudreaus, family meant more than blood ties, more than DNA. They were a family by choice and protected those they considered part of their clan. He kind of envied them that kind of bond, since he'd never had brothers or sisters.

A curious tingle raced across his skin. Derrick turned his head and heard the prettiest laugh. Standing across the patio, Daisy stood encircled by the Boudreau women, her smile lighting a beautiful face. He noted the dark blue color she'd added to her almost white-blonde hair, chunky highlights adding interest to the shoulder-length cut. She'd changed it since the last time he'd been in Shiloh Springs. Then it had streaks of bright almost neon pink. He loved that she was spontaneous and adventurous with her hair colors and wondered how far that extended into her personality.

He sighed and turned his attention back to Chance and Rafe, who stood watching him closely. "I have no intention of hurting Daisy. As much as I'd like to pursue something with her, as you've both figured out, right now I must give my sole focus, my attention, to my son. Ian's been through so much the last few months, he's in limbo, and I need to make him my number one priority."

*No matter how much I want Daisy Parker.*

Thank you for reading Chance, Book #8 in the Texas Boudreau Brotherhood series. I hope you enjoyed Chance and Tina's story. I loved writing their book. Even though Chance proved to be a handful and a bit more than overprotective, Tina proved she was woman enough to tame him.

Since so many readers wrote me, asking about some of the secondary characters in Shiloh Springs, I decided some of them deserved to have their own stories told, and allow them to get their *happily ever after*. This doesn't mean you won't be getting the rest of the Texas Boudreau brothers, it simply means you're getting additional books about the folks living in Shiloh Springs and their interactions with the family.

The first one is Derrick Williamson, the head of the FBI office in Austin, who's been present in several of the books in the Texas Boudreau Brotherhood series. He's been fascinated with Daisy Parker, the owner of the diner, from the beginning. Now that his nine-year-old son is living with him, he isn't sure he can juggle a kid, the job, and his burgeoning feelings for the pretty diner's owner. Keep reading for an excerpt from his book, Derrick, Book #9 in the Texas Boudreau Brotherhood. Available at all major e-book and print book stores.

# DERRICK

(Book #9 Texas Boudreau Brotherhood series) © Kathy Ivan

## LINKS TO BUY DERRICK:

www.kathyivan.com/Derrick.html

"**A**re we getting the cake?"

"Why not?" Derrick waved at Jackie and ordered two pieces of the cake Ms. Patti mentioned. He was familiar with Jill's baking, having sampled more than his fair share of How Sweet It Is goods every time he visited Shiloh Springs. When the two huge slices of cake arrived, he inhaled deeply, wondering if he should have ordered one piece to split with his son.

Ian attacked his piece with gusto, shoveling the chocolatey gooey treat into his mouth, only pausing long enough to take a drink before getting another. He cleaned his plate in less than two minutes. Where did he put it all? Oh to have the metabolism of a young boy, he'd be able to eat anything he wanted too.

He managed to eat half of the huge piece of cake before pushing the remainder across the table to Ian, who demolished it in under a minute.

"You ready to go?"

Ian nodded and grabbed his game and slid from the booth. "Are you gonna see Daisy later?"

Derrick halted halfway out of the booth, surprised by his son's question. "I don't know. Why?"

"Come on, Dad, I know you like her."

"I like lots of people."

"Geez, Dad. I know you *like her* like her."

Derrick hadn't realized Ian had caught onto the fact he tended to spend a lot of his time at the diner when he visited. Guess he hadn't been subtle in his interest if his nine-year-old son noticed.

"Busted. Yeah, I like Daisy. A lot. She's nice. She's funny."

"And she's pretty. I like her rainbow hair."

Walking to the door, Derrick pulled it open and he and Ian headed toward his truck. Climbing inside the cab, he settled in and clicked on his seatbelt, and pointed toward Ian's. Once buckled in, he turned to face his son.

"Would you be upset if I asked Daisy out?"

"You mean like on a date?"

He nodded, waiting for his son's answer. With them working their way toward a semblance of a family unit, he would never do anything to upset the applecart, no matter how much he wanted to get to know the irrepressible diner owner.

"Do you think she wants to date you? I mean, you're kind of old and all you do is work."

"Old? I'll give you old," Derrick reached across the seat, wrapped his arm around Ian's neck, and rubbed his knuckle against his scalp, with Ian squirming to get away, giggling the whole time.

"Dad!"

Turning Ian loose, he straightened behind the steering wheel. It looked like Ian wasn't opposed to him asking Daisy out, which lifted a weight off his shoulders.

Things were starting to look up—not only with his son but with his new start in Shiloh Springs.

LINKS TO BUY DERRICK:
www.kathyivan.com/Derrick.html

# NEWSLETTER SIGN UP

Don't want to miss out on any new books, contests, and free stuff? Sign up to get my newsletter. I promise not to spam you, and only send out notifications/e-mails whenever there's a new release or contest/giveaway. Follow the link and join today!

http://eepurl.com/baqdRX

# REVIEWS ARE IMPORTANT!

People are always asking how they can help spread the word about my books. One of the best ways to do that is by word of mouth. Tell your friends about the books and recommend them. Share them on Goodreads. If you find a book or series or author you love – talk about it. Everybody loves to find out about new books and new-to-them authors, especially if somebody they know has read the book and loved it.

The next best thing is to write a review. Writing a review for a book does not have to be long or detailed. It can be as simple as saying "I loved the book."

I hope you enjoyed reading Chance, Texas Boudreau Brotherhood Book #8.

If you liked the story, I hope you'll consider leaving a review for the book at the vendor where you purchased it and at Goodreads. Reviews are the best way to spread the word to others looking for good books. It truly helps.

# BOOKS BY KATHY IVAN

www.kathyivan.com/books.html

## TEXAS BOUDREAU BROTHERHOOD

Rafe

Antonio

Brody

Ridge

Lucas

Heath

Shiloh

Chance

Derrick (coming soon)

Dane (coming soon)

## NEW ORLEANS CONNECTION SERIES

Desperate Choices

Connor's Gamble

Relentless Pursuit

Ultimate Betrayal

Keeping Secrets

Sex, Lies and Apple Pies

Deadly Justice

Wicked Obsession

Hidden Agenda

Spies Like Us

Fatal Intentions

New Orleans Connection Series Box Set: Books 1-3
New Orleans Connection Series Box Set: Books 4-7

## CAJUN CONNECTION SERIES
Saving Sarah
Saving Savannah
Saving Stephanie
Guarding Gabi

## LOVIN' LAS VEGAS SERIES
It Happened In Vegas
Crazy Vegas Love
Marriage, Vegas Style
A Virgin In Vegas
Vegas, Baby!
Yours For The Holidays
Match Made In Vegas
One Night In Vegas
Last Chance In Vegas
Lovin' Las Vegas (box set books 1-3)

## OTHER BOOKS BY KATHY IVAN
Second Chances (Destiny's Desire Book #1)

# ABOUT THE AUTHOR

USA TODAY Bestselling author Kathy Ivan spent most of her life with her nose between the pages of a book. It didn't matter if the book was a paranormal romance, romantic suspense, action and adventure thrillers, sweet & spicy, or a sexy novella. Kathy turned her obsession with reading into the next logical step, writing.

Her books transport you to the sultry splendor of the French Quarter in New Orleans in her award-winning romantic suspense, or to Las Vegas in her contemporary romantic comedies. Kathy's new romantic suspense series features, Texas Boudreau Brotherhood, features alpha heroes in small town Texas. Gotta love those cowboys!

Kathy tells stories people can't get enough of; reuniting old loves, betrayal of trust, finding kidnapped children, psychics and sometimes even a ghost or two. But one thing they all have in common – love and a happily ever after). More about Kathy and her books can be found at

WEBSITE: www.kathyivan.com

Follow Kathy on Facebook at facebook.com/kathyivanauthor

Follow Kathy on Twitter at twitter.com/@kathyivan

Follow Kathy at BookBub
bookbub.com/profile/kathy-ivan

DISCARD

Made in the USA
Monee, IL
11 June 2021